# That Recoil of Nature

by Craig Grimes

Canadian Cataloguing in Publication Data
Grimes, Craig
That Recoil of Nature

.

1-895166-08-X
1. Fiction. I. Title.

Cover & book design by Greg Thompson

Printed and bound in North America.

First published 2011

Published by Charivari
Toronto
www.charivaripress.com

## *Acknowledgements*

Thank you to family and friends, Lennox Wilde, Allyson McBryde, and particularly Mei Shi, for their encouragement and great suggestions.

Thank you to Daniel Kernohan, my editor at Charivari Press, for his close line readings and many ideas about how to develop the novel.

☙❧

# PROLOGUE
## *Lawrence*
## 1971

DEE AND I MOVED back to Vancouver from the farm and got a couple of rooms in an old wooden two-storey in Kitsilano. There has to be some gap in my memory, some rose-tinted revision, because I think of it as idyllic and I can't imagine any area that was actually well kept up and old-fashioned, the way I recall this place, that would have been renting, dirt cheap, to the dozens of hippies living in the area.

What I liked about the place was that it was only a few blocks from a beautiful beach. We'd head down there, watch the sunbathers, and when someone went into the water, lift the bag holding their wallet and clothes. I didn't give much thought to how the person would manage to get home, in a bathing suit, with no money.

The bulk of our income came from Welfare. Dee went three times and got emergency assistance under three different names. Each time, she dyed her hair a different colour and tried to change her appearance. I'm amazed it worked. She was fairly distinctive looking, paper thin, almost six feet tall, and nine months pregnant to boot. Maybe the Welfare workers were too bored or overworked to look at her closely, or they didn't care (my preferred option). Maybe Dee was really that good. I don't know, but the ruse worked fine.

One afternoon we ran into Jewel on the sidewalk outside our house. She was someone we knew from the farm, more Dee's friend than mine. All I remember after all these years was her long, dark kinky hair, which hardly gets to the essence of her personality, but when I think of all the women with straightened hair I see these days maybe it actually does say something significant about her or the times. We invited her up to our place.

It wasn't a self-contained apartment, just a kitchen and bedroom with a balcony, on the second floor. There were hippies living in the two other bedrooms on the floor and the five of us shared a bathroom.

While I sat on the balcony and read an article in the *Georgia Strait* about the cops cracking down on dope smokers in the city, Dee and Jewel talked in the kitchen and eventually started rooting around for something to make for dinner. Dee announced that all we had was brown rice, so a plan was struck to head to Chinatown for some bean curd and vegetables.

It was early on a summer evening. The three of us caught a bus downtown and decided to walk to Chinatown by way of Gastown, the historic old centre of Vancouver, so Jewel could see it.

When we got to the Gastown town square—more of a hub really, with several streets leading away from it in different directions—we found a contingent of hippies and assorted others, of all ages, sitting cross-legged on the pavement in the centre of the square.

Jewel asked what was going on.

"Oh shit, yeah, I forgot about that." said Dee. "It's the smoke-in."

"It's a protest against the mayor and his crackdown on grass, but it kinda misses the point," I said to Jewel. "It's crazy here lately. They've got narcs everywhere and the pigs have been busting people and sending them to jail for even a single joint. Campbell—that's the mayor—is a conservative prick who hates hippies. I don't think it has anything to do with grass. I think he's pissed about the idea of dirty hippies converging on his beautiful city and squatting in Gastown. He wants to send a message to them to stay home. Using drug and vagrancy laws to throw hippies in jail is the only way he can round 'em up."

There weren't many people protesting, all told. Two or three hundred I'd guess…if that. Others milled around. Someone played a guitar. There was a mellow laid back kind of atmosphere. Hard to believe any of this threatened the state's power.

The smell of grass was in the air but no one offered us a toke and none of us asked; the smoke-in was simply a matter of curiosity we'd come across. We had no interest in stopping.

I noticed some police vans pulling up and parking on the side streets, along with a few mounted cops dressed in riot gear. They weren't really ominous, as odd as that sounds. They were just standing around and watching. The dope smokers were pointing and talking about them.

As we walked past the group in the square the buzz began to intensify, and when I turned and looked I could see more cops, also draped in riot gear, piling out of the vans and taking up positions by spreading out across the streets. Other police—these ones on horses—began to appear and were lining up behind the guys on foot. Effectively, they were creating a wall of riot-clad, shield and baton buttressed cops, on all but one street leading into the square.

Many of the protestors began to get up and walk away from the smoke-in, in the same direction we were headed, towards that one open street. We all funnelled down it. Only a few people remained sitting and smoking.

## PROLOGUE

And then, unbelievably, the cops charged the square.

"Here come the pigs!" someone roared.

People began to run and squeeze into the unblocked street. The pedestrian traffic jam slowed people down and made the cops' job of cracking heads easier. There was yelling and crying, swinging batons and panic.

We were near the front of the pack and ran like the rest, but slowly because Dee was pregnant. Jewel and I each had her by an arm, hustling her along.

At one of the first stores we passed, Jewel yelled to us to stop. She ran to the store and tried the door. It was locked. The proprietors were watching from inside, an elderly couple who mouthed the word 'closed' to her, shaking their heads 'no'.

"She's pregnant!" Jewel mouthed back, pointing at Dee's stomach.

I could see the pair inside consulting and then the old woman went to the door and opened it a crack.

"She can come in," she said, pointing at Dee, "but no one else. Otherwise we'll be swamped."

Jewel and I each grabbed one of Dee's arms and shoved her through the door. The owners then locked it.

I stood with Jewel outside the door in the archway while Dee watched through the glass door. It was dusk, but the street lights had come on and the ethereal radiance gave an even more surreal quality to the events in front us. Foot police, running, waded in among the protestors, hammering them with their billy-clubs—you could hear the smacks and thuds—and dragged them across the pavement to the vans that had followed the cops into the hub.

Cops on horses chased some of those trying to flee. Lots of people just dove into doorways, behind cars and anywhere else that looked safer than the open street.

A young guy, a clean-cut college type, ran in front of a mounted cop who looked like he was playing polo the way he rode up on his cantering horse, wound up and swung his billy-club, driving the kid face first into a newspaper box with a blow to the back of the head. After all these years I can still hear that soft hollow thump, like when you kick a football perfectly. It's sweet to hear on the field but was bloody sickening in this case. The guy lay there immobile, his face covered in blood where it hit the pavement. The cop dismounted. With one hand he held his horse and with the other clubbed the poor bastard. This cop was a very brave man indeed with his club and someone who couldn't fight back.

Directly in front of me, a Molotov cocktail exploded at the feet of a police horse. I thought it might have come from an apartment above one of the stores but maybe it was lobbed from the sidewalk. A ball of flame shot directly upwards and the giant horse reared, his hooves chattering on the pavement, the noise blending with the chaotic screams, crying and the sound of smashing glass. The air was now permeated with the acrid stench of smoke that made your throat constrict.

I'd grown up in this, the era of the Vietnam war, but the reality of a protest was something new. Looking back, over thirty years later, I realize that some of the hippies were probably hardened veteran protestors versed in Real Politick who'd come knowing what to expect. At that moment though, I was thinking it was incredible how people could cobble together the stuff to whip up a Molotov cocktail in such a short time span.

Somewhere, bordering the square, a huge plate glass window of one of the larger stores, Woodward's, was shattered, and people began to pile into the store for safety. A cop on horseback actually picked his way through the gaping opening and started up an aisle on his horse.

"Come on, lets go! Let's go!" shouted Dee, who had come out of the store behind us. "I can't leave you here by yourselves."

The action was still in front of us, with the last of the protestors trying to escape. Again, we joined others running away from the square.

"A bus!" yelled Jewel, pointing up ahead. A cross town bus sat at the corner stop a few blocks away. There were already huge numbers of people piling in, and piling on. The driver had opened the middle doors and there were at least a dozen people sitting or standing on the back bumper or otherwise attached to the sides of the bus. It pulled away as we approached.

The three of us crossed the road and continued up the street, just walking now. We were far enough away from the riot to know it wasn't going to touch us.

'Riot' was the word the media would use for it — the Gastown Riot — but I can't hear the phrase without wanting to yell in frustration; it was the bloody cops who rioted! The protestors were flaunting drug laws but they'd been acting peacefully until the Mayor and Chief of Police decided that the proper response was to bust as many heads as they could. Expunge the bloody hippies from their lovely middle-class city.

This was the State in action and the first time I'd ever experienced anything like it. The State kept order by violence, even in a country like Canada.

In my own life I had experienced a father who called his explosions 'discipline' and I had the ever livin' shit kicked out of me by guys who didn't like the attention their girlfriends paid me. I was sick of violence.

I had never thought, really, about the idea of pacifism. The peace signs I wore were an aesthetic choice and a challenge to my parent's generation but, as a Canadian, I wasn't going to be conscripted to participate in an imperialist adventure in Vietnam, and so knew little about the war. If pressed for an honest opinion I suppose I would have said that there are times when you have to fight back; that pacifism is a naive idea. But after the Gastown Riots I decided that one had to take an idealistic, intentionally naive and categorical opposition to violence, at all times and forever, as tough as that might be. Only then could our acceptance of violence against each other come even close to being eradicated.

As PLANNED, A FEW days after the police siege in Gastown, we flew back east. On the flight—with fortuitous timing—I first read *The Cenci*.

In 1818, in Rome's Palazzo Colonna, the English Romantic poet, Percy Bysshe Shelley encountered Guido Reni's portrait of a beautiful girl-woman; purportedly Beatrice Cenci. Shelley was captivated by the portrait and wrote about Beatrice's story in a verse drama called *The Cenci*.

Some 200 or so years before, also in Rome, Beatrice Cenci, at the age of 16, had participated in plotting and carrying out the murder of her father Francesco.

Francesco Cenci was a sadistic, evil man, who repeatedly abused his family and raped his daughter. Although the Catholic Church was aware of his criminal behaviour, through appeals from his family, it had refused to take action. Eventually, with no respite from his brutality in sight, Francesco's children and wife murdered him.

After the plotters were convicted, many Roman citizens protested their death sentences. Beatrice Cenci had become a figure representing resistance to the licence and brutality of the nobility. Pope Clement VIII, however, was not moved, and in 1599 Beatrice Cenci was beheaded. (In Shelley's drama the petitions to the Pope that would have freed Beatrice and her mother from the rule of Francesco were variously withheld by a lustful prelate and returned unopened from the Pope until, ironically, shortly after the father's murder, a successful petition arrived.)

After researching the events of *The Cenci* tragedy, Shelley wrote a full-length play that, because of the subject matter, was only first publicly performed a hundred years after his death.

Shelley did not agree with Beatrice's decision to kill her father, even though he showed in his drama that neither friends nor authorities were willing to help her. (*The Cenci* was an indirect attack on patriarchal authority, especially that of the Catholic Church.) At her trial she argues that she is innocent. For Shelley however, she remained innocent (the evil moral decisions of others did not reflect on her moral character) only until she rejected forbearance and passive resistance, choosing instead to act in the same evil and morally corrupt way as her father.

Of course the play reinforced my morally absolutist position about violence and murder, but, more importantly, because of that alignment of perspective, it became my guide through the moral quandary I would soon become engulfed in after reading my mother's journal—and then again, especially, after realizing the actual manner of her death.

℘℘

# PART 1
*Robert*
# Autumn — 1951

THE HYDRO CAMP SAT in the middle of a clearing amid the squat pines found near the tree line. At night, the line crew would laze around a huge bonfire and laugh, spit, smoke, and bullshit about the war. Most of the men had fought or lived overseas, so war was a currency they shared and the stories were a way to remake memories; memories that other people, who hadn't been there, thought the émigrés and ex-soldiers should have long since gotten over. The war had ended 6 years ago after all. But it was the adventurous or funny things that got told and twisted, not the horror and nightmares.

On this night Stan Ivanchuk, a mammoth man who came here following the war feeling he had no reason to stay in the Ukraine after the murders of his family members—first by the Germans and then by the allies, until every last one was obliterated—was holding court. "So we hung him by his ankles over the opening to look inna thing and see if it was dry."

Tommy Locke was taking a leak into the runty trees a few feet away at the edge of the clearing—guys would do that rather than miss any part of a good story—and was hanging on every word. Silhouetted in the darkness, Tommy stared back over his shoulder towards the warmth and illumination of the beckoning sacred circle.

"Then the boiler exploded and blew him clear across the room!"

The group howled. A punchline like that told in a thick Baltic accent always got a good laugh.

"Shit!" Tommy swore, as a coda.

"You piss on yourself again?" someone called.

Another big laugh.

"Go to hell," swore Tommy, which got more laughs.

A multitude of public private conversations started up. "Did I ever tell you the one…" "There was this bastard who was always crying in the night…" "Same thing with that Polish Major who was with us." "One time at this pub in London…" "Just slap some bitters in it."

Robert MacQuigau's stories were the same sort as those told by the rest of the men; usually dark humour. And it was no different at home in Wegebow. The ones he told at the dinner table weren't about the stuff haunting him. There was some bragging for sure, laying it on a bit, but you didn't have to do too much of that to make a good story.

Robert's bad dreams would awaken him, sweating, in the middle of the night, and his memories followed him everywhere, at all times. There was a soldier at the Scheldt whose feet were blown off by a landmine. Robert remembered the screams that continued until someone from the medical corps pumped the kid full of morphine. At Normandy he watched another kid's face melt away, amid flames, until the skull was exposed and the soldier all too slowly died. These things don't leave you. Still, he figured he was luckier than the many traumatized and shattered who would be years before they could live a normal life, if ever.

But for all of the war's negative impact on his life, for the endlessly replayed memories he worried would never be behind him, the war had been life truly being lived. It was the opposite of life back home, where every day was much the same as the last and moved at a crawling pace; the exact things he'd enlisted to escape.

After the war, he wanted mostly to get married and have a family. He longed for the uneventful and normal.

Robert had lived in Wegebow for his first 10 years. His father had come north to work in the nearby mill, decided to stay, and soon built a small house in town, by himself, gradually adding to it, outwardly and upwardly, as the family expanded. Robert was the oldest child. There were four more of them by the time they moved to Sudbury, the ancestral seat as it were. But Wegebow was the place he would think about during his most miserable moments overseas—slogging through mud or sleeping in the rain. He'd remember laying on his back as a kid, on the floor beside the woodstove, his head in his cupped hands, listening to the old radio, to *Fibber Magee and Molly*, the big boxing matches and, of course, *The Shadow*. When he saw the posting for a Hydro job in Wegebow he'd jumped at it. Wegebow meant good money and a nice place to raise kids.

Now, despite the dream having come true, he was happy to be in the camp where they came after a day of work installing power lines in the bush, and away from the frustrations of family life. It surprised him. He thought before he came north he'd seen enough bunk beds and barracks for a lifetime. But this was the society he understood.

A gangly young man he knew only as Tony came over to where Robert was reposing on a big log by the fire. Tony bummed a light and sat down beside him.

"Geez, I'd love a steak. A thick juicy one," Tony said dreamily.
"You got a millionaire's taste."
"Yeah. Too bad I don't have a millionaire's wallet."
"You and me both."
"I could use a drink too."
"Umm."
"You too?"
"I'd love a beer."
"My old lady's probably drinking one now down at the Empire or the Legion," he said wistfully.

So, he had something on his mind, Robert realized. "That's Laidlaw right?"
"Yeah."
"You can't get her to stay home?"
"Not without tyin' her up…Yer old lady drink?"
"She's a teetotaler I'm afraid." Robert almost said she was too classy to drink but caught himself.

"Wisht mine was like that. Don't much mind the drinkin' but there's always guys at the Empire movin' on her. I hope I don't go home and find some bugger in bed with her."

"What would you do if you did?" Robert asked, sitting up, suddenly serious. He'd heard guys say stuff like this before, many times, and always ignored it, but tonight he was curious.

"Don't know who I'd kill first. Her or me."

This was the thing with DPs, Robert thought, his fatigue quickly returning, they're incredibly stupid. Why did he waste his time talking to them?

Tony had actually moved to Canada as a kid, but lately, despite his lack of an accent, got lumped in with the Displaced Persons immigrating here from Italy to escape the post-war devastation, and was subject to the same resentment.

"Wisht I'd never gotten married." Tony added. "I wouldn't need to be here if I didn't…"

Robert couldn't relate. He didn't regret being here, or getting married, those were what he wanted, but still, he sometimes lay in bed and thought of all the things he could be doing if he hadn't become an electrician, met Maddy and got caught up in a life as husband and parent. If he had stayed single he might've been a travel writer, seeing the world and writing about things he came across along the way, really experiencing new places and not just marching past them. None of that would ever happen now.

# *Maddy*

The 80 year-old woman in rubber boots and checked man's shirt with rolled up sleeves had evidently come to the doctor's office straight from her garden. She was short and stooped yet nimble, whippet thin with pulled back grey hair, and her weather-darkened skin was spotted leather. A widow with six sons who knew something of what it took to be heard in a man's world, the old lady beamed at Maddy and squeezed her arm, "You're terrific," she said in a firm, clear voice, on her way out the door, "we're so lucky to have you here."

Dr. Madeleine MacQuigau, Maddy, was a tall woman in her thirties with short curly hair and straight angular features. 'Mannish' she'd been inaccurately called by some in town; probably not a comment about her femininity so much as a way to explain the eccentricity of mind that would lead a woman to want to become a doctor. How, it was wondered, had her husband ever allowed such a thing and what was wrong with him that he couldn't support his own family?

Obviously, in 1951, a female doctor was unusual. Many guys refused to see her. They'd rather drive to Hartley to be treated by a man. They'd have gone to a vet first. There were women too who shunned her, the sort who defer to their husbands no doubt, but there were others who disapproved on their own. It wasn't a woman's place to be working and not looking after her family.

Some, like the old lady, supported Dr. MacQuigau and there were others who weren't patients but still wished her well. A few simply saw her as a doctor.

Business was slowly growing so Maddy clung to the idea that she was doing something of value with her life; bringing modern medicine to a remote town.

It was 4:30 in the afternoon, and with no more patients to see, as it was on most days, she left for her usual walk to Waverly Market to get some groceries, fresh air and time to herself. From the doctor's house at the corner of town it took ten minutes to get downtown.

Maddy walked briskly. It would have been nicer if she could wear pumps but she had to settle for flats because of the dirt roads. She liked the feel of her skirt swishing against her legs, and she enjoyed the wide-eyed looks of some of the men from Wegebow, as if they were witnessing an exotic big-city creature. A few would stop what they were doing to watch her pass or stare at her from some window. There were no covert glances here. Robert had stared blatantly at her like that the first time he saw her in Toronto when she came walking through the doorway at a mutual friend's. Not expecting to meet anyone new, he wore a wrinkled shirt with the sleeves rolled up to the biceps, and was sitting on a stack of empty beer cases with a cigarette in his hand. His response wasn't subtle. He stood up, dropped his smoke, and stumbled backwards with his mouth open.

She liked to replay that sort of memory. Every night in the city there were firemen who would hoot and holler at her from an upstairs window of the fire hall as she went past, on her way home from the evening shift at the candy factory.

It was funny, even late at night Toronto felt safer than Wegebow, although people in the north talked about small towns as if they were pastoral and idyllic, while cities, by comparison, were described as dark and dangerous. Yet here, she'd been followed by men in cars a couple of times when she was walking to house calls after dark. Once, coming home in the evening from a patient's, an obviously frightened young woman had run out from between two houses and asked Maddy to see her home. Two young guys emerged from the same spot but hung back in the shadows when they saw the doctor. Idyllic indeed!

It was lonely when Robert was away. At home he'd follow her around, solicitous to help, yet looking for attention, and every hour or so he'd try to nudge her to the bedroom the way he had after they were first married.

When she was 18, in Toronto, her father had called her into the dark interior dining room of the tiny English style row house that dimmed all hopes and told her, in a matter-of-fact tone—as if the girl having ambitions of her own was of no significance—that she had to quit school. Her mother had found Maddy a job in the candy factory where she worked.

Hoping for support, Maddy looked towards her mother standing at the window, but saw only her back, shoulders slouched in guilt.

There was a depression on, Maddy's father continued, and money was scant. As a girl she didn't need an education anyway. No, it didn't matter she had all A's and wanted to go to university; she'd get married and be taken care of. Her brother was the priority.

So she quit high school and helped to support her family for two years until her brother graduated. Then she moved out and went to night school. Getting your own place wasn't something nice girls did. Her father said there was only one reason she'd want her own place. He called her a tramp and cut her out of his life. It would be a long time before she saw her father again. Even longer before she wanted to see him again.

When he came into her life Robert provided the companionship she'd lacked during those years of handling both school and work. To her mind he was handsome, rugged and dashing. He'd been a soldier, and no one in her circle had done that. Yet he read books and understood there was culture in the world. He came from Wegebow but was much different than the locals in many ways. And he saw her not as the daughter of two factory workers, but as cultured and refined, the way she wanted to be seen.

Four doors away from Maddy's, a squat, middle-aged woman in a faded housecoat, with a dour look on her face, was sweeping her front steps. She turned her ample back on seeing the doctor approach. The stares from some of the men aside, most of the Wegebow locals greeted Maddy with silence and averted eyes. A couple of young girls though, weaving along the shoulder of the road on their way home from school, their heads conspiratorially together as they talked animatedly, smiled at her and said hi.

On the next block, the last one before the sidewalk began, Maddy said hello to a substantial man, whose name she somehow knew was Jacques, as he got out of his car after almost running her over while turning into his driveway. He said nothing, just scowled as if she was a great inconvenience and had planned it that way by using the shoulder in front of his house at this exact moment. The coldness and hostility of his manner made her look back over her shoulder three times to make sure he'd gone inside.

Maddy saw Paul Desjardins at the market, smiling in her direction as he did every day when she arrived. He was maybe forty with a nice head of wavy hair, a deacon in the Catholic church, father of a large family and the esteemed Mayor of Wegebow.

As always, Paul began to follow her up and down the aisles while she picked out groceries.

"I went by your house yesterday," he said, in front of the laundry detergent, "and I noticed you don't have your storm windows up yet."

"That's true. Robert's going to put them up in a couple of weeks when he's back home."

Maddy manoeuvred her cart around some cases of Klik and Kam stacked on the floor.

"The Indians up north call that 'Indian steak,'" Paul said and laughed heartily.

"I'm surprised they even eat it with all the wild meat up there."

"Yes, yes, that's true." Paul dropped his voice and added, "some of them are too lazy to hunt anymore."

"I need some flour," Maddy said, as if she hadn't heard, and pressed on without mentioning that Wegebow's citizenry were obviously quite fond of canned meat themselves.

"You know Dr. MacQuigau, I have lots of commitments," Paul said, exuding benevolence, as they passed the tins of fruit, "but Saturday afternoons are yours if you need a hand with your windows or anything. I know your husband is out of town for weeks at a time."

PART 1

This would be upsetting to Robert, Maddy thought, and not something she'd consider. Even though he was away a lot, Robert would still want to do anything that was needed to look after his family. There was something disturbing about Paul Desjardins anyway. He lived in a large house outside of town and Maddy had developed an impression of his family as a sort of monastic religious order, brainwashed with a degree of fanaticism, and kept away from the rest of the world so the kiddies stayed untainted. If his proposal to help her was meant the way she sensed it was, he was a hypocrite and should be ashamed of himself, a married man with all those kids!

Maddy tried not to look offended by Paul's offer. "Oh thanks," she said. "I'll keep it in mind."

Paul beamed.

Maddy quickly found her way out of the market and started for home. She would have to reconsider the time of her visits.

If most of the other people in Wegebow didn't like Madeleine the feeling was becoming mutual. Not that she told anyone how she felt. When Robert wanted to move north it hadn't sounded like a problem. There was a bigger town nearby, a city a couple of hundred miles away, and there'd be trips back to Toronto. But once you actually lived in the place and were settled, with the commitments of running a practice, even getting as far as Hartley was a rare adventure.

But she soon discovered that she didn't like: a) camping (too much work for the pleasure of sleeping on hard ground); b) fishing (when you cleaned fish the scales stuck to everything and their fins slashed your fingers); c) boats (too loud, and they left a smelly rainbow gas slick on the water); d) the gossip (usually pernicious). And most of all she hated Bingo, "twenty-five cents a card and eighty dollars first prize." She'd given them all a chance. Her only social activities now were The Tea, Apron and Bake Sale and the odd square dance.

Don't be uncharitable, she often thought, but even small things about Wegebow were starting to annoy her more than they should. Some of the names for instance: Eustace, Aloysius, Napoleon. Who in their right mind would name a child something like these?

At one of the houses Maddy always passed, she often noticed a girl watching her from a window, or the front steps, or peeking around a corner of the house. The girl looked to be 12 or 13 years-old, so you'd think she should be in school.

The house was an old one, covered in the ubiquitous grey rolled shingle of the north, torn in spots, with cracked white paint around the windows and doors. A sheet, looking like it was tacked up in a few places, more or less blocked the front picture window. One of the bedroom window panes was covered in plywood. Neither the wooden porch (just a platform really) nor the front steps had a railing, and the dark grey paint on them had been worn down to the wood, splintering in deep furrows along the middle of each stair. There was no sidewalk across the yard, just hard-packed, fawn-coloured dried clay, sprinkled with long tufts of brown-scorched scratch grass. It was a sad and dreary house that looked to have long since stopped crying to be cared for and resigned itself to its fate. Maddy was afraid to do more than glance at the place as she went by, as if the owner might be looking back and become angry at the intrusion. Part of it was pity too. Who, living in such a house, would want their neighbours to be looking it over? Best treat it as if it were as normal as any other place.

The girl always wore the same grubby-looking clothes. She was a bony kind of skinny, with long wispy blonde bangs hanging in front of her eyes. It was shyness, Maddy figured, since the girl's watchfulness showed an apparent curiosity for the life passing by.

The doctor called out hello one day and the girl looked up, her head cocked to the side with one hazel eye visible between strands of hair, and nodded in return. From then on she ducked out of sight before Dr. MacQuigau got too near.

Once, Maddy had asked her friend Emelie about the girl and gotten only her name; Denise. She was 14, maybe 13. Emelie knew her mother had died a couple years before or so and the story was that afterwards her father had gotten permission to take Denise out of school. "They do that, ya know, when kids are needed at home to help." The father didn't work apparently, just sat around all day on some sort of army pension. "I don't know," an uncomfortable Emelie answered every additional question.

"But don't you think it's strange? Don't you want to know what goes on there, that she's being treated okay? She's looking after a man, but she's only a child. How does she know what to do? Who's looking after her?" Maddy stared at Emelie, incredulous such questions even had to be asked.

"It's not my business."

And Maddy gave it up. It wasn't the first time she's seen this turn-a-blind-eye kind of attitude in Wegebow.

As Dr. MacQuigau walked, she could see Denise straight ahead, also returning home from the market, trudging along in no great hurry, a bag of groceries in her arms. She was a couple of blocks from her house and unaware of the doctor coming up behind her.

"Denise!" Maddy said, falling into step beside her.

The girl looked up wildly at the mention of her name and appeared ready to run.

"My name's Maddy. I've wanted to introduce myself for awhile."

"Hello," Denise mumbled, slowing and then stopping entirely.

"I've seen you around and thought I'd like to get to know you."

"I have to go," the girl said surprisingly loudly, looking at the ground and then suddenly hustling away.

"Oh, okay. Do you know where I live?" Maddy called after her, but received no answer. "It's the brick place at the end of this road, the last one. I'm a doctor. If you ever want to talk to someone come and see me."

Denise turned and nodded several times.

"No charge if you need a doctor!" was hollered to the retreating back.

## *Paul*

Visibly prominent in Wegebow was the white wooden Catholic church, standing on the town's one rise of ground, casting an omnipresent and stern look of moral reproof over the two thousand or so inhabitants. Father McNeil performed the equivalent oversight for anyone who didn't venture outdoors to admire his church by hovering over the dances and wherever people gathered indoors.

Wegebow was the end of the line, literally. It squatted beside Lake Wegebow at the end of a road running north from the Trans Canada Highway. Further north still were thousands of square miles of sub-arctic muskeg and one would have to think that, surely, a good portion of it had never been seen by any human eye.

It was an ugly town of mostly small wooden houses, painted grey, beige or some other nondescript shade, or covered in dark grey rolled asphalt or white aluminium siding. Brick houses were a rarity because it was expensive hauling the bricks to such a remote locale, but there was a smattering of them, and most were now covered with several coats of paint in advanced stages of degeneration. A couple of architectural rebels had gone so far as to do their houses in pebble dash.

Built around a Canadian National Railway roundhouse which had trimmed its operations of late, people still stopped when a train whistled and puffed her way through town, and waved at everyone appearing in a window, who usually waved back. Men were now also employed in the local businesses or in the paper mill eight miles away in Hartley, and most of them spent their spare time honing exceptional hunting and fishing skills.

Originally French speaking, the town had been infused with the blood of Scottish trappers and Ojibwa. Like the dogs who interbred to the point of resembling no breed in particular, the townsfolk were now virtually all related to each other. The word 'family' was heard a lot here, spoken of reverentially as a sacred trust. "You gotta stand by family," people would say, "nothing matters more."

Hartley was different. Since the war had intruded, it strove to be part of the world outside. They'd just put up two sets of traffic lights and had a movie theatre and bookstore, but they voted out their mayor after he dared to suggest they invest in parking meters that would charge a nickel to park. How much money did a government need anyhow? One could take highfalutin modernity too far.

People from Wegebow seldom ventured to Hartley, and when they did, would rush home from the big unpleasant place as soon as possible. Wegebow was a town too isolated and small to notice its own smugness and closed mindedness.

Mayor Paul Desjardins was the leading light of the group of men who owned the largest businesses in town and were prominent in the church. It was a happy consolidation of power in the same hands—economic, familial, religious, political—which saved everyone the messiness of it being spread around.

Paul was a man blessed by many happy coincidences.

He always began his daily constitutional by touring his empire, Desjardins' Tours and Motel. The former consisted of three boats and two small planes flying tourists in and out of the bush. He'd learned to fly in the military but joined the air force late and never went overseas. It was Archie, an ex fighter pilot, who did most of the flying.

The tour company used part of the office of Desjardins' Motel which was conveniently located beside the town dock where the Desjardins' planes and boats were moored; they being the only tour company licensed to use the public amenity. Paul liked to spend most of his time each day circulating around the two businesses, chatting to people, or sitting at his desk reading newspapers left by guests.

Yvonne Graves worked the front desk during the day shift at the motel and Paul was in love with her after a fashion, although he called it friendship. He would lean over the counter, obviously buoyed by being in her presence, smile steadily, and ask about everything in her life. Yvonne usually lied in response. Paul would have called his actions friendly flirting if he acknowledged any kind of intention in them, but it appeared to Yvonne—who knew something of these matters—that he was doing his best to get her into bed. Paul didn't realize Yvonne had slept with a good percentage of the men in Wegebow. He maintained a romantic image of her as innocent, even virginal, so didn't press his attentions.

Paul lived two miles from town with his wife and their nine kids; devout Catholics all. The happy coincidence of this location let him keep his kids away from other, less religiously pious, children, while allowing himself the freedom to socialize with women and all those needing redemption. The kids would be dropped off at school and picked up immediately afterwards, not by bus but by their mother, the friendly and severely doctrinal Gracie. She preached to her children, with obedient and fervent conviction, of a woman's subservience to her husband—doesn't old-time religion of any stripe always yearn to set the clock back to a time of unrestrained male authority in all things?—yet she managed the household, the kids and did the books for the Desjardins' business ventures. Her opinions and ideas directed every successful decision concerning the family business. Gracie was the ultimate happy coincidence in Paul's life.

Being mayor also gave Paul a reason for drifting around downtown Wegebow during working hours, nipping into local businesses and chatting to citizens, which, at that time of day, consisted mainly of housewives. He had developed a daily routine. At 2 p.m. he stopped for coffee at Woolworth's, served by the beautiful Claire Laframboise. From there he popped in to speak to Cheryl at the cleaners, Betty at the restaurant, Maria at the variety store and ended up at the Waverly Market late in the afternoon. Paul saw nothing wrong in this. He was just being friendly, proselytizing even. He made constant references to scripture and what was 'right for families.' Everyone knew Paul stood for moral rectitude and tradition.

It so happened that Dr. Maddy MacQuigau almost always arrived at the market around the same time as Paul. He had taken a liking to her lately.

The same couldn't be said though for the way he felt about DPs, who were about the only patients the doctor had. He had little exposure to foreigners, so picked up on the usual small town prejudices (they were different and poor so, of course, took advantage of their hosts). It was said that Dr. MacQuigau treated some of the DPs for nothing. That just wasn't right. He couldn't imagine what sort of person would give preference to foreigners over their own people. Still, the town having a doctor was good for business, as Gracie said, so he remained committed to encouraging Dr. MacQuigau in spite of the bad example of having his daughters see a woman working and taking away a man's job.

As mayor, Paul had come to realize that more citizens meant more business, and the priest liked DPs—who were Catholics after all—so Paul did his best to lure them to Wegebow. He got the mill to pay for want ads in the Toronto papers. His motel built some monthly rental units and the town footed the bill for a bus (although the mill paid the driver) to carry workers back and forth between Wegebow and the mill. It was sweet business.

## *Marcel and Emelie*
## Winter

Thursday night was Marcel's payday and he followed Emelie up and down the aisles of Wegebow's one tiny supermarket. They each pushed a cart that Emelie filled with groceries after getting her husband's nod of approval for everything going inside them. To taunt the large clumsy hands guiding it, Marcel's tiny cart would veer towards the shelves, or a wheel would wobble or lock. At one point, in frustration, he picked the whole damn thing up, although it was filled with groceries, and put it back on course in the middle of the aisle. He was a tall, rotund man, and the cart was like a toy when he got his big mitts around it.

The kids, René and the baby, who was now almost 5 months old, were at home with a sitter. Grocery shopping was the only time Marcel and Emelie were ever out by themselves.

At the checkout Marcel paid for the groceries while a 16 year-old kid bagged them and smiled at Emelie like he'd been taught to. He even helped haul the bags outside and carefully passed them to Marcel over the January snow bank, dirty and brown from idling car exhaust and the grit thrown up by passing tires.

The couple drove the few blocks home in silence, as if they didn't know each other. When they got there Marcel paid the babysitter, a girl who lived nearby, and she left while Emelie put away the groceries in the kitchen.

It was a cheap and dreary room. Pieces from a brown circular burn in the counter's maroon top were flaking off like crusty bits of scab. Two chairs of the heavy, gold-flecked black and chrome kitchen set had tears in the plastic seat covers and there were now small lunar pits where little René had pulled away chunks of the exposed foam rubber thinking he could eat it.

It was only when Marcel said nothing in response to Emelie's comment about how cold the night was, that she could feel his controlled rage. She began to speak more and more of inconsequential things, of the price of beef and the size of the oatmeal box. Her voice was higher than normal and quavered slightly.

"So what was that shit?" Marcel finally spat out.

"What shit?"

"The thing with the kid."

"What kid?"

"The one at the market. The one you were flirtin' with. The one you wanna fuck!" He was getting very loud. The baby started fussing in the bedroom.

"What're you talking about? You mean the boy bagging the groceries?"

Emelie stopped putting groceries away and sat down at the kitchen table. Marcel gripped a bag of potatoes firmer and firmer and began to pace.

"Of course 'the guy baggin' the groceries'," he said, caricaturing her voice. "The two of you smilin' and flirtin' with each other. It was bloody embarrassin'."

"He's a kid. He's just smiling at people. I'm sure he smiles at everyone."

"Don't gimme that bull. You're all the same. You say one thing and you're screwin' around with guys behind our backs."

"I don't know what you're talking about."

"I'm talkin' 'bout you and Vincent Pretty Boy Lavoie and God knows how many other guys you screwed. And that slutty sister of yours who's shacked up in Toronto. Youse are both the same. I shoulda listened to everyone, to keep away from the LeClairs."

"I was a kid. I didn't have any parents. I made mistakes. But I married you. I thought you understood."

"Well I don't! You lied to me about bein' Miss fuckin' Innocent."

"I didn't lie. I never said anything like that. And leave my sister out of this! Is your family so perfect? Your mother got pregnant by a man who wasn't her husband. Who wasn't your father. You shouldn't be talking about my family."

That was enough. It was way too much. Marcel strode to Emelie and slapped her so hard on the back of the head that she and her chair went over sideways. He had to kneel down to keep slapping her as she balled up with her hands covering her face. He hit her over and over.

AN HOUR AFTER HER husband's attack, Emelie lay curled up in bed in her nightgown, in the same foetal position she'd taken on the floor of the kitchen. She didn't sleep, just lay there silently, in shock.

Marcel came to her bedside and sat down. Emelie didn't move.

The Jesus of fertility, who was always busy in this Catholic part of the world, a yellow aura glowing around his head, watched them from a cheap white frame above the bed.

Marcel had tears in his porcine eyes, squinting through the flab. "I don't know what happened," he blubbered, aggressively snorting back the snot starting to run down his upper lip while rubbing the back of one of his meaty hands across it. "It's just I love ya so much."

Marcel took her hand while he spoke, gingerly, as if he was picking up shards of broken glass. Emelie didn't resist. She was afraid to move.

He cried and swore he'd never hurt her again.

A little later, where he sat on the front steps, Marcel slumped forward with elbows resting on his knees. It was dark and cold—that miserable biting January cold that comes from a wind blowing in over the frozen lake—and he wore no coat. That was okay, it was his punishment, he thought. Orange sparks flew in the blackness from the cigarette protruding from the fist he was slowly tapping against his forehead. How could this have happened? What kind of man hit a woman? Was he a coward? A sudden rush of anxiety made him lose his breath, like a punch to the gut. What if word of this got around? He'd never live it down!

Shit, it wasn't his fault! He was under a ton of pressure at work because of a new Wop supervisor who didn't like him and always blamed him for everything, and since the war there was a flock of damn immigrants hovering around, like turkey vultures, looking to take your job. No one liked him at the mill anyway and there was no chance to get ahead. The pay was crummy and he had a wife and two kids to support.

Emelie was to blame, any fair person would say that. Since the baby had been born they never had sex anymore. She didn't want to go near him. They'd lost the thing that was there when there was just the two of them. He didn't know what to call it. She didn't look after him anymore, ask about his life, or take care of him. It was all about the kids all the time, just talk, talk, talk. All she wanted to do was go to Francine's or the doctor's to drink tea and gossip. "All she does is run the roads," his grandmother would've said.

Marcel was only 24 years-old. His life was over. Even here in Wegebow, you could see some good-looking women, but he'd never know any woman except Emelie.

IT HADN'T ALWAYS BEEN like this. Things had only begun to change a few months earlier and it started over nothing. Or at least Marcel didn't know what it was. He'd look at Emelie as she talked on and on, his face becoming taut and severe while Emelie looked back at him with growing puzzlement and alarm. It was some time before she could put a name to his look. She finally found the words: he hated her.

Marcel didn't understand what was happening. Sometimes the general frustration just grew too intense. Trying to open a stubborn bottle top or some other inconsequential thing would make him crazy. He didn't want to get mad and fought it so hard, trying to stay calm, but what he really wanted to do most of all was to take the bottle and throw the damn thing as hard as he possibly could against a lousy wall. Emelie saw the tension in him when he tried to control his fury and she became afraid of it, not that she thought, really, he would ever hurt her.

Things deteriorated to the point that Emelie needed to ask Marcel several times before he'd do anything around the house, like fix a broken window or cut the lawn. He was spending his free time, almost exclusively, tinkering with his boat motor, tying lures for fly fishing or pursuing one of his other hobbies. Emelie tried to negotiate her requests by modulating her voice and making them sound matter of fact.

"I'm sorry I'm not perfect like your old boyfriends!" Marcel yelled at her one day after a repeated request. It was a few weeks before the attack in the grocery store.

"I'm sorry too," Emelie snapped back in retaliation before thinking.

Marcel pushed her as he stomped by and slammed the door on his way out. He then walked around the town until he calmed down. When he came home he apologized. Emelie said she'd provoked him, and she forgave him. She didn't think he meant to hurt her, only that she happened to be standing between him and the door when he marched out of the house in anger.

In the days after Marcel beat her up, he thought about that incident the previous month. It had all started after Emelie wouldn't stop bugging him. And this time she'd made some remark about his mother. She'd provoked him again, just like before. It was so unfair. She caused these things yet he was the one who would be humiliated if word ever got out.

# *Maddy*
# April — 1952

Emelie had been Maddy's friend since the previous spring, and was still her only friend in Wegebow, but with a twelve year age difference Maddy would have described their relationship as being more like mother and daughter. They were both outsiders who grew up in cities so had quickly discovered a natural camaraderie.

They first met on the beach that runs for a mile or so along the southernmost shore of Lake Wegebow. Both of their houses overlooked the beach. Emelie was wandering with René and came across Maddy and her 4 year-old, Lawrence, engaged in attempting to skip stones. The boys started playing together, making roads and digging in the sand while their mothers sat on a big driftwood stump, talking and looking out over Lake Wegebow. A small boat, with a pair of men in it, sputtered across the water in the distance. One of the men was her husband, Emelie pointed out. He was heading for Fisher Island in his cousin Bernie's boat with the new Johnson motor. "There's snapping turtles there and lots of bass in the reeds. When he has any free time, him 'n Bernie are off together."

Maddy heard a counter melody of empty loneliness in the words and thought how tedious life must be when stuck at home with a baby in this desolate place. Robert was often working in the north for long periods of time putting up phone lines, but it wasn't the same; she had her work and a babysitter.

Over time, Maddy welcomed having gotten to know someone and René was a little friend for Lawrence to play with. Throughout the summer Emelie and René stopped by every day to pick up Lawrence and the three of them would head for the beach.

After Emelie's baby was born in the early fall there was only a short break before the visits resumed. When winter came they would pile on to a sled to be pulled across the snow and if Maddy had no patients she would come too.

Once, shortly before Christmas, Emelie uncharacteristically didn't appear for 2 weeks and Lawrence looked futilely out the window several times a day waiting for his friend to arrive. Calls to Emelie's house weren't answered. She finally showed up, providing no explanation for her absence, and acted as if there was nothing out of the ordinary. Her visits had been sporadic in the months since then. She'd stop in every day for awhile and then disappear for several days in a row.

Lately, Maddy had noticed Emelie becoming withdrawn. She'd stare off while the doctor talked, clearly far away, and then suddenly look at her with rapt attention as if Maddy's words had broken through the distraction and she was now struggling to catch up to the conversation and comprehend. There was a sterner topography to Emelie's face too but it stubbornly refused to reveal any secrets about itself. At times, Emelie would rock nervously back and forth or answer in a sarcastic tone that didn't fit with her usual demeanour. When asked one day if something was wrong she muttered, "Nah, everything is just so hunky bloody dory."

Maddy wondered if the source of Emelie's unhappiness had something to do with the new baby, or if, maybe, she wasn't getting along with Marcel. She prodded her a couple of times to talk about it, like poking something with a stick to see if it reacts, but got only silence in return.

"Oh, I have some clothes for you," Maddy interjected into the conversation one day in the early spring. She and Emelie were sitting by the lake.

"No! I can't take them. Marcel got really mad at me the last time you gave me some," Emelie's voice drifted off as if remembering the conversation.

"What?" Maddy looked bewildered. "Why would he get mad?"

"He says it's charity."

Maddy snorted, despite herself, and rolled her eyes.

"It's not charity! They're just clothes I won't be wearing anymore and I'm so huge by the time you get finished cutting them up and re-sewing them it's like you made them yourself," and after a pause added, "and don't forget you have to teach me how to sew some day."

"I don't want to get Marcel angry," Emelie said in a panicky way that made Maddy look at her with a question on her mind.

"Well that's that then…too bad."

Maddy considered Marcel to be a boor with the loutish attitudes of a backwoods' hillbilly. On the few occasions when they were in each other's presence, he had made digs about DPs and 'Newfies', the citizens of Canada's newest province, and how they were all dragging the country down, apparently in contrast to the Marcels of the world. The comments were aimed at her because she was the doctor for the 'Polacks', 'Ukes' and all the others whom Marcel disapproved of.

"I really do appreciate the clothes though," Emelie qualified contritely, "it's so nice to get something that didn't come from a catalogue."

She almost never got anything from that source either Maddy knew.

"But I'll get something new anyway, don't worry, I always do. Marcel says, 'We can't afford your fancy habits'," Emelie said, imitating his voice and laughing.

"You? If he thinks you have expensive habits it's a good thing he's not married to someone like me!"

Emelie was a small woman with a fawn, freckled complexion, who didn't look much older than a child. In the pause that followed, Maddy found herself studying Emelie's face. Today the freckles weren't visible because of a layer of make-up.

"Did you hit your eye?"

"What? Oh yeah, I left one of the cupboard doors open, turned 'round, and bang!" She giggled.

Emelie didn't stay long. She had to go home and make Marcel his lunch, she said.

After Emelie had left, Maddy called Lawrence and held out her hand. "Let's go make our lunch too."

"Isabel'll make it? She knows what I like."

"It's her day off."

Maddy hated these type of comments, suggesting he was closer to his babysitter than to her. During the day, and if Maddy went out on a call in the evening, Lawrence would stay with Isabel, who lived with them from Monday through Friday. It was an arrangement he still wasn't used to. Maddy felt the same desperate guilt, several times a day, when leaving Lawrence or the house. She had thought that having an office in her home would be almost the same as staying at home, but it wasn't. Lawrence still hated it whenever she left for the office and he'd cling to her, crying. Maddy felt derelict as a mother and would often end up in tears herself.

As Maddy collected up Lawrence and took him inside, she wondered why Marcel resented her giving Emelie some used clothes. Maybe money was getting to be an issue with a second child. Could be it injured his pride. Typical of a man, to feel emasculated by something like that. It was silly.

On first getting to know Emelie, before the new baby was born, it sounded like Marcel was very happy but now Emelie gave the impression their marriage was feeling some strains. She often said, when showing up at Maddy's, that she was there to give Marcel a break, but maybe the break was meant for herself.

Ah well, it wasn't right to be too hard on the guy. They would sort it out over time. You don't get much sleep with a new baby. Maybe they were both just exhausted. A guy like Marcel would leave everything to his wife, but the fuss could still wake him up. Maybe fatigue was the reason Emelie wouldn't show up for days at a time. Maddy told herself to try and find the time to go over and take the kids off Emelie's hands for awhile.

Maddy was lucky to have a husband like Robert, she thought. He loved babies and was always willing to help, especially with a boy. That was important. Who else would a boy imitate if not his father? He needed to have a father who was active in his care if he was going to learn how to be a man.

# *Emelie*

Sweeping was difficult for Emelie this morning because any kind of vigorous movement sent pain coursing through her recently separated shoulder. And, anyway, it didn't make the house look any better with its run-down furniture. The pillows of the maroon couch had lumpen spots where the springs pushed through, and sunken areas everyone tried to avoid sitting on. The upholstery was flattened, with a sheen, and was even worn right through in spots. And there was a clammy and musty tobacco smell that came off of it, too deeply embedded to get rid of no matter how much airing out the house got.

# Part 1

At the market, Emelie liked to look at pictures in magazines of newly decorated homes and fantasize about the way she would do up the place if they could only get a few dollars together, but Marcel refused to listen to her pleas to buy even a new couch. He'd say things like, "It's luxuries like that, we don't need. You're a spoiled, pampered rich girl from the city." And he would use the occasion to launch into an invective about the mill and how he was underpaid and what a burden his family was, riding the gravy train he provided. They'd just bought a new boat for Marcel's fishing and a new motor as well, but Emelie was too afraid to point out the double standard.

She was ashamed of the place and wouldn't invite Francine or Maddy over because of it. They both had such beautiful furniture. She didn't want them to see what her life was really like. The one thing I CAN do, she thought, is to keep the place just as spotless as theirs. Even if it hurt to clean on some days, it meant having some dignity.

She watched little René running his toy trucks around the faded linoleum floor. They were a present from Francine. René made engine noises and staged conversations between the imaginary drivers. He needs new jeans, she noticed. She was good with a sewing machine, of necessity, and had already patched the pants several times, but Marcel would accuse her of neglecting the boy if she asked for money to buy new ones. "Are you too busy to sew them?" he would say, meaning to be sarcastic. Or, "Let him get a little more use out of them, he's not in a fashion show."

Asking Marcel for anything was like planning an assault on Normandy. A wrong step and you got shot down. Diplomacy was better. Or maybe a tactical advance. Anticipate his objections and eliminate them first. She wouldn't have minded his miserly attitude if that's all it was, but asking for money gave him a chance to be lord of the manor and go on and on about what a crummy wife she was, and she couldn't disagree or he became even more upset. If he got himself worked up there was danger. When he said 'no' about new clothes for the kids, she just let it go, dragged out the sewing machine and fixed the old ones so they would last a bit longer.

The important thing was how the kids were always clean, she thought with a good deal of satisfaction. There was no way they would look like orphans and be a source of ridicule for other kids. Marcel could do what he wanted behind closed doors but the neighbours didn't need to know. If they kept things private, she and the kids could keep their self-respect.

# *Maddy*

After wringing out the laundry, Maddy, carting the basket under one arm and Lawrence's tricycle under the other, made her way up the basement stairs and out to the backyard to hang the washing on the clothesline in the spring sun. It was warm enough for her and Lawrence to be comfortable wearing light jackets.

The little boy climbed aboard his trike and laboriously struggled over the grassy ruts they called a lawn. It stretched away from the house until reaching an incline where bits of exposed rock served as steps, running two metres down to the beach. To the east and west, the yard was bordered by dense pine forest. Below the trees was a thick ginger carpet of dead needles. Today, a southern wind blew in the freshness of the water and decay of the beach but on still days the air was permeated with a heavy pine fragrance.

On the east perimeter stood a wooden shed constructed by Robert on one of his weekends at home. Along the opposite side, a vegetable garden with a low, protective wooden fence was the product of another home visit.

"Did you see the fence your father put 'round the garden?" Maddy called out over the wind to Lawrence, pausing between pinning up laundry.

He stopped riding, looking earnestly at the short pickets surrounding a damp patch of ground still waiting to be tilled.

"What's that for?"

"To keep the rabbits out so they don't eat all our carrots and stuff."

Lawrence got off his trike to inspect. "Rabbits..." He paused in mid-speech to stare directly upward as a flock of geese, madly honking at each other, flew low overhead. As if nothing had happened, he resumed. "...are bad buggers."

His mother answered something about this not being a good word. She caught only bits of his speech as he got back up on his trike, dropping his voice and talking to no one in particular. The rabbits had better not come around and eat the morning glories he had helped plant on some rocks by the lake or they'd be sorry. They could run "lickety-split" like some bunny or other in a book but he'd get his dad's gun and shoot them. He was an amalgam of Beatrix Potter-tempered, little boy innocence, with the unsentimental harsh sentiments of the northerner living in an antagonistic environment.

Maddy didn't approve of parents who bragged about their children but, even so, she would still tell people how her son was the most sociable little boy she had ever met. He would instantly warm up to anyone. And she told how he was a curious kid who knew how to read by the age of 3, but she declined to point out that there wasn't even a library in this desolate, God-forsaken town, not to mention there being nowhere to see a concert, play, or movie. In her mind the place was ignorant. No nice way to put it.

"Hello," Emelie loudly announced herself while still managing to sound tentative. She peeked around the corner of the house, and smiled broadly at Maddy in the way a little one does when they wake up from a nap and first see somebody.

"Come in! Come in!" Maddy's voice, muffled because of a couple of clothes pins in her mouth, beckoned her forward.

The rest of Emelie rounded the corner struggling with a padded, dark blue monstrosity of a carriage, piggishly resentful at being turned on the grass. The little boy by her side squealed and ran in the direction of Lawrence.

Emelie hesitantly looked back and forth as if waiting for some non-existent dogs to be set loose. "This carriage is too big and heavy," she said in annoyance, "it's impossible most of the time." Picking up the baby, she staggered to the back steps and sat down at Maddy's feet. "I should leave the stupid thing at home, and just carry Cecile."

"The crummy dirt roads around here…" Maddy sympathized. "I don't know how you manage to push a carriage. But anyway, nice to see you. And on a Saturday too!"

"Oh…yeah…I thought Marcel could use a break from us, you know?"

Under her short jacket Emelie wore a sun dress whose pattern had almost entirely drained away adding to the general impression she conveyed of insubstantiality and ethereality. Pulling the hem of the dress over her knees with her free hand, she smoothed it in a slow, deliberate way. She looked so slight that Maddy wouldn't have been surprised to see her whole body swept up by the breeze.

"A break? He doesn't get that from being at work all week?"

"Well, you know what I mean; time to himself." She shook her head, frowned and avoided Maddy's eyes. "He's under a lot of pressure at work." It sounded pat, rehearsed, meant to convince herself or her friend that any problems Marcel was experiencing weren't his fault. She looked childlike, Maddy thought, small with an earnest look on her face, like Lawrence. The mill's a bad bugger.

"When he's home René's all over him, you know. I think it gets on his nerves lately. It'd be hard on anyone's nerves." She pushed back her short hair, crisp with too much hair spray, and patted it in place as if it were an expensive perm. Her hair hadn't seen one of those in a long time

"He's a kid. Happy to see his dad…"

"I must be hard to live with too…"

"You? Oh, please."

"I'm always saying things without thinking. I provoke him."

"Don't talk like that."

Maddy had no idea what sort of pressure a janitor in a mill could be experiencing and she hadn't noticed René being particularly more vivacious than any other normal kid, but what are you going to say? She hung the last bit of laundry on the line.

"Anyway, I'm glad to see you Emelie…So, apart from annoying your husband, what have you been up to? I haven't seen you in a couple of weeks."

"Oh, you know, the usual. Busy, busy. And the baby had a cold so I was keeping her inside."

Maddy sat down on the steps beside Emelie. "Let me see this little punkin," she added, carefully taking the sleeping baby. "Give your arm a break. Hello Cecile," she whispered and gently, so as not to awaken her, stroked a round cheek with her forefinger.

Emelie smiled, rubbing and flexing her arm. The baby was no trouble, she said, very quiet, but heavy. "It looks like she's going to be big like her dad. She's the same weight as her brother was at twice her age."

"Oh my god, look at the dust on my shoes! They're grading the road today," Emelie said, blushing, acutely self-conscious as she always was in Maddy's presence. "I hope it doesn't get dirt all over your washing."

"No, the wind's blowing the other way…They say they're going to pave it. It'll be easier to walk but the cars will go by even faster. Six of one, half dozen of the other."

Emelie got up and took a tissue from her purse laying in the sullen carriage. She busied herself cleaning up her shoes. "Maybe I should put some fly dope on René."

"I think he'll be fine with the wind."

Across the yard Lawrence had helped René up on to the trike and was giving him a lecture about how to ride, all the while pushing from behind, trying to get him moving across the bumpy ground.

"No, not that way!" Maddy called to the two as they approached the rock steps by the lake. René get off the trike and the boys turned it around to point in the direction of the house.

The mothers resumed their conversation.

"Give me that you little bastard!" René could suddenly be heard screaming at Lawrence, and he began to slap him over and over. By the time Emelie and Maddy had rushed across the yard, Lawrence was sitting on the lawn, crying and rubbing his eyes with his little fists while René sat benignly on the tricycle.

"René!" his mother cried. She strode over to him and hauled him off the trike with a struggle. René roared and kicked at her.

"I'm sorry. I'm sorry," Emelie said to Maddy interspersed with, "I don't know where he's heard language like that." To René she was saying, "Look, you made Lawrence cry. He's your friend. You never hit your friends!"

"Don't worry. It's okay. You're fine, aren't you?" Maddy soothed Lawrence, who'd upped the volume of his crying because of the attention.

MADDY STOOD AT THE front window, thoughtful, and watched as Emelie and her kids passed from view. Was René imitating his father's behaviour, she wondered? He could only have heard language like that from Marcel. Is that the way his father talks to him? It wasn't unusual to scold your kids, parents do it all the time, but calling them names like 'bastard' was way too much. Or maybe those types of words had been directed at Emelie and the little boy just overheard. Emelie had indeed said how Marcel was acting different lately; that he was under a lot of stress.

But it wasn't just the language. There was René's aggression and violence. Was that imitation? And then she remembered the black eye a few weeks earlier that Emelie had tried so hard to hide. Had Marcel done that? Was it possible the bastard hit her; that his bad behaviour consisted of more than just language? Good men usually didn't hit their wives but these things happen often enough.

She caught herself. Violence didn't fit with Marcel's personality. He was slow and awkward, giving the impression of a pokey stumblebum. On the other hand, she'd discerned from some comments of Emelie's, about being afraid to look at men on the street, that Marcel was the jealous type.

Maddy suddenly wished she had tried harder to get Emelie to open up. Who else was Emelie going to confide in if not her, as she appeared to have only one other friend? The problem would be how to broach the subject of Marcel's behaviour. Or should she? It was none of her business and if she said something and was wrong, or if it was something Emelie wasn't ready to talk about, then their friendship could be jeopardized, and how would that help?

And what would she say if they were to talk about this and her suspicions were accurate? What advice could she give her? All the doctor could do was to make sure Emelie knew, if she needed someone to talk to or go to bat for her, that she could rely on Maddy.

It would be best, Maddy told herself, to counsel Emelie not to do anything too rash. There was nowhere for her to go if she left Marcel; not that anything so extreme was likely. She was an orphan. Her only family was a sister in Toronto who sounded like she could barely take care of herself and their relationship was strained anyway. Things would sort themselves out over time Maddy concluded.

# *Marcel*
# May

Following his big explosion in the winter, Marcel made an honest effort to curb his temper but there was no way to not get pissed off at certain things. At times he got to the point where he was going to blow up but slammed the door instead and marched out, or threw something against a wall, or pushed Emelie.

Marcel would apologize after, even though he thought it wasn't right. Sometimes, when he was silent, Emelie would ask him what was wrong but it couldn't be explained. It was just that at times he felt so angry there was no way he could talk until he had slammed something or yelled. Afterwards, the anger was gone and there was no point talking about it.

But lately Emelie was getting mouthy. She had told him that if he ever hit her again she'd leave.

"No you won't!" he'd yelled back. He wasn't going to take that kind of shit. A man's wife doesn't just up and leave without making him look ridiculous. Everyone would know what had happened.

"So where you think you're gonna go?" he added. "Your slutty sister's? The priest's? If you ever leave I'll go there and make sure you regret it for the rest of your life. I'll take the kids and you'll never see 'em again."

Violence looked to be the only way to keep order. If a few weeks went by and he didn't do something to keep Emelie in check, things would just go off the rails and she'd start acting like she was in charge or complain about how he treated her.

She got mad at him once, about his hitting René, but the kid needed it and he'd be damned if he was going to let anyone tell him what he could or couldn't do with his own son. If it took getting loud and putting Emelie in her place so she'd shut up and let life go on with some peace, then that's what he had to do.

# *Maddy*

Ewa Lampa let Maddy into Unit 3, a small hotel room with a kitchenette. A cross and a large painting of the virgin Mary with glowing heart had been hung on the wall hooks originally put there for the framed cardboard reprints of cowboys on horses that Paul Desjardins had personally selected, although thinking they were a little too good for DPs, but which were now stuffed under the bed.

It was close to midnight, and Maddy had already gone to bed when she got the call to make her way over to the motel to treat someone who was hurt. The source of the injuries hadn't been specified.

Ewa's husband Henryk, as Maddy found him, sitting on the bed in a sleeveless undershirt, was badly bruised on his face and arms.

"I'm okay," he said several times looking embarrassed by the attention.

Henryk Lampa was 61 years-old, Maddy ascertained, as she moved his limbs and looked at the bruises. He was lucky he hadn't been more seriously hurt.

"I tried to fight but three, four guys jumped me so I rolled in a ball to protect myself."

"You should have called the police."

"I did, but he just got mad on me when I called him. Same as last time." Henryk sounded disgusted.

"You mean this happened before?" Maddy was incredulous.

"Not me. My friend, Konrad. But the men always yell bad things at me too and call me Polack. The constable came and he got mad and talked to us in a way not right. He said maybe we should go live in Chicago where they got lots of Polacks."

"Did you recognize any of the men who jumped you?"

He hesitated. "No, it was too dark and it happened fast. I don't think those were boys from Wegebow. Maybe Hartley."

"Maybe you should travel together. Maybe you should fight back!"

"It's not so easy Doctor. You come back from the dance. You go visit your friend. You can't always have someone with you. They find you. Better to just try not to get killed."

Mrs. Clay, who was on her way out the door, had been Maddy's last scheduled patient of the day. It was only 10 a.m. the next morning. Maddy was tired and frustrated from her late night. How, she wondered, did you challenge a cop who obviously hated foreigners?

She thought about Emelie who had stopped coming by again. A week had passed and now a second.

It hadn't been a conscious decision to leave it to Emelie to choose the time and place when the two would get together, their friendship just developed that way. But they were friends after all so there was no reason why Maddy shouldn't pay her a visit. With no more patients and Lawrence being with Isabel, Maddy walked the several blocks to Emelie's house.

She knocked at the door and waited. No one came. She knocked again. Still no answer. When she was about to leave she noticed the door knob slowly turning. The door opened a few inches and René's face appeared around it.

"Hi sweetie, is your mommy here?"

"She is but she can't come to the door. She's sick."

"What's the matter with her?"

"Don't know. She just stays in bed."

"Well I guess I better have a look at her. I'm a doctor."

"Oh." He sounded uncertain.

"Maybe I can make her feel better."

René pulled open the door and stepped back.

Inside, Maddy walked through the livingroom. Had there been a fight? The furniture was pushed around. An end table was turned over. A lamp and an ashtray, along with its spilled contents, were on the floor in the middle of the room as was one of the beat up cushions from the chesterfield. The musty, stale smell was stifling.

"Emelie?" Maddy said tentatively, poking her head through the bedroom door.

Emelie was reclining on top of the covers, leaning against two propped up pillows, and Maddy had obviously just awoken her.

"Maddy, what're you doing here?" she slurred.

"My God! What happened to you!" Emelie's face was badly bruised in several places.

Maddy rushed to the bed to take a closer look. Emelie turned her head away. "Now don't tell me you banged your face on a cupboard door!"

"It's not a big deal." Emelie shifted her weight to sit up and winced in obvious pain.

The doctor sat down beside her. "Let me look at you." She cradled Emelie's chin in her hand.

"No. I'm okay," said Emelie pulling her head away.

Maddy withdrew her hand. The two women stared at each other. The conviction Maddy had let herself feel, that Marcel simply couldn't hurt his family despite the evidence, finally disappeared.

"God Emelie, when did this happen?"

"When did this not happen? It happens all the time. It was yesterday and last week and maybe the week before that." Emelie's tone was sanguine. She shifted and winced feeling the pain of resignation; of her last hope for privacy fading.

"All the time? So it wasn't just an argument? He does this regularly? The son of a bitch!" It came out as a loud whisper because even in her fury she kept René in mind, who was in the other room, and the baby who was likely sleeping. "I should go to the mill and scream at the bastard! Let the other men know what a coward he is for beating up a woman! Emelie, why didn't you tell me what was happening?"

"Because it's my problem. Please keep this between us."

"It's your problem? What about your kids? I can help."

"Things'll calm down. Marcel's just going through a bad spot. He's a good man at heart. He really is." Her tone was defensive. "I don't know what to do. I try to take care of him but he explodes about everything. We walk on eggshells. I don't know what it is we do that sets him off!" The volume of her voice had escalated and she began to cry.

"What you do? You think this is your fault? Goodness Emelie, wake up, Marcel's not right in the head. He should be in jail! You have to go to Bernie. He'll stop this stuff."

"But I don't want Marcel going to jail." She seemed jolted by the ugly sound of the word 'jail'.

"Then don't press charges. Bernie will talk to Marcel and straighten him out. It's the secrecy that's the problem. As long as he thinks he can do this and no one knows about it he'll keep doing it."

"No, absolutely not," Emelie said firmly. "This is my family, my life and my problem. Leave it to me."

## *Robert, Lawrence & Maddy*

*A beautiful Sunday, I wish it would never turn Monday*
*'Cus I lie between the sheets my bed adorning.*

Lawrence poked at his cereal while sitting in his high chair at the kitchen table and watched his father frying his own breakfast. Robert was singing along to the Harry Lauder record playing on the hi-fi, dropping his voice to a hopeful baritone, with comments to Maddy interspersed between the lyrics. He talked to her back because her hands were in a sink of soapy water. Sometimes when they played out this scene he'd wrap his arms around her and grope. Maddy would withdraw a soapy hand and push his arms away saying, "Lawrence" as the only explanation for why he should desist, and despite the fact that Lawrence was unaware of the sexual aspect of what he was watching.

"And the Major says, 'Youz should do it. There's some good prizes'."

He was telling Maddy, for maybe the fifth time, about his boxing career in the army.

"And of course you said, yes…Eat your breakfast Lawrence."

She didn't understand the male fascination with violence; couldn't even comprehend the violence in the cartoons they played before the movies where people had safes land on them or got chased over cliffs. Why would anyone laugh at someone else's misery?

"It wasn't the prizes, all you won was a razor and shave cream, that kinda stuff. It was just somethin' to do. I had three fights and won the camp championship in my weight division."

Maddy was only half listening. Emelie was on her mind, as she was almost all of the time lately, but this wasn't something to discuss with Robert. They were married but she wouldn't talk about her patients with him.

"Eat your breakfast Lawrence," was said with a quick look over her shoulder. "Do you have to use every dish in the place?" she added with startling vehemence as Robert dumped some cutlery and pots into the sink.

He paused, plate in hand on his way to the table. Her comment was somewhat of an affront because it had been said in the same tone used to speak to the little boy. It made him angry but he let it go.

"Don't fool around with your cereal," he said as he sat down, taking it out on Lawrence, who'd been watching his parents.

*Oh it's very nice, oh it's very, very nice*
*To have your breakfast in your bed on Sunday morning.*

Lawrence swayed. He liked this part and wished he could eat his cereal in bed on a tray, the way he did when he was sick. He swung his arms to the music until one hand bumped the cereal bowl. Most of the milk betrayed him and splashed across the floor.

"Look what you did," barked Robert, reaching over and cuffing him across the back of the head. "I told you to eat your breakfast and not play with it."

Lawrence howled.

Maddy spun around, deeply inhaled and then exhaled a loud cry. "What are you doing?" She slapped her wet hands against her apron as she went to comfort Lawrence. The hi-fi needle jumped with the force of her steps causing Harry Lauder to slide from *Beautiful Sunday* into the middle of *Stop Yer Tickling Jock*.

"I told him to smarten up! He doesn't listen!" Robert yelled, his temper having leapt up quicker than Maddy's. It frightened Lawrence even more. "He needs some discipline. In the army…"

"In the army? Listen to yourself! He's just a little boy! You're too tough with him."

"Kids need discipline. It'll make a man of him…Okay, fine, if that's what you want," he added, dropping his voice and feigning complacent surrender, "it'll be your fault when he gets older and we have no control over him."

Robert sat down to demonstrate complete indifference to the fact that, due to Maddy's indulgence, their son was destined for ignominy and disgrace.

In the face of Robert's aggression, and perhaps from some idea that a father had a right to discipline, however stupidly, Maddy said no more.

While buttering his toast, Robert softly sung along to Harry Lauder to prove he wasn't upset in the least; at peace feeling he had colonized the moral high ground of parenthood.

It wasn't so bad when you first went to bed. There was always a big fire and someone would cram as many logs into the stove as it could hold so you'd get suffocating heat for a few hours but by the time you woke up in the morning the wood was just ash and the air was frigid. You'd freeze your ass off if you didn't get out of bed at 5:30 a.m. or so when the men first began to stir. The smell of frying bacon was a lure. Some guys would get up early just to be the one who got the chance to sop their bread in the bacon grease.

Robert, lay on his bunk bed early the next morning, putting up with the cold, while visiting one of his personal demons—his sense of failure as a parent—to reach a temporary accommodation in order to get on with his life. He was a lousy father, he thought, maybe too rough on the kid, but he didn't like Maddy talking to him like she had the day before. He was within his rights to do what he did, but how do you ever get to the point of not feeling guilty for every stupid thing you do? To be fair, Maddy was too soft on the kid. She spoiled him and, in the long run some discipline was the best thing.

He should be home more. The kid was too attached to his mother and she to the boy. Robert didn't know where he fit in anymore.

He knew the war had changed him. The impulse was there, to lash out sometimes, but the more he thought about it the more he realized that getting after the kid wasn't about his short temper. It was about discipline and respect. The proper rationalization of his actions brought some peace on these mornings of self-recrimination. Once he'd reminded himself it was all in the kid's best interests, he could get up and take on the day.

# *Emelie*
# June

"Yes, yes, I understand what you're saying…you don't know when she'll be back."

Maddy opened her office door a few inches while she spoke on the phone to smile at Emelie, mouse-like and hesitant as usual, standing with her kids just inside the front door. René was absorbed in watching his friend, Lawrence, sitting on the tiled kitchen floor having his shoes tied by Isabel. Emelie held the shoulder of René's jersey to prevent him bolting into the house.

As she listened to the voice on the other end of the line, Maddy made a sweeping motion with her hand to tell Emelie to come in further; into the kitchen laying between them.

"Mr. Legross," she said, with her voice dropping as she pulled the door almost closed, "your wife made the appointment only two days ago…uh huh, uh huh."

Emelie, obediently shuffled her way forward to stand a few inches inside the kitchen, still restraining René in front of her while holding the baby with her other arm. She turned her attention to Isabel and Lawrence rather than continue listening to Maddy's conversation. In a moment Lawrence would be ready and they could head for the lake. Maddy's voice rose and fell. There was a stir of motion from the doctor's office and the sound of the phone being put back into its cradle.

"Sorry," apologized Maddy, pushing the office door wide open and coming into the kitchen. "It's the strangest thing, Chantal Legross made an appointment with me, now she's suddenly left town and all her husband says is 'something came up.'"

"Oh," Emelie replied flatly, because everyone knew what Chantal's husband was like. It was best not to think about where she'd gone. Just hope for the best. Still clutching René she turned and looked out the kitchen window and made a comment about what a nice day it was, not wanting to be talk about Chantal.

"Yes, it's lovely out," agreed Maddy. "That's why I wanted you to wait. It's a slow business day and I was hoping I could convince you to walk down to Main Street with me. Isabel said she'd keep the kids."

PART 1

# *Maddy*

In the centre of town, where the road dips down by the lake, the businesses catered to American hunters and fishermen. There was a marina and the town dock, where local kids in bathing suits could usually be seen kneeling with fishing lines wound around a short piece of wood. They would peer into the blue and then violently yank up a little bass or sunfish. From the dock, you could see Desjardins' Motel, an equipment shop, and Desjardins' Tours. Jean's Live Bait, Minnows & Gunsmithing was in a lop-sided building covered in tarpaper but announcing its presence with a vivid and cracked metal Coca-Cola sign showing a perky Santa slugging back a Coke.

On Main Street, one block up, was a bank, cleaners, supermarket, barbershop, beauty shop (with a four dollar perm), hardware store, restaurant (specializing in moose steaks and tortiere) and a Woolworth's. At the western end of Main was a gas station and coal yard. Such were the commercial interests of the town.

The two friends covered the creaking, crooked hardwood floors of Woolworth's. Maddy convinced Emelie to accept a present. Some underwear. Something pretty. Something for her. Marcel wouldn't notice a thing like that.

They sat at the lunch counter, gently twisting from side to side on the round stools which rotated on silver pedestals. Maddy had an orange pop and bought her friend a chocolate milkshake. Emelie loved the experience more than the drink, she said. They brought out a silver canister, filled it with ingredients and snapped it into place on a green blender with one of the thick threaded arms in the middle of the mixture. Turned on, the blender roared and the angry arm whirled. When peace fell again and they brought you the milkshake the thing that would make or break the experience for Emelie was whether or not they gave her the silver canister holding the liquid that wouldn't fit into the glass.

On the wall behind the lunch counter were tall mirrors running its entire length. The friends talked about some plastic flowers in a rack behind them, visible in the mirrors. They noticed a couple of Catholic matriarchs approaching so turned and smiled in their direction. The two walked past, averting their eyes.

"You better get used to being treated as if you don't exist Emelie, if you want to sit with me," Maddy said, laughing lightly.

"Don't worry. I'm used to it. I get the same thing and have since high school. The witches around here don't like outsiders. We're not as perfect as them. They're nasty, these damn women! I hate them and everything about this place. They're the reason I quit school and now I only wish I could get out of this town and away from them altogether."

Maddy was startled by the aggressiveness, but felt she understood. She seized upon the comment as an opening to talk about the subject she wanted to get to. "It's too bad you had to quit school to get away from people like that…Did you ever think of going back? You know, for yourself? You could take correspondence courses." Her voice rose with excitement despite wanting to make it sound as casual as possible, like the idea had just occurred to her. On the two occasions when she had tried to speak to Emelie about Marcel's violence she had been aggressively rebuffed for intruding into private matters so she knew she couldn't speak directly to that again. Her plan was to offer a solution without acknowledging the problem.

"Ah…no, never thought about it," Emelie said as if barely taking in the remark.

"Obviously, being a mother is terrific, and that wouldn't be affected by you finishing school. You have so much potential Emelie. It seems such a waste if you don't do something with it. You're only 23!"

"I couldn't be a doctor like you."

"No, no, you don't have to be a doctor. You could learn any profession you like. It would give you something of your own when the kids get to school. It would give you your own money."

Emelie frowned. Maddy's intrusion into her life wasn't going away, like a mosquito that eventually demands attention.

"Marcel'd never give me the money."

"I'll give you the money!"

She desperately hoped Emelie would say yes. Please, she thought, do this, make your own life and get away from this guy. She knew there was nowhere for Emelie to go as things were now, but with an education she could head for Winnipeg or Toronto and support her family on her own.

"No you won't! I couldn't take money from you!"

"Call it a loan."

"Marcel wouldn't let me I'm sure."

"You could just tell him you're taking them, don't mention the cost."

"You can say that Maddy. You never had anybody knocking you down whatever you tried to do." Her voice was rising. Tears were imminent. "I want to get the house looking nice or get decent things or go to the dances but Marcel stops me."

"But I do know what opposition is. I know it's not easy." And she told Emelie about her own parents forcing her to quit school.

"You didn't have kids when you went to school."

"No, but I had to work full-time and go to school at the same time. You could do it if you wanted."

Emelie just shook her head.

"You don't understand what he's like. He wouldn't let me."

As the two friends sat and spun back and forth, the subject turned to Maddy's fears for Lawrence's future. She confessed that after only one year here she was ready to move back home. It was a subject she'd avoided before but felt emboldened by Emelie's tirade about the nasty women in Wegebow to unleash a bit of her own frustration.

Emelie listened attentively to what the doctor said. She figured Maddy was just about perfect and had begun to try to be like her, even imitating her speech mannerisms and pet phrases. The things Maddy worried about for Lawrence — a good education, opportunity — were things she had never even considered with respect to her kids but now saw they wouldn't be getting them in Wegebow.

Emelie admitted wanting to move back to the city too. She hated everything about Wegebow and the people. And when she spoke, Maddy saw a shadow of isolation much darker and more futile than she'd imagined.

Emelie confessed that her husband expected his wife to spend her whole life at home preparing a sanctuary for him.

"When Marcel comes home from work he goes on and on asking about what I did all day. Like he's suspicious. Like I got a boyfriend," she snorted, "with two babies to look after. Jesus! He wants to know why I'm spending time with you. He says," and she parodied Marcel's voice, "'That woman figures she's smarter than us. She'll give you grand ideas about gettin' a job and tellin' you to waste your time readin'. Like there's something' wrong with that. Or, he says, 'she'll be givin' you advice about how to raise my kids'. He even hates me doing stuff with Francine — and she's Bernie's wife so she's his own family. He says, 'That woman runs the roads'."

Maddy didn't tell Emelie what she thought of her husband. What a lout! But she understood better why Emelie assumed there would be opposition to her taking any school courses. "Well, please keep the idea of correspondence school in mind. If it ever comes down to it and you worry about their future you could move back to Fort William with your kids." She was just planting the idea in Emelie's mind that she could get out on her own. She felt convinced that in the end Emelie would need to get the hell away from Marcel. There was no reason to think their kids wouldn't be better off if their parents lived in peace, and if they spent less time with a father who was an ignorant hillbilly.

# *Emelie*

Had she been right to tell Maddy what Marcel had said about her? She knew, when saying it, that Maddy would dislike him more, but so what, Maddy was her friend and she should be on her side.

The kids were having their afternoon nap and here she was, with a bit of time to herself, and all she wanted to do was lay down. Such was her life. She was exhausted.

It felt like she was in prison, confined mostly to this house, always to this town, and with only a bit of adult contact that she reached out to in desperation. But it wasn't like a jail exactly. More like one of the prison camps for soldiers she'd heard about. You could see the open space all around you, all you'd have to do was cut through some flimsy wire and make a run for it, but you didn't do it because even if you weren't cut down immediately you were in the middle of the bush and there was nowhere to run to. The citizens would hate you and hunt you down. Their language and yours were totally different. You couldn't even fake it. And if you got as far as a hostile city, well what would you do then? So, the reality was, all you could do was accept the loneliness of your situation.

She looked down at René who lay beside her, at his sleeping face, and she stroked his hair. In the dim light he looked angelic. She began to cry. That morning Marcel had been at him again, cursing and slapping him. All the boy wanted to do was to go for a ride in the car with his dad. Marcel had to go to work sure, but he didn't have to act like that!

What the hell was the matter with him? And what was the matter with her?

First time he pushed her she felt she'd provoked it, so she forgave him. Maybe that's what got her thinking everything was her fault. But it wasn't. Marcel loved her! She must have done something to make him forget it. If he could only feel those feelings again everything would be good again. She was tired of forgiving him. It seemed that's all she did and it didn't make him appreciate her. Just made him think he could get away with whatever he wanted. She'd spent too many hours over the last few months wondering what she could do to make Marcel's life easier so he wouldn't explode.

Maddy told her that Marcel should respect her but what did she know of such things? Emelie had listened and tried to lay down the law with Marcel. Enough was enough! But all it did was make him angrier and he slapped her.

She'd get out of here if she had anywhere to go. That was her only option. Marcel wouldn't stand for her going to school, so she'd have to go and work at any crummy job she could find.

It was a good thing Maddy found her all beaten up that day. It made her ashamed for Maddy to know what kind of husband she had. It made her furious he would humiliate her. Maybe her anger would help.

# *Marcel*

It was lousy outside one Saturday. It was pouring and a fishing trip with Bernie had been cancelled. Bernie was stuck in Port Arthur where he'd been testifying. It was a murder trial. The biggest crime in Wegebow's history. An Indian had been drunk and killed his drinking partner. For weeks it was all anyone in town talked about. There were stories it was a ritual killing. Some kind of Indian thing. People were saying the killer had tried to cut his victim's heart out.

There wasn't a boy in town who hadn't learned things about the bush from an Indian friend in school. There wasn't an adult who wouldn't ask one of the Cree men for help if he had a skunk under his porch or any of a thousand other problems that required some knowledge of nature. But even so, these same Wegebow adults continued to be imbued with the ideology of imperialism: Indians are children.

Marcel had things on his mind when Emelie, in apparent frustration over having previously asked him three times said, without her usual diplomacy, "Will you PLEASE take out the garbage?"

He lost control. This time he didn't slap her. He punched her, and when she curled up on the floor he kicked her repeatedly in a flurry of rapid, brutal blows.

Marcel didn't apologize after. Those days were past. Emelie wouldn't quit bugging him about crap. That's all it was. The only reason he went to see her where she lay on the bed afterwards was to tell her that this had been her fault for bothering him.

"Something's broken Marcel," she whispered through clenched teeth. "I think it's my shoulder. I need to go to the doctor."

"Shit! You're just imaginin' it. I barely touched ya. Get it out of your mind. You're not goin' to no fuckin' doctor."

But Emelie continued. She was afraid to move. She told Marcel he had to see to the kids and then take her to the doctor. There was no choice. Even Marcel eventually realized this wasn't just stubbornness; something was wrong.

They'd never been to Dr. MacQuigau. Marcel hadn't visited a doctor in his life and Emelie had seen Dr. Paisley in Hartley when her babies were born.

But it seemed best to Marcel, that if they had to see a doctor, they should go to someone who'd keep their mouth shut, even if it was a woman. She and Emelie were already best pals or something, and the doctor was married to Robert MacQuigau. Rob's a good man, thought Marcel, he'll understand that a man has rights within his family. If the doctor gave him any lip he'd go see Rob.

Dr. MacQuigau hustled to turn on the lights in her office. Emelie came in supported by her husband, the two of them doing a slow shuffle, pain tightening Emelie's face with every movement. Dr. MacQuigau told them to halt and stuck a chair under Emelie.

On examination, the doctor gently poked and prodded and asked several questions. It seemed possible, she said, that Emelie had a broken collarbone. No wonder she was in so much pain.

Throughout the exam, unprompted, Marcel interjected his version of events. What happened to Emelie was an accident. She fell off a chair while changing a light bulb. He'd told her about chairs tipping over when you don't stand in the middle but she didn't listen. She knew everything.

"You need an x-ray", Maddy said. "Let's get in the car and drive to Hartley."

Marcel cut her short, "We ain't going' to no Hartley. This is a private matter. I expect you to keep it private."

Dr. MacQuigau glared at him.

"Nothing is private Mr. Gagnon. Being married to someone doesn't give you the right to do whatever you want to them. Assaulting somebody is a criminal offence. You should be in jail!"

"Bernie? Yeah, go ahead and call him," Marcel scoffed, his face flushing despite the sarcastic tone. "I told ya she fell off a chair. You don't know what you're talkin' about. No wonder no one comes here. You're a crackpot. Come on Emelie," he announced, grabbing her wrist, "we're gettin' the hell outa here."

"Please," Emelie begged Maddy, pulling her hand back. "I fell off the chair."

Maddy said flatly, "You need to go to the hospital."

"No hospital," said Marcel.

"Please, just do what you can for me here," Emelie whispered between her clenched teeth.

PART 1

# *Maddy*

Maddy said nothing further in front of Marcel about assault charges—let him think nothing would come of this. But something had to be done. The injuries were shocking and disgusting.

The next day she went to the local O.P.P. office to see Bernie Boudreau and report Marcel's behaviour. She wasn't betraying Emelie's confidence. She was a doctor who knew directly of an assault.

Bernie and Marcel were close. Emelie once told Maddy that Marcel worshipped Bernie because he was a little older than him and had been in the war. Emelie sounded fed up, like she was being jilted for another lover, and her sour expression showed a distaste for the whole thing. She felt that Marcel's friendship with Bernie was the relationship that seemed to matter most in the world to him. He wanted Bernie's approval for every step he took.

"Marcel thinks they're comrades in arms. It's his chance to play soldier. He talks about Bernie all the time like he's in love with him, you know? Bernie this and Bernie that. He goes on about every detail of their stupid hunting and fishing trips. All I hear before they go is about their bloody plans and afterwards I have to hear about every boring thing that happened."

In spite of his friendship with Marcel she felt sure that Bernie would take some action. Most men would act gallantly when it came to violence against a woman, she was sure, and anyway, a crime reported by a doctor wasn't something you could ignore.

"Ah, welcome, come in, come in. Sit down Mrs. MacQuigau," Bernie said when Maddy arrived at the downtown storefront that people referred to as the police station. He butted his cigarette and waved away the smoke hanging in the air between them. "Whadaya got for me?" His uniform was the starch and polished leather of an ex-soldier, but his voice was so soft you had to strain to hear it.

Maddy went through the events of what happened.

Bernie shuffled papers as Maddy spoke, barely listening and with a half smile on his face, as if sharing a joke with an invisible someone about Maddy's concern for Emelie. She continued on, becoming increasingly angry.

"But you tell me both Marcel and Emelie say she fell off of a chair, eh?"

"Yes, that's what they said, but I'm a doctor. You don't get bruising all over your body from a simple fall. Emelie was repeatedly struck by someone or something. I'm reporting an assault to you as a doctor should and I expect you to take action on it."

"Mrs. MacQuigau…" Bernie sighed as if addressing a recalcitrant child.

"It's Dr. MacQuigau!"

"Dr. MacQuigau," he said, with emphasis, as if he were indulging a silly whim. "You've told me what you think but you aren't the police, right? When we get a complaint we investigate and determine what happened." His tone was condescending. "We know a little bit more about assaults than you…don't you think?"

"I know Marcel's your cousin, Constable, but that doesn't mean he didn't break the law."

Bernie began to frown. His voice became severe and surprisingly, to Maddy, it sounded officious and formal.

"Emelie's my friend as well. But I am fully capable of detaching myself from my feelings and looking at events fairly and accurately. If I weren't, I'd have someone from Hartley investigate…Righto," he said abruptly, with finality, lightly slapping his palms on the desk, suggesting decisiveness, "leave this with me and I'll look into it."

For a brief moment Maddy was seduced by his tone into thinking he would do his job.

A WEEK LATER THE doctor phoned Bernie to follow up.

"Ah, yeah, Dr. MacQuigau. Been meaning to call. We've concluded our investigation. Emelie has no interest in laying charges. She says Marcel didn't do anything to her. I don't know if she told you different or if you're just reading into things. My advice Doctor is that if Emelie ever comes to you with something like this again, and says Marcel did something or other, you send her home to her husband and tell her to stop bothering him. Marcel's a reasonable, hard-working man who looks after his family."

"Let me ask you something Bernie. As a man, doesn't it make you angry when you see a man beat up a woman?"

"That's not what happened here," he said with resignation. "Good-bye Doctor."

She slammed down the phone. Bernie was a coward. She'd held on to the faint hope that going to him would stop Marcel, that Bernie would grab him by the scruff of the neck and make him smarten up, that even if he couldn't do anything as a cop he'd at least be offended enough as a man to do something. But he protected Marcel the way he protected boys who preyed on Polish workers.

The men of Wegebow were all cowards! If she was able to she'd go to Marcel and beat the hell out of him. Let him know how it felt! Just the idea of administering some justice gave her a momentary reprieve from the sense of frustration. No wonder people sometimes took matters into their own hands. What were they supposed to do when the police showed themselves incapable of, or uninterested in, doing anything to stop a crime?

MADDY FELT HER HANDS were tied. She had to go outside of Wegebow for any results. She told Emelie about her talk with Bernie. Yes, she understood the distress it caused, but it had to be done, and now she was going to the O.P.P. in Hartley on her behalf.

Emelie begged her not to, and refused to go and file a complaint herself. She said she'd deny what happened if Maddy went on her own.

"Bernie works for the O.P.P.," Emelie said. "They'll listen to him. He'll come and tell Marcel you're still trying to make trouble for him, and Marcel'll slap me around again and threaten to hurt me and the kids if I ever tell you anything else. And he'll do it! If the cops did do something—say they charged him and he went to jail—the day he got out he'd come and find me and then I'm done. I'm sure of it. He told me he'd kill me if I ever went to the cops and I believe him."

Maddy didn't know what to do with those kind of statements. They were incredible but she was certain they were true. Going to the police in Hartley was out, but this son-of-a-bitch had to be stopped! There had to be some way.

# *Maddy*
# July

Emelie told Maddy how Marcel went on crowing about what he obviously saw as vindication. He'd only taken Emelie to see the bloody doctor, he would say, because of her whining so much, saying she had a broken collarbone or something. He knew it was bullshit. And it took this so-called doctor a whole day to figure out Emelie only had a hairline fracture (not that he had a clue what that meant) when anyone could see she was exaggerating. He, of course, had known it right away and tried to tell the doctor from the beginning, but she wouldn't listen to him. Figured she knew his wife better than he did. No way was it okay to go there again. The quack was just out to make trouble for him.

But Emelie hadn't listened to the prohibition. She told the doctor about Marcel's speech while standing in Maddy's kitchen.

Dr. MacQuigau practiced her own version of Medicare as did many doctors who lived in small, rural towns in the fifties. She overcharged those who could afford her services—not that they were aware of it—which allowed her to undercharge those who couldn't afford them. Because Emelie's visits had to be hidden from Marcel, Maddy charged her nothing at all.

The next week Emelie showed up first with cracked ribs and then to be treated for a partially dislocated shoulder. It seemed to Maddy that Bernie's lack of action had made Marcel bolder. It appeared he felt immune from prosecution, or maybe there was no longer any question in his mind he was doing anything wrong. Emelie told her how Marcel had lost it on one of the occasions which prompted a visit, beaten her up, and said afterwards, "Don't you ever move my toolbox again!"

It was only a matter of time, Maddy thought, until Marcel put Emelie in the hospital with some sort of critical injury.

As time went on Emelie's face grew thinner and more gaunt. Almost skeletal. And that appearance was compounded by the darkness around her eyes which made them look like two deep cavities.

The doctor was becoming adamant, Emelie had no other option but to go to the police in Hartley. Despite convincing arguments, Emelie was equally adamant, there was no way she'd go.

"It keeps my floors clean at least," Emelie said during one visit (demonstrating the black humour she was developing). And she continued on to tell how, when laying on the kitchen floor being kicked, she could smell the wax and knew by how strong the smell was whether the floor needed to be waxed again soon. She would try to remember when it was last done and pick a date to do it again.

Emelie's friend Francine would stop by and watch little René, the 4 year-old, when his mother went to the doctor. He couldn't be trusted not to say something in front of Marcel which would tip him off that they had been to Maddy's. The way it was going though, according to Emelie, she'd have to start bringing René to the doctor to be treated as well. Marcel was slapping him around more and more and talking about what he should do to cure the kid of his lack of respect.

"I should kill him!" Emelie said to the doctor one day. "He said he'd kill me if I ever left…One of us has got to die it seems."

"You don't mean that. It's crazy. We have to find some way to stop what's happening but that's not a productive way of thinking. You're sounding just like him and it's because you're scared."

"Maybe I should be acting like him," Emelie replied. There were tears of anger coalescing in her eyes. "You push me to fight back and go to the cops. So I try to stand up for myself. I threaten to leave. I demand he treat me like a human being and it just gets worse. I need to think about my own survival. I'm in a war. It's kill or be killed."

"It's not a war though, really. In a war there's no other options. Negotiations aren't possible. We just need to find another way to resolve this."

"I never felt like this before Maddy! My stomach is in a knot whenever he's at home. I'm sick with worry every time I talk to him because I don't know which Marcel I'm gonna get. Months have gone by and nothing's changed… Dogs get treated better. I always thought he loved us and wondered how he could act like he does. I tried to make him love us. But now I think if he loved me even a little bit, or loved those kids, he couldn't treat us like he does! I give up. I have to be tough and do whatever it takes to save myself."

"You know I'll try to help you Emelie, with whatever it is you do."

"I know. Thank heavens I have you. If I didn't I don't know what I'd do."

## *Maddy & Marcel*

Maddy had never specifically promised Emelie that she wouldn't speak to Marcel but it was something that had to be done. She knew there could be no mentioning details of a recent beating or Marcel would know his wife had been to see the doctor against his wishes. It would be tricky but Maddy felt she had to confront him all the same, to try and appeal to his humanity. It must be there somewhere. Emelie would never have married him in the first place if he'd always been violent. But she was now trapped in the life she wanted with Marcel, with no place to go for help and no way to escape. If Marcel was so determined to hurt her, the way he seemed to be, then he would. Emelie's only chance of survival was for him to stop attacking her.

So Dr. MacQuigau went to see Marcel Gagnon one Saturday afternoon after Emelie took the kids down by the lake. It was her chance. She considered the options ahead of time and her plan of attack was to approach the subject of Marcel's behaviour in general terms. Maybe make reference to the attack in June when he'd carted Emelie up to the doctor's. He couldn't wonder how she knew about that occasion. She'd play it by ear.

Maddy hoped that he might be out cutting the grass or working in the yard. Somewhere public. But, nearing the house, she remembered Emelie once saying how the yard and lawn were left to her to look after. Maddy wanted to stop and go home, suddenly struck with the gravity of her plan. No one was making her do this. It would be easy to turn around she thought, but she didn't.

To her good fortune she found Marcel standing out on his driveway. It had once been gravel, like the other driveways in town, but most of the rocks had wandered off and left two hard-packed clay ruts where the wheels of Marcel's huge Chevy traveled in and out.

Only Marcel's legs, protruding from a huge pair of rubber boots, and his behind, were visible. The rest of him was bent under the raised hood of his car as if it had unsuccessfully tried to digest him and was now in the process of regurgitation.

Maddy cleared her throat and said, "Marcel?"

He yanked his head back at the mention of his name. His sandy hair was trimmed in a close-shaven brush cut, like Bernie's, and his pale forehead glistened with sweat and oil smudges. He had a wrench in his hand. His first two fingers were nicotine stained and there was black grease caked across the knuckles.

"Whadaya want?" He stared coldly at Maddy.

She tried to take a calm, reasonable approach.

"I want to talk to you about Emelie?"

"Whadabout her?" He looked serious, like he was half anticipating to hear the doctor had come with new medical results.

"I was looking out my window and I saw her down on the beach. I couldn't believe the way she's changed. She's pale and thin and wobbly. She can't take any more of this. You're killing her."

"Bah! She come to see you? She tell you that bullshit?" He spat inexpertly. The spittle ran out of his mouth and he had to bend his head so it didn't dribble down the front of his shirt. It landed on his rubber boot.

"Fuck," he said.

"No, I told you, I saw her on the beach from my kitchen. She looks like a wreck. We both know what's happening. People treat their dogs better! And she was with your kids…"

Maddy waited for a rejoinder but Marcel shook his head, cursed and reached back under the hood as if to say, enough of this. He'd ignore her.

"She's a good mother and those kids need her," Maddy said to his broad backside, "and they need their father too. You have to take care of them, not treat them the way you treat Emelie. They love you…"

"This is my family!" Marcel bellowed, standing up and twisting around. He'd had it. "It's none of yer damn business! You call yerself a doctor. Women don't do stuff like that unless they're dykes or sumptin'. They look after their own families and don't meddle in other people's business. Keep the hell away from my kids and my wife bitch or you'll fuckin' regret it."

Maddy could smell his beery breath, his face was so close. She was 5'10" and not used to being afraid of men, but the tension in Marcel made her own muscles instinctively tense, to protect herself or flee. He raised the wrench. She stared back, refusing to let him see he could intimidate her.

Partially, he didn't hit her because she was a woman, but the bigger reason was that he was a coward.

"No! You keep away from your wife Marcel or you'll regret it." She attempted to say it slowly and deliberately, but her voice quavered.

Marcel suddenly pulled back his arm and hissed. His arm shook so badly did he want to hit her. Maddy involuntarily flinched, turned and walked away.

As she shakily made her way home, she thought about what Emelie's life must be like, being so afraid all the time, and having an out of control thug like Marcel thinking he could beat you with impunity. But it was impossible, she knew, to really put yourself in her place and understand.

# *Maddy*

Twenty years after the events of that spring and summer, Madeleine MacQuigau began a journal to record her version of what happened.

She wrote:

*After my visit to Marcel's I began to seriously consider the possibility that he might kill Emelie some day. She was broken, dispirited and weak. She couldn't stand much more. Even the kids were vulnerable.*

*I don't think he ever told Emelie I'd gone to see him. She never mentioned it anyway. Maybe she couldn't stand to argue with someone else, or just needed me too much to get angry.*

*The week following my visit, Marcel pummelled her so badly she suffered a miscarriage and broken ribs. He kept a closer watch on her after that and made more threats. Now he said he'd cripple her if she didn't keep away from me. He'd lost all control and was trying to isolate her.*

*My heart broke for Emelie. I felt so sorry for her. It was unbelievably frustrating, I had no idea what to do.*

*I'd been to the police and was branded an hysterical female, despite being a doctor.*

*I'd faced up to Marcel to no purpose except to make things worse.*

*He threatened to find her if she ever left him and to take the kids...and she believed him.*

I had used every form of persuasion I could think of to get Emelie to go to the O.P.P. in Hartley but it made no dint in her armour. It seemed her self-esteem was too shattered to believe she could go back to school and build a life for herself somewhere else. But when I think back I wonder if she was just being realistic; that she was too fatigued to take on any more.

And the unfortunate reality was that she couldn't leave. She had nowhere else to go. She had no family who could help — her aunt was dead by then and her sister was just scraping by in the city — and there were no social services.

Since Marcel wasn't about to stop the violence on his own, someone had to convince him to change his behaviour, and the only person I could think of who might have a chance of doing that was the priest. At least, everyone in town professed to be obedient Catholics, so it was worth the attempt.

I went to see Father McNeil to beg for his help.

The priest was in his seventies, a thin man with deep hollow cheeks but protruding Adam's apple and cheekbones that made his head look like a skull with only the flimsiest of flesh covering it. He was tall, slightly stooped, and his face pointed downward when he walked, giving him a birdlike appearance, as if he was about to start pecking the ground for seed.

Father McNeil showed Maddy into his tidy little office at the back of the church, cheerfully ushered her to a chair and asked how he could help.

"I wanted to tell him everything, so started in with stories about how I had first discovered Marcel's violence. How Emelie's bruises and long absences had made me suspect something was going on.

He sat there smiling at me for some reason while I talked. I think it was a sort of practiced pleasantness that meant he wasn't really listening. You could tell when what I was saying began to sink in because he started to look very stern.

I told the Father about finding Emelie beaten up in her home one day. The priest tsk tsked, shaking his head. And then I told him about the night a few months before when Marcel had supported Emelie up to my front door with a suspected broken collar bone. That's when Father McNeil looked most severe. I told him about the multiple injuries and the numerous times I had tried to convince Emelie to go to the police in Hartley. He winced. I told him about my fruitless efforts to get Bernie to address the violence and even my visit to Marcel's.

I wanted to continue with Emelie's recent visits to my office (they say confession is good for the soul) but something stopped me. The Father's manner made me distrustful. His most severe expressions only accompanied those times when I spoke about going to the police. Quite possibly, he wasn't angry because of what I was relating, about a distaste for Marcel's behaviour, but because he was angry at me for making a public fuss about it.

He picked up on the fact that the events of my history had stopped months before (I wasn't about to give it away that Emelie snuck over to see me against her husband's wishes).

"Why are you coming to me now? Why not back when this happened?"

"Well, I told you about Bernie," I said. "I was waiting to hear back from him."

"But you don't know if these things are still happening…"

"A tiger doesn't change its stripes."

His face relaxed and he smiled condescendingly at me in a way that looked too well rehearsed. I was getting tired of idiot men doing that.

"Poor girl. Poor girl," he added, shaking his head and looking off into the distance. That gave me a bit of hope.

The Father said he would speak to Marcel.

"Leave it to me, please," he said, with emphasis on the word 'please'. "I would appreciate if you didn't speak about this to anyone else. That won't help this family to heal in the long run. They'll do better in the future if they can maintain some privacy. I'll talk to Marcel and I'll talk to Emelie, somewhere away from her husband so she feels comfortable enough to be open with me and tell me the truth. And don't worry, I won't tell them where I heard about this."

For the next few days I hung on to the slight hope he'd inspired; that he would actually do something.

I should have known that my going to him wouldn't change a thing. Father McNeil acted as Bernie had before him.

Eight days later Emelie called and asked me to come and see her because she was so badly bruised that she didn't want to be seen in public.

I should have been prepared. The priest had concluded our meeting with a little talk about the sanctity of family and how necessary it was to preserve it.

Where is the morality of the Church? Father McNeil's hypocrisy was astounding. He talked about the sanctity of family, yet was making it clear he would stand by and watch a mother killed. I could only conclude his failure to do anything showed that his only interest was in protecting a man's right to do whatever he wanted with his family. What should I have expected differently from a church run by men, for men? The whole town was this little cozy place where they did whatever the hell they wanted.

For thirty years the priest had been assigned to this backwater. It was because of his lack of talent, I decided. This was likely where the Catholic Church garaged its worst talent. Then again, maybe they had kept this clown here because it was a place stupid enough to let the Church run their lives. And what was most scary was that there were people on earth who would give a man like this such power over their lives. The Church was all powerful here. I once had a patient, a Mrs. LaFlamme, who told me her husband had wanted to run for Mayor and get some rule changed so that other motels, besides the one belonging to church deacon Paul Desjardins, could open near the town dock, and the priest had gone to him and said that what he was doing was against the Catholic Church.

I was convinced that the one moral position I was sure of was that it was wrong to kill a helpless woman. If the Catholic Church didn't agree, then the Catholic Church was immoral. To not do everything in my power to stop Marcel would be to act immorally."

☙

# *Maddy*
# September

Robert always slept late on his first Saturday back home, so Maddy held off on the laundry until after lunch.

Lawrence ran his tricycle around the cement floor of the basement while his mother forced dripping laundry through the ringer of the washing machine and then tossed it in a basket. The basement was like one you'd find in any new house on the outskirts of Toronto where Maddy grew up. The new was always at the edge of the city, like the proverbial tree that added a ring to its trunk every few years. And the further out you went the bigger the houses got, and even more so, the yards. The nearer the offspring stock of the original British immigrants got to the countryside it seemed the closer they were to the dream bred into them; that of being gentry with their own estates.

Maddy had a passion for houses. As a girl she'd forever be looking at them and drawing floorplans of the sort of place she'd like. When she and Robert moved to Wegebow and looked around, they saw only the unattractive dwellings of the north. They were just a cheap means of shelter. "I don't want a house that looks like a hunting camp," she told Robert. So she did a drawing and they took it to an architect. Their new house, with built-in doctor's office, stood at the outskirts of town, the last house at the east end of Wegebow, right on the lake.

"What's that?" Lawrence asked, pointing to a piece of clothing he'd run over.

"A brassiere."

It was inconsequential but there was something in her voice that caused a puzzled look on his face. It was a mundane question; still Maddy felt uncomfortable by it. But she'd previously made the unusual decision of deciding not to be shy about anything her son asked in curiosity, about sex or any other subject, and to answer him openly.

"What's that?" Lawrence asked, for further clarification.

"My underwear."

He lost interest and rode on.

Maddy was satisfied with the unremarkable response. A brassiere was an ordinary thing after all. Here was the point of being open. Bodies and sex wouldn't be so sensationalized if people weren't afraid to talk about them. Kids would get the adult version of bodies, as sex objects, soon enough. Let them be kids as long as possible.

She could hear Robert up in the kitchen, back from the hardware store. She heard him coming downstairs and could tell from his walk and then his face that something was bothering him. He had a reddish, freckled, Viking complexion, inherited from a Scottish trapper who came to the area many years before, but his face flushed crimson when he was upset.

Smiling, she said hello.

"Why've you been makin' trouble for Marcel Gagnon?" he asked brusquely, squaring his stocky frame and planting his hands on his hips.

"Did he tell you that?"

"Yeah, he said you tried to start a conspiracy against him. You figured he hit his wife after she fell off a chair, so you been trying to turn his wife and the town against him. He said you even went to the police and the priest! Is that true?" His tone was incredulous and accusatory.

Maddy was furious, Robert of all people should have supported her! He always had in the past.

"Fell off a chair? Emelie has been coming to see me every couple of weeks or so for the last five months. The bastard beats the hell out of her regularly. Who's side are you on? Are you trying to justify his actions?"

Robert hesitated, confused by this version of events. The volume of his voice dropped. "You know I'm on your side. I always am. I'm not trying to justify anything. If he's treating his wife like that there are ways of dealing with it. If Bernie won't help, go to the cops in Hartley. You can't attack a man here in Wegebow. Three quarters of them are bloody related to each other. They all stick together."

"Oh, and you're so different? Listen to yourself! You're so ready to believe them. That's the trouble. You're all family here. I couldn't talk to you about this because I can't discuss my patients, but I always wished I could. I figured if I ever did say something you'd be a man and grab Marcel by the scruff of the neck and make him smarten up!"

"Hey, I'm not related to that clan! Don't lump us together. I stick up for my family too but if I was like the people around here I'd be living in Sudbury, on the same block as my parents. You don't get it do you? I have to live here. We have to live here. Our son has to. Attacking Marcel in public, telling people what you think is going on, will only backfire. It'll just mean we're ostracized. Shit goes on here like it does anywhere else. People don't want their dirty laundry hung out in public, or their neighbour's dirty laundry either. They'll just hate the messenger."

"This whole town is filled with hypocrites then. Bloody pious Catholic backwoods' types who ignore anything they don't want to admit exists."

"Maybe. But most towns are like that, right? As much as I'm on your side Maddy, this isn't the way to change it."

Lawrence had begun to cry watching his parents. His mother picked him up and said nothing further to Robert as she brushed past him on her way upstairs. Let him do his own dirty laundry! She was furious with him and the gutless men of this town. What he had in fact been saying, she thought, was that there wasn't a single one of them who'd raise a finger to protect Emelie. They all respected each other's right to get carried away and treat their wives however they saw fit. It was something to note for the future.

"I always take your side," Robert's voice rose as he followed her up the stairs and into the kitchen. "Marcel wouldn't do anything so extreme. There's gotta be more to this than him just beating her up. People don't suddenly turn into something they're not and Marcel was never like that his whole life. He was always this big stumblebum who plodded around with a stupid smile on his face. I'm sure he loves her…Maybe Emelie is just really fragile and her bones break easily." He was getting louder.

Maddy let it go. When he got loud he was intimidating. It was a bully's way to win an argument. She stopped talking when he did this even though she knew he figured when she shut up that he'd won; as if her silence meant she was in agreement.

PART 1

# *Maddy*
# Mid-September

Six months had gone by since a broken collarbone had forced Marcel to bring his wife to Maddy's office. During that time Emelie had been to the doctor, as a patient, fourteen more times. She was slowly being killed. Two days ago, little René had come in with a broken arm, courtesy of his dad.

Emelie never left the house any more except to see Maddy for treatment. She was lethargic when dragging herself into the office, as if she'd given up on the idea there was any way to stop what was happening.

It was pointless, Maddy concluded, to continue badgering her about going to the police and it would be pointless to see the police on her own when both Marcel and Emelie would deny any story of abuse.

Maddy refused to give up. Robert had been away for the last two months. Hydro was trying to get as much work done as possible before winter. But even if he'd been there she doubted she would try to put it on his shoulders to stop what was happening. He was away too much. Even if she convinced him to go beyond his don't-get-involved-with-families attitude and intervene, things would just start up again after he left town. It had to come from, and could only come from, the law and the church. It was their responsibility, but she didn't know how to get them to accept it.

So Maddy had twice more gone to see Bernie. He threatened to get a restraining order if she went near any of Marcel's family again. She saw the priest again as well and he told her she wasn't a Catholic so should stop attempting to interfere with Catholic families. The authorities of the town, the men whom Emelie needed to uphold morality, did nothing. Inexorably Maddy felt that if Emelie was to be saved she would have to do it herself but had no idea of what more she could possibly do.

MADDY WROTE:

> *Taking the law into your own hands wasn't something one could justify, yet it was a sign of my desperation that it was something I eventually came to consider. Of course I dismissed it. It was like the thought of suicide when you're down. It's not something you seriously contemplate, but the idea makes you feel better, as if there's actually a solution out there. But now, for the first time, I thought seriously about the morality of it. I wanted simple and clear moral absolutes to guide me but couldn't find them.*

*Taking the law into your own hands shouldn't happen, I realized. That's why there are laws and police, to stop people from doing whatever they please. But in Emelie's case the laws and police had failed. They took the side of the criminal.*

*So would it be wrong to intercede? Marcel would never stop the violence. There was no hope. The church wouldn't help. Emelie had no family to rely on. I'd been holding on to anything I could. I kept thinking Bernie would physically intercede to stop Marcel from terrorizing his wife, but the truth was that the only one she had on her side was me.*

*She'd been driven to the point of saying she wanted to kill Marcel. It was 'kill or be killed', she said. It was a war. Marcel wasn't a Hitler — to suggest it would have been ludicrous — but there was a principle there. If you could have killed Hitler before the war and prevented all of the carnage, wouldn't you have done so? I would have. So, if you knew someone was about to kill another human being, even one, didn't the same principle apply? Emelie had to protect her children however she could. It was moral to do what ever you could to stop someone from killing another person.*

*Marcel was actively engaged in violence. Making sure he didn't kill Emelie and her children wouldn't even be a proactive act, like killing Hitler would've been. It would be an act of defence of her children and an act of self-defence. I didn't think Emelie could really kill her husband, but I understood the anger and frustration. If I was Emelie, driving a car, and Marcel was walking across the road in front of me, I would be hard pressed to make myself stop, I told myself.*

☙

IN HER 1972 JOURNAL Maddy could still remember the precise details of Emelie's visit to her office that fall day.

An emaciated and exhausted Emelie sat facing her across the desk while the baby slept in her carriage and the little boy lay on the floor where his left arm with the cast on it rested. He ran a toy car around the legs of a chair with his good arm, and only paid attention to where his mother was, looking at her, when she shifted her position.

Dr. Madeleine MacQuigau sat behind her heavy wooden desk, watching Emelie.

"He had his rifle out," Emelie was saying, "'cus he'd been sitting out back cleaning it."

"René was crying. I put him in bed and he didn't want to take a nap. Three or four times Marcel stuck his head in the backdoor and yelled, 'shut the kid up!'. When René wouldn't stop, Marcel came slamming his way into the house and pointed the damn rifle right at him. His hands were shaking and I thought, oh my God he's going to kill him, I really did, and I begged him to put the gun away."

"You know the way I think," Maddy said. "You only have one option. I'll drive you to Hartley right now."

"No," said Emelie, her voice dropping back into the soft register of resignation. "We've skinned that cat. They'll call Bernie who'll say it's just two hysterical women being crazy and they'll believe him and Marcel will kill me afterwards. Maddy," her voice took on a more plaintive tone, "I'm so afraid he's going to keep hurting the kids, I have to do something. I really do, in all seriousness, think I have to kill him no matter what that means for me. A mother has to protect her babies."

Maddy's face reddened, but she wouldn't have been able to explain why she felt embarrassed. Emelie had made similar comments every time they'd gotten together for the last three months.

"That's crazy Emelie! You can't think that way."

"I've got to. I could shoot him." Her voice was still weak but the hate in it was palpable. "He's got a lotta guns. Maybe use the same damn rifle he pointed at René. That'd be bloody fitting! Just put it to his head. Put it to his head and fire. Problem with making it look like an accident though is that I don't touch the guns. I wouldn't be cleaning it. I wouldn't be playing with it. I guess I could say I was moving it. I'm not just talking. It shows you how bad it is that I've thought about it for real."

Maddy hesitated, uncertain if Emelie was serious or not. "And you know what would happen after?"

"What? I don't ... Yeah I do, they'd hang me."

"And then where would your kids be?"

"They'd be alive!"

"And they'd have no parents…This is absolute madness to be talking like this, as you well know. Look what he's done to you…got you thinking like him. I've been thinking of something for awhile. It's the only solution I can come up with." She paused for the dramatic effect that would ensure Emelie's attention. "Go to Toronto."

Emelie smiled and shook her head at the impossibility of the idea.

"No, no, wait, listen to me. I have relatives and friends there. I'm sure if I asked I could find someone to put you up. You could get some kind of job and then a place of your own. I'll give you money in the meantime to get by." She was brightening with the thought of it. "Think of it, a whole new life, with no fear for you or your kids."

She watched Emelie for an answer. René got up off the floor, stood beside Emelie and put his head in her lap, the tone of the discussion possibly conveying to him that something odd was happening and he needed comfort because of it.

"That's unbelievably kind," said Emelie, "but I can't impose on people's lives. It'd be too much. It could go on for a year or two or three. But I know Marcel. The son of a bitch wouldn't stop until he found us and then he'd kill one or all of us…God I hate men! I shoulda been a goddammed nun."

Neither woman spoke for awhile.

"I wouldn't care you know," Emelie said. "It's funny, you're telling me this is crazy. For me, it feels like my only way out. If I have to kill his father to protect little René I will, and I'll let 'em hang me."

She looked fierce.

Maddy tried to remain calm by controlling the movement of her hands, slowly and deliberately straightening the pen, blotter and papers on her desk. She thought, yes, if Emelie could kill the bastard she probably should. Here was the perversity of the situation in its starkest form. No one had the moral integrity to protect this woman or her kids, but if Emelie were to do so herself she'd become a criminal and they would probably kill her!

"Okay, let's say you killed Marcel. Now you're in jail. What'll happen to your kids?"

"They'll end up with his family." Emelie answered immediately. She had no family who would press the issue. "Actually, I don't know if that lot would even take 'em. They don't want anything to do with Marcel."

"So where do they end up? Orphans? With some family somewhere. You need to improve their lives, not hurt them."

"That'd still be better for them than being killed."

Maddy sighed. She hadn't planned to do what happened next. She watched Emelie for a moment, then got up and went to a glass-doored cupboard, withdrawing a key from the pocket of her skirt. She hesitated before slowly unlocking and opening the doors. The doctor ran her fingers along the large bottles on the second shelf from the top before they stopped on one containing a very strong sleeping draught. It was seldom given to patients because a large dose could easily be fatal. She hesitated again, then removed the bottle of pills, set them on the front of her desk and sat back down.

"We're friends," she said. "You may hate me for doing this but I love you dearly. I'm not suggesting you do anything, just telling you I'll support you whatever you do. The bottle of pills on the desk contains enough drug to be lethal. Ten or so of these crushed up in Marcel's food would kill him. I guess he'd eat them if they were in something like a meatloaf where he couldn't taste them. Bernie would come and so would I. I'd be asked to examine the body and issue a death certificate. If I said it was a heart attack, it would be believed, especially if you told everyone that Marcel had been saying for an hour or two beforehand how he had chest pains. They'll curse me later, talk about how he would've seen a doctor if there was a real one in town and not just this woman."

Emelie looked dead calm, as if she hadn't heard.

"As I say, I'm not telling you what to do. Not even offering. Just telling you about a drug. The bottle is there. We've finished our appointment now. If I turn around and the bottle is gone I won't report it. I won't even know it's missing. If it's still there, I'll wonder how it got left out, put it away, and make sure it stays locked up forever. Bye Emelie."

Rising, Dr. MacQuigau turned her back to Emelie and looked out the window. Not twenty feet away was a thick stand of trees, impenetrable and dark, despite the fact it was a bright day. Maddy couldn't see the house next door through the bush even though it was only a hundred feet up the road. That was the trouble with this place. Not so long ago, because of the war, the realities of the outside world had intruded into life here, but now the town was drawing back under cover, to a place where unspeakable things happened but no one talked about them or did anything to stop them.

Nothing was said. There was a long quiet while the bottle cast a beckoning come hither look at Emelie; a seductive promise of a less brutal life.

Maddy heard Emelie get out of her chair and pick up the little boy. There was movement and unknown noises. A purse opening? Hair being brushed? A purse closing? The door opened.

"Bye Dolly."

Maddy hadn't been called that since she was small. When the door closed she turned and saw that the bottle was gone. There was elation but dread. Despite coming to the conclusion after a year of watching Emelie become a punching bag that anything she might do to protect herself and her children was moral and warranted, it had still been a sudden decision to facilitate the deed herself.

The implications of what she'd done began to register. If something happened to Marcel, she was directly involved! In a few minutes she'd gone from someone sympathetically watching Emelie's fate unfold to being an accomplice in a murder!

She sat down at her desk, shaking. How could this have happened? What was going to transpire in the near future, that Marcel would die, was now inevitable. The adrenaline rushed through her body and she felt she was going to vomit.

In the moment of madness, just passed, Maddy hadn't thought of what would happen to her if the murder was discovered. She would hang the same as Emelie! How could she have done something so insane, on impulse?

She tried to calm herself and think dispassionately. What had she done, really? She had turned her back to Emelie. There was a bottle of pills on the desk. She hadn't advised murder, just let Emelie know what the pills could do. It was Emelie's doing if they were used to kill Marcel! If caught—and Maddy suddenly grabbed on to the thought—she could say Emelie had stolen the pills. But who would believe it? Everything we do has ramifications she chided herself, we need to consider the consequences of our actions before we take them, and she hadn't.

There would still be time to stop Emelie. It had to be done! She wrestled on her coat and boots, but something made her stop at the small mirror by the door and begin to fiercely brush her hair. For someone in such a great hurry she brushed her hair for a long time, the strokes gradually slowing down. She thought about Emelie. Without some sort of extreme action she, and maybe her son too, would soon be dead. Undoubtedly, what was meant to be would now happen. All that Maddy had done for Emelie was to offer her the means to fight back. What Emelie chose to do with that power was her decision. She must support her, whatever she did. What Maddy had done in giving Emelie the means to end her suffering was to act in the same way she always had, for the same reason she'd become a doctor; to preserve life. Maddy slowly took off her coat.

IN THE DAYS AFTER Emelie's visit there were no phone calls to say her husband had fallen ill. Maddy felt so terrified every time the phone rang, thinking it might be Emelie, that she wanted to pull the phone out of the wall as if it had something to do with her misery.

Over and over Maddy reviewed the reasons why she'd acted as she had. It swamped her thoughts as she tried to work and carry on her life.

While examining a patient, Julie Frechette, Maddy looked up when Julie's droning recitation of her symptoms suddenly stopped. The patient was studying her face because Maddy hadn't been listening. This type of thing was happening over and over. And she was uncharacteristically curt at times when something was said to her.

Maddy couldn't grant herself peace from guilty thoughts about abandoning her family. If Marcel was murdered and she was caught, what would happen to them? This was horrible! How could she have not thought of them until after the fact?

PART 1

PERVERSELY, MADDY'S ATTITUDE BEGAN to change as a week went by and nothing happened. Why was Emelie doing nothing? Was she about to stand by and let Marcel kill her and René? Maddy had risked her safety and the future of her family to help her and now the foolish girl was doing nothing.

Maddy vacillated daily in her thoughts. At times she was glad Emelie had done nothing and hoped she wouldn't. That would give Maddy some peace. That's what mattered. She hated Emelie for being a weak, stupid girl who had other options but was too cowardly to take them. Her refusal to go to the O.P.P. has led to this disaster. Maddy got angry at herself for getting dragged into such a girl's life. She should get the pills back for her own safety and that of her family. But, as with all of her resolutions, Maddy didn't act on them.

Quickly going off to sleep had become a thing of the past. Each night she would eventually decide that on the next day she would retrieve the pills from Emelie. That was the only thing that would calm the anxiety enough to let sleep come. But it was just a lie to find some rest because in the morning she'd remember why she gotten involved in the first place and then she would do nothing.

Maddy flipped back and forth a hundred times between guilt and regret on the one hand, and vindication for her actions on the other. She didn't know this was a conflict she would struggle with for the rest of her life.

IT WAS 1 A.M. when the phone call came.

"Marcel's dead! He had a heart attack. Come quickly."

Dr. MacQuigau awoke Isabel and told her she was leaving before rushing off to Emelie's house.

Emelie was watching out the window and pulled open the door before the doctor was halfway up the walk. The second Maddy came into the house Emelie clutched her and started to sob, bouncing up and down in her nervousness.

They stood like that for a whole minute before Maddy stepped back and took a firm hold of Emelie's arms.

"Stop...stop...stop. Breathe deep. Stop. Where's the kids?"

"Asleep. Oh my God Maddy, what did I do? This can't be happening!"

"Sh. Sh. It'll be okay."

"I gave him..." Emelie gasped for breath, "the pills..." and she paused again to find some air, "you know? I didn't think...I thought nothing was going to happen. A long time went by...Then I heard it. There was a thump." Emelie put her hands on her cheeks and then over her eyes as if she were watching a violent car crash and couldn't bear it. "He fell. I knew it then. It happened. I came in and he was on the floor." She waved her arms low, back and forth to illustrate. When she tried to continue. Her mouth moved but no words came out. Her lips gaped before she burst out with, "Oh damn, Maddy! I shouldn't have done this, you pushed me to it! Why did you do it? I wouldn't have done this on my own! Oh God! Why did I bloody listen?"

"Listen? To me? It was your idea in the first place Emelie and it was always your decision."

"It's okay. You meant well. You meant it for me." Emelie wasn't listening. "I just can't believe it's really happening…Oh Maddy…they're gonna hang us! They're gonna kill us! There's no way we're gettin' away with this. Oh my God! Oh my God!"

Maddy was furious with the suggestion she had pushed Emelie to kill her husband, but instead of showing it she wrapped her arms around Emelie saying, "Sh, sh. Just wait here till I go look at Marcel. Okay?"

Marcel was slumped in the crummy easy chair in the livingroom. One of his legs was buckled beneath him, twisting itself as the body had slid towards the floor. As Maddy examined it and felt for the non-existent pulse, her hands shook violently.

She rose to her feet and stared at the body. "Damn, damn, damn," she muttered under her breath. Could this possibly turn out okay in the end?

Next step would be to go back to Emelie and calm her down. Go over the story. Make sure the girl could remember. Geez. Here it was…the fatal flaw. Potentially. In all of the frustration and wonder as to whether she would or wouldn't give her husband the pills, the question Maddy should have been asking was whether Emelie was capable of doing this without giving them away?

Maddy took Emelie by the hand, led her into the kitchen and sat her down in a chair.

"You have to listen to me and remember what I'm going to tell you about the symptoms of a heart attack. When Bernie gets here you need to tell him Marcel experienced all of these. We can go over them until you feel you can do it. Okay?"

"Okay," Emelie said. "Yes. Oh thank you so much."

"If you do this well maybe Bernie will believe Marcel had a heart attack. Listen to me very closely. We'll go over this until you can repeat it…First, put on a long sleeve blouse to cover the bruises."

A HALF HOUR LATER they called Bernie and waited. It was amazing to Maddy how easily things went. They told Bernie what happened and Emelie's performance was flawless. As she spoke the doctor appeared to re-examine Marcel.

"Yes," she said, touching his neck and pushing his face slightly to one side as if examining him, "the symptoms and the condition of the body makes it pretty obvious. He died of a massive heart attack."

It was nonsense but Dr. MacQuigau saw that Bernie believed everything. She was amazed at his reaction. He cried.

It wasn't so surprising to her in retrospect. It was a small town and Bernie was inexperienced in these things. And Marcel was family. Bernie sputtered out how if there'd been a real doctor in town this never would have happened. Marcel would've been seeing him and the doctor would've recognized Marcel was sick just from looking at him.

Soon, Bernie turned professional and called the funeral home.

## *Maddy, Paul, & Emelie*

The funeral service for Marcel Gagnon was held in the Catholic parish church.

Mayor Paul Desjardins was there imagining the eyes of the parishioners were on him, posing in his regal way, as the model of the sort of upright Christian man who was needed in Wegebow. The Desjardins were an impressive sight as they filed into their pew; nine scrubbed and well-dressed children, hands folded and serious looking. Paul and Gracie were not exceptionally prolific producers by northern Catholic standards but their 9 offspring were, still, a nice haul of new souls for the church.

As expected, few of the people that Maddy saw as she climbed the steps to the church returned her gaze or said hello. They looked stiff and awkward in their dressy 'Sunday clothes'. The men's suits—from the Sears or Eaton's catalogues—were mostly ill-fitting. Hems dragged on the floor and cuffs rubbed against the backs of hands. The women wore dark hats and incongruously bright red lipstick. Some of their dresses had come from catalogues or Woolworth's but most were made from patterns. They were a community still poor enough to be able to look after themselves.

When Paul Desjardins saw Maddy sitting alone he momentarily deserted his family to slide into the pew beside her. He kept a more than polite distance but sat sideways, facing her, with his left elbow leaning on the pew in front of them.

"Thanks for coming," he said, as if speaking on behalf of the town.

"Oh, not at all. Emelie's my friend and neighbour…What a tragic day."

"Yes, yes, terrible for the whole family, but they'll get support here. We value families in Wegebow. It's not like the south—beggin' your pardon—where people don't do what they have to do to make families work. Here we stand up for Christian families."

Paul looked smug. He liked to address women in a way that demonstrated his commitment to family and religion. He wasn't entirely conscious of it. It was just that he felt women deferred to him when he took the role of pontificator on family values.

"It's true. People often don't put forth the effort," Maddy said vaguely, looking about for Emelie, annoyed at this platitudinous line of conversation. She understood his point, sometimes people do walk away too easily from a marriage, and some do take a cavalier attitude to commitments, but she had just spent a year watching Emelie almost being killed because she stayed in a Christian Wegebow marriage and wasn't inclined to agree about the virtue of sticking it out when things got bad. Paul's diatribe sounded self-righteous and naïve but Maddy wasn't going to argue with him and disclose anything of Emelie's life.

Paul looked at Maddy intently and expectantly, waiting for her to say something more.

"Well," he said, breaking the silence, "I should get back."

"Yes," Maddy said, and looked past him at his family. "They all look so lovely," she said of the kids, "so well-behaved, like angels."

"Thank you," he beamed.

Maddy had grown up as a Catholic but left the church at marriage. Either she or Robert needed to convert and Maddy decided to make the choice for both of them. Her decision to leave the Church came after hearing a priest say at mass that a dead child was unfortunately going to be denied heaven because he hadn't been baptized as Catholic. Maddy had missed the anti-ecumenical section of the bible; the one saying that the Catholic Church was the one true faith.

In the first row of pews an older woman dressed in black was being comforted by a younger woman; or at least the young one was holding her arm. The elder lady was looking around, checking out anyone coming through the door, and looked to be coping rather well. Was that Marcel's mother, Maddy wondered? The people near the lady would be his extended family. She recognized some of them from having seen them around town and even knew a few of their names, but there were many unfamiliar faces.

Emelie was already there, sitting in the front row of pews on the right, also dressed in black, with her two young children beside her. Bernie's wife Francine held the baby while the little boy stood on the bench curiously looking around. Maddy got up and made her way down to the front to sit beside Emelie. She took her hand. Emelie smiled appreciatively and dabbed at her eyes when the service started.

In his homily, Father McNeil sounded subdued, perhaps even bored. His head bobbed gently from side to side, like a dove's, as he spoke of how Christ had died in order that our sins could be forgiven and our souls have eternal life. He emphasized the importance of the Eucharist on this day. "'Whoever eats my flesh and drinks my blood shall live forever', said Jesus".

'Family' was the subject of the priest's message. Family above all. Marcel was a devoted family man who understood this. Apparently, there's a special place in heaven reserved for men like Marcel, the parishioners learned. Men of exceptional familial devotion.

The priest pointed to the Gagnon family from which Marcel sprang, sitting there in the pews, and to the wife and kids whom he so obviously adored. It would be a great comfort for Marcel to know his family would provide support for each other, the Father said. He spoke directly to them and looked benignly at Emelie.

Did this mean that she would have to provide emotional support for Marcel's clan, Emelie wondered with some panic? It was a group she barely knew. Looking over she saw his mother stoically staring straight ahead. None of the other relatives cast a reciprocal glance back at her either.

"The family, for Catholics, is holy because it's symbolic of the body of Christ," continued Father McNeil, now warming up, leaning forward and proffering the tone of a lecturer. "The father of the family is the symbol of the Lord himself. He's the father who leads, rules and decides by his wisdom and mercy. God the father. The mother is symbolic of the church, bringing to mind Mary, the blessed virgin. Holy mother church. She creates a home and life that can be lived in accordance with the wisdom of the father. The children are like you, the worshippers. The lost sheep for whom mother church functions. Children should be obedient and unquestioning. They need to honour their father and mother.

"Marcel Gagnon stood firm for the values of family when it is lived as the mystical body of Christ; as a devoted husband and father who wanted his family to grow up in the ways of the Lord. As such, his life must be celebrated."

Emelie began to feel comforted by the priest's words because of their fantastical nature. It would be good if her kids and the town all thought of Marcel as a good man. Who then would suspect what she'd done? But, as Father McNeil twittered on, Emelie increasingly felt the urge to shout that it was all a lie; that she'd killed the bastard because the men of Wegebow refused to acknowledge what he was. She suppressed the suicidal impulse — what was wrong with her? — yet it would be good if men knew what could happen when they beat up their families. Marcel wasn't the only violent one by a long shot.

"We must remember brother Marcel," continued the Father, getting louder and more passionate, his voice taking on the squawk of an avian predator. He waved his right hand with his forefinger and thumb spread apart, as if he were a kid making an air pistol who would soon cock his thumb and shoot the doubters. "Let his life have meaning for all of us. Let it help us stand against all the things that weaken families.

"First among these is our recent experience of the war where many women worked outside of the home while their men were overseas. Women performed heroically, but the war is over and they need to return to their houses. They forget that the central fact of their existence here on earth is not their selfish desire for individual acclaim, or the material goods they can obtain from a second income, but to be a wife and mother." Anyone could see he was clearly choleric at this intrusion into the male domain. "A woman who works, when she doesn't have to, shames her husband. It tells him he is incompetent to provide adequately for his family. It turns God's directive, that man is the head of the household, upside down. And the working mother does irreparable harm to her children. They're left with babysitters as she neglects her motherly duties. These children suffer a lifelong lack of self-esteem and confidence resulting from being abandoned by their mothers."

Maddy looked attentively at the priest as he spoke, wondering at what point the speech had switched from being about Marcel to being an attack on her, or maybe women in general.

"Catholics are correct to be concerned about this tendency; to put individual attainment ahead of their spiritual duty. This has led to the disintegration of morality. It has led to the devaluing of the family as a whole. To the use of contraceptives. To the neglect of the central reason for families, which is to reproduce and expand God's family.

"Everywhere I look, I see the signs of moral decay." The priest paused and shook his head at the trend. His voice dropped into a deep sort of sadness. "I see it in the movies playing in Hartley. I see it in the music and dances we have right here in Wegebow. I see it in the increasing tendency of women to indulge an obsession with fashion, to wear pants and immodest swimwear, inciting the lust of men around them, making them forget their marriage vows and causing them to sin in their thoughts. We must shelter our children from these things and refuse them in our own lives." His voice rose again and spittle flew from his lips as he warned of the vileness of loose women.

"Let the recent inoculations that science has discovered to protect us from disease serve as a model for our lives. We must inoculate our families against the disease of moral depravity. To do this end we must cut them off from the sources of immorality. We should not allow them to wear provocative clothing or to dance lasciviously."

Paul Desjardins nodded in agreement.

"Monitor your children's friends and especially who they date. Increasingly we are faced with the difficult situation of mixed marriages, of Catholics marrying non-Catholics. Non-Catholics simply do not have an understanding of the strict moral rules that Catholics abide by; of our profound adherence to family and morality. Such marriages become a battle for the souls of the children, and these are struggles we must win in order to ensure the children are brought up in the one true church.

"Let me remind all of you parents of the central importance of providing discipline. 'For if a man know not how to rule his own house, how shall he take care of the church of God?' it says in First Timothy 3:5. If you spare the rod your children will be spoiled. It is they who will pay with their eternal souls for your negligence."

Father McNeil looked accusingly at Emelie, and paused. He had stated the morality of families and even Emelie, who didn't worry about such things, could see he was saying that the moral high ground belonged to Marcel. She and the Father stared at each other. Emelie dropped Maddy's hand and stood up, still staring at the priest. She took her daughter from Francine, and grabbing René's hand, shakily squeezed her way between the mourners' knees and the pews in front of them. At the end of the row she straightened herself, squared her shoulders and marched down the middle aisle, and out of the church. She had turned her back on the priest and the altar without even blessing herself.

"Let us all, on judgment day, be able to say, like Marcel Gagnon, that I provided a strict set of rules for the behaviour of my wife and children, and insisted they live their lives in accordance with them; to compel them to live their lives in the way of the Lord." The priest's voice intensified to something like an eagle's scream so that Emelie could hear his words as she marched away from him. The shocked parishioners didn't dare to turn their heads and watch her go.

CR SO

# PART 2
## *Marcel's Love*

WHEN HE WAS YOUNG, 6 or 7 years-old, and it was winter, Marcel, accustomed to no breakfast, would rise early, get dressed, put on three grubby sweaters and a cloth coat with two buttons missing, take his brother's mitts, knowing he would have them back before Guy needed them (although Marcel would still catch hell because the mitts would be wet), then he'd head for the bush.

He loved roaming the trails. The trees are pretty stumpy by the time you get as far north as Wegebow, with slices of Canadian Shield granite protruding through the dreary terrain, making it almost impassable, but the bush teems with wildlife because, unlike the south, there are very few hunters in orange vests blasting every creature out of a tree or off the ground who dared to move its unfortunate head.

Marcel lived a solitary existence with no real friends. Sometimes, much younger kids would attach themselves to him for periods of time, until he lost his mystique. He was a big awkward guy, 5'10" by the time he was in grade 7, and, on meeting him, smaller boys would be in awe of his size and immediately defer to him.

The band of boys, following Marcel's direction, would creep around the forest floor with slingshots and pick off partridge with unbelievable accuracy. One of the Ojibwa kids had taught them all how to call geese so perfectly that members of an overhead flock would swoop down, directly in front of them, to look for their lost member. It's the kind of thing one needs to see to appreciate the skill involved.

The Gagnons lived in one of the wooden houses on Second Avenue. It was grimy and dreary inside. The exterior had once been white but eventually became grey. The paint had begun to peel as if the wood was shedding its veneer of civilization and returning to primeval forest. It was a house that even the neighbours in their own little wooden houses looked down on, lived in by a family they saw as primitive.

Sometimes Marcel's dad, Francois, would take his oldest son Guy out hunting, but their trips never included Marcel. He longed to join them and would lie to the younger boy that, yeah, the three of them were going on a hunting trip, yet it never happened. At first the story was that Marcel was too young, but when he was older, Guy and his dad would just take off when he wasn't around and not even bother with the nicety of pretence.

After a time, Marcel would have been happy just for the chance to accompany the men to shoot off a .22 at the dump or the gravel pit.

Francois sat on his porch every night and put back four or five beers. Not violent but incoherent, he would slur his words as the beer took effect.

"Little bastard," he'd drunkenly mumble at Marcel sometimes. "Why can't you be like Guy. He's a real man that one, my son Guy."

Marcel had no idea how to please the old man nor understood why he so much preferred his older brother. Sometimes Marcel expressed an opinion of his own, demonstrating he was a functioning human being. This drove Francois to bring out his belt and wail on the kid long after he made his point of how displeased he was at Marcel's uppitiness. Marcel got to be terrified to say anything and of being around the old man at all.

MARCEL ALWAYS KNEW HE wasn't going anywhere in school, even on his first day there. It was another world, one he was just visiting for awhile. He was awkward and shy around kids his own age. It was hard for him to get his large fingers to work, to learn how to handle a pencil, or to muster any kind of co-ordination and grace when playing sports, even though he was rugged enough.

Kids kept away from him. They called him names. 'bushboy' or 'retard'. His lack of co-ordination got him beaten up a couple of times by smaller kids but his sheer bulk helped him knock down a few others, so eventually kids didn't call him 'retard' any more, except from a long way away.

At age 16, Marcel quit school, and his father got him a job at the paper mill as a janitor, sweeping, shovelling and picking up mostly. It was 1944 and there was a shortage of workers because of the war. He was making decent money for a 16 year-old and began to save in the hopes of one day buying a car.

MARCEL HAD NEVER BEEN comfortable with girls since first encountering them at age 5. They were odd creatures with small damp hands you had to dance with sometimes in kindergarten and he wasn't sure he liked them very much. They were little but they were intimidating. He had almost never touched a female before, only very occasionally his mother. She would sometimes hug Guy and call him her "handsome young man," but such a thing would've been ludicrous with a huge lump like Marcel.

With age, Marcel's interest in girls developed but he was too terrified to speak to one, even when she spoke to him first, extended some kindness, or treated him as if he was just another guy. He held court a bit with some younger boys, boasting of his imaginary exploits with the opposite sex. They drifted away from him as they realized the stories were lies.

Marcel didn't like to go near the high school after he quit, but was drawn to the town hall on the Friday nights when they had dances, wanting to be around people of his own species; other kids his own age. From time to time he'd develop a crush on one of the girls of Wegebow. It was a pointless exercise in frustration since he didn't know how to proceed to even speak to the poor thing.

At the dances, Marcel would stand by the door looking ready to run like a deer at the sound of a rifleshot. He always wore his one pair of dress pants and the short-sleeved shirt that he liked because his brother Guy wore one similar. Guy watched movies and knew how to dress sharp. Marcel was growing his hair like his brother's and combing it back with something they called 'slickum'.

MARCEL GAGNON NEVER TOOK his eyes off Emelie LeClair, 17 and doll-like, wearing some flowered spring dress. He watched her at the Legion hall as she danced, laughed and chatted to her friends. Everything about her was like a dance, her smile, her laugh, her walk, the way she flicked her sandy hair and even her serenity when she sat by herself.

The LeClair girls had moved to Wegebow and started at the high school shortly after Marcel quit. Their parents had just died or had died earlier and they were living with one of their aunts. Marcel didn't know the full story.

He thought about Emelie every night as he lay in bed. It was always the same fantasy. There was a forest fire and Marcel would rush in and rescue her. He'd embellished it over many weeks. First he just had to run through smoke to get her. Then he added flames. One night he threw in a bear, and then a rushing river to be crossed. Emelie's ankle became twisted and he had to carry her. Marcel imagined his shirt had become torn and his muscles were exposed, like the pictures in one of those men's magazines he would clandestinely look at in the store.

The two girls wore city fashions, and seemed exotic to the boys, who lined up to dance with them. They were 'easy' guys said. If you wanted to get lucky try one of the LeClairs. Marcel felt nauseous on first hearing that. His faith in Emelie's innocence had almost been shattered when he heard the remark, but it was Chester who said it and he was a fool. And as soon as he said it his girlfriend Viola had fired back that boys thought that way because the LeClairs were from Fort William. This made sense to Marcel. Everyone knew there were bars and lots of people in Fort William. It was a city. People always thought the worst of anyone from the city; they were so experienced. Marcel clung to Viola's comment like a lifeline.

Rumours began circulating that Emelie was seeing Vincent Lavoie. It was crushing news, at first, but it became something that didn't matter. It wasn't as if Emelie would ever have noticed him anyway, a girl like that.

AT A DANCE ONE night in April, Marcel stood by the door and stared at Emelie as she danced. But then, in the middle of his trance, she looked back at him. He reddened and averted his eyes in panic. Could she have read his thoughts? He glanced back and saw her preoccupied, talking to another girl and even though they walked in his direction he continued to stare, hypnotized.

When Emelie passed by with her friend she looked at Marcel again and smiled. Caught, he blushed once more and quickly bowed his head. When he raised his eyes, angry at himself for being too shy to smile back, he didn't see her.

"Why don't you move inside a little more?" she asked, suddenly right beside him.

"Er. Uh."

"Aren't you cold?"

Marcel went from chilly to frozen. "Ah, no."

And then she moved off.

Marcel attempted to appear interested in the others at the dance while he struggled to breathe. It hadn't been much of a conversation but he consoled himself that he'd at least answered.

It was almost too much to bear when Emelie later strode purposefully across the room and said, "Dance with me?"

"I...I don't dance."

"I'll show you how," she said and held out her arms in the position of a dancer.

To his eternal pride, Marcel danced with her. Twice. First time was a quick number. They went round and round in a heady kaleidoscope of disorienting colour. Marcel's step was just a shuffle and his knees regularly banged Emelie's thighs she was such a tiny thing.

They stayed on the floor for a slow dance and it was an even more dizzying experience for Marcel with Emelie's head pressed up against his chest. She smelt good, like lilacs, the way the drawers in his grandmother's dresser smelled.

When it was over Emelie smiled at him and said thank you.

"Thanks," he mumbled back.

"I'm Emelie. You're Guy Gagnon's brother aren't you?"

Oh damn! What had she heard about him?

"Yeah."

"I've seen you before," she said. "Maybe I'll see you again. Maybe we can dance again." And she smiled, walking off back to her friends.

THE TWO BROTHERS SHARED one bedroom. Unlike others their age who had tacked felt pennants on their walls from exotic locales like Port Arthur, North Bay or Sault Ste. Marie, the only decoration in the boys' room was a picture of Betty Grable that Guy had clandestinely torn from a magazine in a store rack and hung up with a finishing nail. He'd kept it folded up in his pocket for two weeks so it had ridges across the important parts and you had to look at it straight on or you couldn't tell what it was a picture of.

After the dance, Marcel pretended to sleep when his piss drunk brother came home. He wanted to stay in his dreams with Emelie and knew that if Guy noticed him awake he'd start to drunkenly ramble at him, something like, "When I was a young puke like you I didn't have a car or a girl but now I'm the sharpest guy around this town. You never gotta worry 'bout that though, eh."

Guy wasn't overstating his popularity. The local kids saw him as hugely admirable because of his carefully slicked back hair, with a tail that looked like it'd been sliced off a wet muskrat, and the fact he'd kept a pack of smokes tucked in his sleeve since the age of 15. When he got a car it was loud, rusty, sullen and refused to start. Often the smaller kids on the street would have to gather behind it and push. Guy would pop the gears and rev the hell out of the thing. Huge belches of smoke were emitted from the exhaust pipe. Guy's success at getting the car running was a victory they all shared.

Marcel didn't play the usual fantasy reels in his head that night, but relived the dance, recalling every detail about Emelie's appearance, her touch and her smell. She was so angelic, how had it happened she wanted to dance with him? Yet, despite the celestial comparisons, for the first time Marcel began to think of Emelie as a real, sentient human being. He wanted to touch her, to hug her or take her in his arms. That'd be enough. He was falling too much in love to want it to be more; to sully it somehow.

AT WORK, MARCEL BEGAN to daydream about walking with Emelie and holding her hand. He'd be her boyfriend. There goes Marcel and Emelie people would say as they went past. Maybe when they were married they'd get a place of their own on Second Avenue, just up the street from his parents.

At night, Marcel began to walk the streets of Wegebow in the hopes of spying his love. He finally saw her, a week after the dance, when she passed him on Main Street walking with her friends. He was ready to smile and wave at her, but she acted as if she hadn't seen him or didn't know him.

One of the people in her group was Vincent Lavoie.

Stupid, stupid puke! Marcel thought about himself for having gotten so carried away. He knew it, he had said it to himself in his moments of daydreaming about Emelie, that there was no chance these things would ever happen. But thinking about her was a pleasure he'd been unable to control, and he had let his fantasies go in the most fantastical directions. Now he was going to pay for his weakness.

In the coming weeks Marcel would remind himself of the horrible feeling of seeing Emelie with her boyfriend every time his daydreams of her started to take over. Maybe they were a sin, he thought. He'd imagined himself with a girl and now he felt worse than before, like he was being punished for it.

AT THE NEXT DANCE Emelie again approached him with her Saturday smile. It was as if she was completely unaware of the tragedy he'd gone through; of his suffering and self-rebuke. But all was forgotten in an instant when Emelie asked him to dance.

It was a slow dance. To be close to a woman was unique and Marcel was intensely aware of even the slightest touch between them, of the least bit of contact of fabric to fabric. The smell of Ivory soap seemed suddenly lovely.

As they slowly turned in their shuffling gait, Marcel looked at several young men reluctantly inching just inside the hall, curious and trying to look inconspicuous, afraid of someone noticing or speaking to them, yet magnetically drawn to the place. But this time Marcel wasn't among the group. He now belonged to the dance and felt triumphant.

This time, when the dance was finished, Emelie held on to his hand, just for a moment too long, just long enough for it to feel like she meant it.

They sat down together and Emelie asked Marcel about his job, what he did at the mill, how he liked it, did he have a car and what were his plans? She was practiced and at ease conversing while Marcel managed to get by with grunts and a few words sprinkled in here and there.

They danced a second time and then a third. It was Emelie who did the initiating.

"Why don't you ask me to dance?" she said to Marcel, and he decided that the next time he would. Not at this dance of course but the next one.

When the music finished for the last time that night, Emelie asked Marcel if he'd walk her home.

Marcel's life was magnificent, he was about to be seen by others, walking home with Emelie LeClair. He'd look after her. It was as if all his dreams had come true. When they got to Emelie's house she told Marcel to phone her if he wanted.

"I have a car," he blurted, "if you wanna go to the movies in Hartley next week we can." It was more than he had said in one fell swoop all night, perhaps the first real sentence he'd strung together around Emelie. And she said yes.

THEY DROVE TO THE Royal Theatre in Hartley. Marcel had only been to the movies once before, when he was younger and some kid's parents had taken him along to a matinee because at the time they drove by to pick up their son he was playing on the road with Marcel.

The movie experience wasn't the same as it had been on Marcel's first visit. There was no popcorn or drinks flying through the air. The usher in the nifty red jacket wasn't coming around turning on his flashlight every five minutes telling someone to pipe down.

Marcel found the movie hard to follow. His attention was too riveted on the fact he was sitting beside Emelie LeClair and even though she stared straight ahead her arm sometimes rested against his. It was best, he thought, not to take notice of the couples around them who'd gone there to neck, since it just terrified him to think he might ever kiss her.

On the drive home Emelie talked non-stop about the movie, others she'd seen, and of how terrific the coming attractions looked to be. The pair decided to go again the next week. They did and they went every Saturday night after that. It was a good place for Marcel since it didn't require any conversation.

WHEN THE SCHOOL TERM ended for Emelie, the two of them saw each other every night and Marcel's ability to converse began to improve. Because he didn't want to talk about his childhood at first, about BB guns and shooting birds, he talked about work. Sometimes he voiced the opinions of the men he heard in the lunchroom. There was an iron curtain in Europe, Mr. Churchill had said, and the Chinese were at war with themselves. Communists were the new enemy. Marcel railed that DPs coming from Europe were sucking the blood out of the Canadian economy and the like.

Emelie was more generous. Everyone deserved the chance at a better life. Fortunately, with her, Marcel didn't need to say much. She talked enthusiastically, going on and on about her life, family, friends and people in the town, commenting on what a good listener Marcel was.

Marcel was in love and he found every commonplace Emelie spoke about, whether it was her family or simply what she did during the day, fascinating. He took her side in everything and found all her quips funny. They were so much alike he felt, neither of them fit in. They understood each other's feelings without even needing to have them explained.

Marcel began to develop some rational opinions about the behaviour of the people Emelie talked about, but at other times he'd bristle and make comments about how women gossiped too much. It was a remark his father mumbled from time to time. Emelie didn't seem to take offence.

Marcel's family and himself weren't subjects he wanted to discuss with Emelie since they were huge embarrassments, but she gradually coaxed information out of him and reacted with sympathy. She was on his side and defended him when he told her how he was treated by his parents and schoolmates.

Marcel had never experienced anything like this. Emelie trusted his version of things and said his heart was a good one. So he told her everything about himself and he was flooded with love.

She was everything he had always lacked in his life.

THE YOUNG PAIR BEGAN to go for long walks in the bush. Marcel was at home there and he showed Emelie how to creep up on a beaver lodge in the early evening so as not to disturb the beavers while they glided across the pond in the dimming light and waddled ashore, grunting to each other. The couple would see who could pull the longest strip of birch bark off a tree, avoiding the holes left by woodpeckers. It encouraged Marcel enough, when Emelie said she was impressed with his knowledge of the bush, for him to go on at length about animals, birds, and wild plants.

"If you're ever starvin' pull out some of these Queen Anne's Lace and eat the root. It's what the Indians do. Tastes like parsnip."

His knowledge was the end result of many hours of trekking about, observing, fishing.

"For pickerel and pike you wanna troll in a boat but bass like the reeds, but reeds'll get caught up in your motor if its runnin', so just drift," he said, as if Emelie was likely to be out on her own in a boat sometime soon looking for a nice place to land some fish for dinner.

And he told her about the legends. Huge muskies that could drag you to the bottom of the lake. Moose that had been hit by cars and killed whole families.

Marcel and Emelie began to talk about getting married, although there'd been no proposal as such, it just came to be assumed this was what they both wanted. And they did. The plan was to rent one of the small apartments on the main street above the stores. There were always vacancies because the single men who worked in the mill came and went.

In September, Marcel said it was time to get married.

"I NEED TO TALK to you," Aunt Estelle said to Marcel two weeks before the wedding. "It's important. Will you come 'round to the house tomorrow and bring your fiancé?" Aunt Estelle managed the town hall where the dances were held and had watched with interest, but detachment, the budding relationship between her nephew and Emelie.

Marcel agreed to the meeting request. The next day was Sunday so he'd sleep till noon, eat, pick up Emelie and then head to Estelle's. Her house on Tenth Street was small and well kept up.

Aunt Estelle had been married to Marcel's mother's brother so she had the good fortune to not be related by blood to anyone in the Gagnon clan.

Marcel felt nothing for her, neither positive or negative, and had gone to her place slightly bewildered. He contemplated not going at all but Emelie told him they should go out of courtesy. The old lady's just nosey, he thought, looking for something to gossip about. Women!

"Come on in," Estelle said, and led them through the house to the kitchen. She still retained her French accent. Originally from Montreal, she met her husband when he'd been there for some kind of course the paper company had sent him on. They never had any children.

Marcel followed awkwardly. Everything was neat and prim. There were lace doilies on the arms and backs of the furniture. He was afraid of banging into one of the little tables with a flower vase or knick knacks on it.

The small kitchen window had been replaced by a picture window, the size usually found in a living room, so it was a bright room and one could see the birds flitting around a feeder in the back yard.

"I've often thought about what I'd say to you when we had this talk," Estelle began, once they were all sitting down around the kitchen table. "I've worried for three years, and I still don't know how to say this. I sorta hoped I wouldn't have to, that I could just settle this in my will. So I think the best thing is to just tell you what happened and what was said."

Marcel stared at her.

"Okay, I see I'm not making any sense…About twenty years ago there was a surveyor who lived at the motel for awhile. He worked for Hydro and would fly into the bush and back every day. Sometimes he was gone for a couple of days at a time but mostly he'd fly back every night around dinnertime, eat at the restaurant, and then go back to the motel. He was a real big guy, like you.

"You won't remember, because it was before your time, but your mom used to work nights at the motel until around eleven. She'd take Guy and he'd sleep on a cot in the back. Sometimes I watched him at your house. Your dad was a teamster up in the bush where they did the logging and he was away for weeks at a time. Your mom used to say she loved her job. I think she worked there for around a year and then got pregnant and quit when you were born. It would've been too hard to look after two babies and work too.

"About three years ago a man came to see me. His name was Jack and he told me he was the surveyor who used to stay at the hotel. This is the part I was just talking about…er, when I was saying that…I didn't know how to tell you what I had to say. So, what I am going to do, is just to tell you exactly what the guy said to me.

"Jack told me that when he was living here twenty years ago he would spend every night sitting in the front office of the motel talking to your mom and playing with Guy. Jack and your mom became close and they had an affair. Keep in mind I'm only the messenger here! They were both already married but they were lonely too. It's no excuse but things like that happen, especially here where men often work away from home. You probably heard stories about some of the women whose husbands were away during the war. Same thing.

"Anyway, what Jack told me was that your mother got pregnant with you, and he was the father. He said your mom wanted to run off with him but he wasn't interested in divorcing his wife. His job finished up here so he went home and hoped his wife would never know what happened. He did some checking later and found out your mother had the child. He guessed she probably never told her husband he wasn't the father because no one ever asked him for money for your upkeep. Jack got off lucky I suppose you could say, your mom never went to see him and his wife never found out.

"When Jack visited me three years ago he said it was because he was dying from cancer. He gave me some money and asked me to give it to you when you got married so you could put it towards a house. If you didn't get married I was supposed to give you the money when I saw fit. Jack said he wanted you to know about him. I don't know why. He said I was the only one he trusted to tell you about the past."

Estelle pulled a large envelope from her apron pocket and placed it in front of Marcel who appeared to have reached a new level of confusion. Emelie took his hand.

"I bought these bonds in your name with the money. If someone finds out about them you can say they were from me, if you like. It'll upset Guy and your parents who'll wonder why I'm favouring you over Guy and not giving him money as well, but I can live with their cold shoulder. They never wanted anything to do with me anyway."

"You mean my dad is not my dad?" Marcel said, staring at the envelope.
"Yes."
"That Jack guy is my dad?"
"Yes."
"Where is he?"

"I think he must be dead by now dear. I'm sorry."

"Why didn't he tell me himself?"

"He told me it was because he didn't know how. You didn't know him and he didn't know you or how you'd react. Maybe he didn't know how to approach you since you were only 14 or 15. I don't know, it sounded like he was ascared of your reaction."

"Do I have brothers and sisters?"

"No. Jack said he had no kids with his wife."

"What's Jack's last name?"

"He didn't say and I don't remember from before."

"So my dad doesn't know about this?"

"I don't know. I don't think your mom told him. Your father was away a lot when your mom got pregnant so he might have figured it out, or maybe there were rumours."

"So my mom was a slut!?" Marcel said angrily looking around the room.

"No, you have to forgive her. She was young and lonely. They both were. Things like that happen."

Estelle talked to Marcel until he calmed down. Emelie had said nothing to him the whole time, just squeezed his hand.

MARCEL AND EMELIE ELOPED. They didn't want their marriage to be a family affair. Marcel wouldn't confront his family about the past, it was better "to let sleeping dogs lie" Emelie said, but he didn't want anything more to do with them. His dad was not his dad, his brother was only a half-brother and his mom hadn't wanted him or was angry at him or something. She'd rejected him. Emelie was the first person who ever really loved him and he'd start a family with her. A real one, the way it should be.

The bonds made a nice down payment towards a little house in the northwest corner of town, well away from both of their families. Marcel was making a man's salary now at the mill. They didn't need anyone except themselves.

## *Emelie's Love*

On a cold day in late March, Emelie removed her sweater at school to reveal a tight sleeveless blouse that she swore looked exactly like the one Rita Heyworth wore in *Tonight and Every Night*. Emelie should've known, she'd sat through the movie three times the year before in Fort William. It was an adult and daring outfit for Wegebow and high school but Emelie loved Rita Heyworth and wanted to look just like her.

It had been necessary to hide the blouse under a sweater that morning during breakfast. Aunt Avril, as proper as Emelie's father had been, didn't have much tolerance for unladylike behaviour. She also frowned on affection and the new tendency to adopt exotic foreign customs; eating spaghetti and the like.

As Emelie walked down the hall, aware of all eyes on her, she went past a group of girls who were watching her approach but whose eyes all simultaneously dropped to the floor at the same moment. One of the coven said to her, like a ventriloquist, without moving her lips, "You look like a slut."

Emelie didn't stop, look at or respond to the girl but walked faster and faster until she reached a washroom and locked herself into a stall where she sat down and cried. Why did life have so many disappointments? She thought she looked so wonderful and adult. She knew by then, because of Vincent telling people about the two of them, that the personal attacks from other girls had little to do with what she was wearing.

EMELIE HADN'T LIKED WEGEBOW since that January day when she first stepped off the train with her sister and aunt into a minus forty degree snowstorm. It took them all of ten minutes to walk the two blocks from the antique station to Aunt Avril's home in the centre of town. The snow banks were a blinding white that hurt your eyes and were piled so high it was hard to see the little houses beyond. The frigid air made your lungs ache and your cheeks burn. There were no sidewalks so the women had to half climb the snow banks to avoid a horse drawn milk wagon squeezing to the right to miss a car passing in the opposite direction.

It appeared to Emelie, as they went by Main Street, that the only store selling anything of interest was Woolworth's. Fort William hadn't been much as cities went, but there were stores, theatres, concerts and all the friends she'd cultivated for her entire life. It was home. This was too much. She'd lost her guardian aunt and now everything else important in her life in a just a few days.

Annette and Emelie LeClair were 17 and 16 respectively. Their mother had died when Emelie was 2 and their father when she was 12. The girls had gone to live with their aunt Sylvie, a prudish and truly passionless woman, until she too had died. And now they'd come to Wegebow to live with yet another aunt, Avril, their last living relative.

Emelie only had one vague memory of her mother, a mental snapshot from her perspective, sitting in her crib, waiting, and then seeing her mother look around the doorframe at her and smile. Why she remembered this detail she didn't know.

On the other hand, she recalled everything about her father. Louis LeClair was a small man with delicate hands and a gentle demeanour, but saddened by life. He ran his own small pharmacy, still called LeClair's, a Fort William institution, until his unexpected death from pneumonia. He'd been non-affectionate and mostly detached. Not so in his opinions of how to bring up girls though; of that he was passionately opinionated. Among other things, his daughters were expected to wear prim dresses and learn the impeccable manners of young ladies.

Still, Emelie missed him. She felt entirely alone.

FINDING VINCENT HAD BEEN a blessing. She'd met him in the autumn at the Boucher's place up on the Row, outside of town. The girls were playing badminton one Saturday afternoon in the huge backyard that stretched away from the house until it dwindled off into bush.

After moving to Wegebow, Annette, always the more outgoing of the two LeClairs, had quickly became friends with the three Boucher girls and Emelie came along as part of the package. The Bouchers lived on Millionaire's Row. It was unlikely that any of the families who lived on the Row were actually worth a million dollars; they were just rich in comparison to the working class of Wegebow.

Emelie was sitting out a game while the other four girls played pairs. She noticed Vincent Lavoie the moment he came around the far corner of the house next door and looked in their direction. Even from a considerable distance she could tell he was handsome, but it wasn't until he was up close she could observe the dreamy blue eyes and decide that he looked exactly like Frank Sinatra. She had something like forty pictures of Frankie, carefully cut from magazines, taped to the walls in her half of the bedroom.

Vincent immediately came over to join them. The badminton game stopped on his arrival. Emelie could see the Bouchers were obviously pleased to see him, especially Francine, the middle girl, who never stopped blushing. Emelie recalled a comment Francine had made to her earlier about how wonderful it would be to have an older boyfriend.

Vincent was introduced to Emelie and Annette.

"Welcome," he said, attempting man-about-town suavity. "We need some new blood in this town. It's a pretty dull place."

"They're from Fort William, so they're the most exciting thing we've seen here in quite awhile," Marie, the oldest Boucher, told him.

"They've been to the latest movies, know all the fashion magazines and are almost the only girls in town who wear what's in style," bragged Francine.

"Have you ever been to the movie theatre in Hartley?" Vincent asked Emelie, looking her up and down.

"No."

"I'm sure it's nowhere near the size of a theatre in Fort William but it's mighty good. I like to drive up there in my new convertible. I make pretty good time. You gotta go to a movie there sometime," he added with intention while smiling charmingly.

Emelie blushed at the attention.

Francine Boucher looked alarmed at the exchange.

The badminton players soon continued their game while Vincent stayed on to talk to Emelie.

LATER, BACK AT HOME, when Emelie told Annette she was going on a date with Vincent, her sister's reaction surprised her.

"You should've said no! Francine is crazy about him. You had absolutely no business agreeing to go."

"But he isn't Francine's boyfriend! If he doesn't want to take her to the movies it doesn't mean no one else should go with him."

"You're supposed to be her friend!"

Emelie didn't know how to respond. She hadn't had this sort of attention before from a young man. She couldn't pass it up, even knowing it was a selfish decision. If other girls were jealous they'd have to get over it. No wonder Vincent had no interest in Francine. She was 16, same as her, but acted two years younger with her constant giggling and staring. Vincent was a man with a car and a job. He obviously wanted to be with someone who was more of an adult.

Emelie decided she'd spend as much time with him as possible.

AT 7 P.M., VINCENT picked up Emelie in his Chieftain Convertible. Aunt Avril had been alarmed by the prospect of her 16 year-old charge going out on a date with a 19 year-old man, and even appeared ready to quash the idea up to the point where Vincent came to the door and was brought into the house to meet her.

The house smelled old and stale. The furniture was heavy oak but the area rugs were worn. It was dreary and cramped.

"What a beautiful house you have here," said Vincent, smiling broadly and reaching for her hand. "It's so nice to finally meet you. I've heard so much about you."

Aunt Avril smiled back at the handsome young man.

The young couple soon went off on their date with Aunt Avril's blessing.

At the theatre, they sat in the back row. Part way through the movie Vincent raised his left arm and slipped it around Emelie's shoulders. She froze. Of course she'd imagined doing such things after noticing this is what couples in the back row did; she just hadn't any experience of them. Her first impulse was to draw away, but she knew how that would make her look; like a teenager. So she didn't move. By the end of the movie she was comfortable enough for it to begin to feel thrillingly dangerous to be near Vincent and to have him touch her.

She hadn't grown up with much physical contact, learning that displays of emotion were wrong. She was taught to act with arms-length, contact-avoiding decorum; but it didn't come naturally. She wasn't like that. The only effect of the training was to make her feel guilty when she spontaneously hugged her father or expressed feelings.

Later that night when she was in bed, Emelie fantasized about Vincent's touch. The creeping hand sliding around her shoulder and over her face, stroking her and exploring her body. She imagined herself in a scene from one of the trashy crime magazines the Boucher girls had found in their parent's dresser, with the lurid drawings of insatiable men tearing away the clothing of innocent girls.

The following Monday at lunchtime, Emelie looked around the cafeteria for Annette and her friends, but they weren't there. She sat down to eat her lunch, expecting the four to show up at any minute, but they never did.

Later she saw Francine during a break between classes and asked where they'd been.

"Oh, Cherri wanted to finish an art project, so we ate in one of the classrooms."

Emelie didn't see any of the girls at the bus stop that night, their usual spot to wait, so she was the first of the group to get on. There was an empty seat beside her but all four of the girls walked past without any acknowledgement and sat together in seats much farther back.

"Is everyone mad at me?" she asked Annette later, back at home.
"About what?"
"About me going out with Vincent."
"I don't know, why you'd think so?"
Emelie mentioned being left alone at lunch and ignored on the bus.
"No, it's just a coincidence," Annette said, "but doing that to Francine wasn't very nice."
"I didn't do anything to Francine! Vincent isn't interested in her."
"Maybe he would been if you said no."
There was no point pursuing this, Emelie thought.
Annette and the Bouchers ignored her the next day at lunch and again after school. It was the same the next day, and the day after that.

Emelie decided she wasn't going to look for the girls any more. She got on the bus ahead of them, sat with a girl she barely knew, and told herself she was still a good person who had done nothing wrong so wasn't going to let them see she felt hurt by being shunned. Especially by a sister siding with girls who were almost complete strangers!

On the weekend after the dance, the Lavoie parents were away from home for the weekend; visiting family. Vincent invited Emelie over to listen to records: The Mills Brothers, Eddie Fisher and Rosemary Clooney.

Vincent got Emelie up and dancing. Later he poured himself a drink and offered her one. She had never drunk alcohol before and didn't much like the taste but she did like the feeling of being an adult.

When Emelie told Vincent about being ignored by the girls, he laughed.

"I can't help it if Francine is in love with me," he said with braggadocio. "But I wanna go out with a gal who's a grown-up woman, not a child."

That made her feel good. Let them do what they wanted, it just showed what kids they were.

Vincent's parents were away for the next two weeks and Emelie went to his place every night. They would sit side by side on the couch and kiss. Each evening they progressed a little further.

"I want to experience everything with you, forever," Vincent whispered.

Emelie pushed his constantly roaming hands away when what he was doing was inappropriate, but knew she was being very slow to say stop. She was stern with herself afterwards, recalling the lectures from her aunt and the priest about the evils of promiscuity. She would think of the terror of unwed pregnancy and promise to be better behaved next time. And so the next time, just as rehearsed, she'd start out with good intentions and try to keep things proper, but she'd then become uncomfortable doing this with Vincent, not wanting him to see her as a callow young girl. In time it became clear her ardour was as strong as his and she told herself to let things go where they would and to accept it. This relationship seemed to be 'the one.'

Sex was strange, uncomfortable and embarrassing the first time they made love. It had started on the couch in the Lavoie livingroom and ended up in Vincent's bedroom. Emelie had to let her mind go elsewhere and close her eyes. It was over quickly.

After a few experiences with Vincent however, Emelie began to think the sex was perfect and she was in love forever. Vincent was the most handsome and perfect man she'd ever met.

VINCENT BECAME ALMOST HER entire social contact outside of school. Annette never even bothered to tell her anymore when she was heading off to the Bouchers' or some other place. It was taken for granted that Emelie had other plans.

But in a short space of time Vincent began to call Emelie less and less. For several weeks she often ended up sitting home by herself, alone in her room reading. Then Vincent would unexpectedly call and tell her what time he was picking her up and where they were going, as if he assumed Emelie was available whenever he needed a date or had his parent's house to himself.

ONE SATURDAY AFTERNOON VINCENT stopped by the house unexpectedly, popping his head through the back door. He was due to come by to pick up Emelie at 7 p.m. but it was only 2 in the afternoon.

"Vincent! What are you dong here?" Emelie asked, rising to her feet from where she knelt washing the floor, and wiping her sudsy hands on her apron. "I mean, it's nice to see you, but…you know, but I thought you were coming at 7."

"Well, sorry. I won't be able to make it. Pop has someone coming for dinner, an important client and he says it would be good for me, career-wise, to meet the fella."

Emelie said she was disappointed but understood. She always said the same thing.

"Oh, and I came by because I wanted to get back the records I loaned you. They're my father's actually and he's been looking for them."

It was a couple of hours after Vincent left before Emelie suddenly became angry. Why was she never invited to his house when his parent were home? Was he ashamed of her? Did he see her as beneath him? They weren't thoughts she arrived at after a long period of consideration; they were just suddenly there, intruders, and Emelie didn't know if she was unhappy with their presence or not. She tried so hard to do things to please him, like spending an hour that afternoon cleaning up the kitchen because he'd be there for ten seconds later in the day. What was the point of it if he saw her as beneath him? Would there be anything she could do to change his attitude? She knew immediately the answer was no. Now she just grew angry at Vincent's idea of his own superiority. What had he ever done? He worked at a business his father owned. It wasn't like he'd accomplished anything on his own.

ONE EVENING EMELIE LAY in bed talking to her sister Annette in the bed across the room.

Annette told her sister about some things she'd heard. Vincent had apparently been talking to his friends about Emelie, including Richard Martin who was Marie Boucher's boyfriend.

"He's been telling people you show him your body and have gone all the way with him." It was stated as an accusation more so than a statement. Annette hadn't really believed it when she was first told.

"He didn't say that!" Emelie was incredulous. "You're making it up 'cus you're all jealous of me."

"That's crazy. I'm just telling you what Marie said. If I were you I'd ask Vincent about it. He's the one who needs to stop making stuff up…if he is."

"He wouldn't be making it up."

Annette gasped but said nothing.

Several minutes of silence followed.

Emelie finally said incredulously, to herself and the darkness as much as to her sister, "I don't believe he'd say something about private moments. They were ours. He couldn't betray us. Those things mattered as much to him as they did to me."

IT WAS IMPOSSIBLE FOR Emelie to sleep that night or to think of anything else the next day at school.

After dinner she began walking towards Vincent's house but saw his car parked on Main Street outside the restaurant. Teenagers preferred the lunch counter at Woolworth's, with its burgers and shakes, to the old-fogey restaurant with its red and white checked plastic tablecloths, the little vase of plastic flowers at each table, and the French Canadian menu featuring baked beans, tortiere, and pork chops. But even so, teenagers frequented the restaurant because it stayed open until 7:30 p.m. to cater to single guys living in the motel who worked at the mill.

Vincent was sitting at a table across from Connie Baxter. Emelie went inside and slid into the empty chair beside him. Connie got up and left, saying she had to go.

Vincent turned to Emelie, smiling, as if pleased to see her, and asked how she was, adding he'd just been going to call.

"Can I see you outside? Can we go and sit in your car?" she whispered.

Vincent looked at her with a slightly bemused look.

"I just bought this Coke. Let's sit here."

"I want to go somewhere private."

"This is private. There's no one around."

"There's lots of people around."

And suddenly, Emelie couldn't constrain herself. "What have you been saying about us?" she said more loudly, her voice beginning to shake. "No, don't bother lying to me 'cus I heard. You've been telling people about things we did that were private and special." She was crying now and sorry she hadn't waited until they were outside.

"I didn't say nothin' to no one," Vincent said, dropping his voice sulkily.

There was a pause while Emelie gained control. The denial had helped. "Then why are people talking about it? Even Annette has heard things."

"Not from me. It's just the same old stuff. You know, about the LeClair sisters being cheap and easy. No one says so to me or I'd make sure they didn't repeat anything like that ever again, but there's nothing I can do about other people saying it."

Until this moment Emelie hadn't known such comments were being made. She stared at Vincent in bewilderment with a sick feeling in her stomach, and no idea of what to say. She wondered if Annette knew what was being said about them. Were the stories because of her? Vincent had to be lying or maybe he was responsible for the horrible things being said.

Emelie got up and left the restaurant.

How could life be any worse? It had gone from bad to unbearably awful. She wanted to be away from Wegebow more than anything else in the world.

The next day, seeing Vincent drive by with Connie Baxter, convinced her that more than anything she wanted to leave this town, her friends, her school and everything else in this crummy life. She had no one and nothing.

EMELIE BEGAN TO BE aware of the pernicious intimidation that came from being labelled promiscuous in 1946. Crude drawings were once found on her locker. Rotting food from someone's old lunch was mashed through the locker's grate. At times, guys pressed against her in crowded hallways or going in or out of a class. She didn't know which behaviours towards her were based on the rumours about her and which weren't. A group of boys at school, clustering around a locker at school, would snicker when she went by or make a comment about her body. Girls didn't sit with her in the lunchroom or on the bus except, strangely enough, Francine Boucher. Perhaps she sympathized about how one could be charmed by Vincent Lavoie.

One time, a boy asked Emelie about an assignment as they left a class. She spoke to him for all of ten seconds and as he walked away a girl in her class, a girl who wasn't even the boy's girlfriend, said angrily to her, "What, isn't there enough guys to screw on the Row?"

EMELIE HAD NOTICED MARCEL Gagnon a few times over the winter during dances at the hall. He stood just inside the door for some reason, like he was afraid to come in. Marcel was very tall and stocky. She thought of L'il Abner. He always wore the same clothes, as if he only owned the one outfit.

Marcel never took his eyes off of her. It was unsettling in a way.

It was the April 15th dance and Emelie's relationship with Vincent was all but over. She didn't look for him and he didn't call her. They had each come to the dance on their own. She wanted so much to dance with someone, to show Vincent she was enjoying herself. When she saw Marcel standing by the door she acted on impulse and went to speak to him.

He was a goofball, she quickly decided. A big lumpen clown. He stammered and stuttered when trying to speak. To approach him had been a bad idea.

A little later, when she saw Vincent dancing with Connie Baxter, Emelie again approached Marcel and asked him to dance. She came away with bruised knees, it was like trying to dance with one of the bears in the circus. But there was something sweet about his clumsiness, she told Francine. The guy had probably never danced with a girl before.

"He's a retard," was the response, and Emelie understood the remark.

"Maybe he's just not used to talking to girls."

Emelie liked that idea. Vincent had been a good conversationalist but was a braggart and never said anything honest. There was something completely without artifice in Marcel's manner

In the time between that night and the next dance, Vincent all but disappeared from her life as if he was dissolving in water, simply becoming less and less present. On one night they'd both been part of a group of people going to the restaurant but it was only because Francine had dragged her out.

Despite her best efforts, she was still struggling to stop herself from thinking about Vincent much of the time and hoping he'd again act as if he liked her. She knew her best remedy would be to get interested in someone else. Maybe just as a friend this time.

AT WHAT POINT IT began she didn't know, but Emelie started to think about Marcel instead. His awkwardness was endearing, the way a big dog's would be. Marcel wouldn't be the sort to try and seduce girls or to run around on his girlfriend, and he was truly enamoured of her. When she thought that way, her next feeling was one of momentary panic. Perhaps Marcel had heard stories about the promiscuous LeClair sisters, or maybe even that's why he was so attentive. Her agitation would calm when she remembered seeing Marcel at the dances, watching her, long before her involvement with Vincent.

"He's a retard," Francine would respond with finality at any attempt to speak to her about Marcel.

"No, I think he's afraid of people. Maybe if they didn't call him names but gave him a chance, he'd be more sociable."

"The way he stares at you is creepy."

"No it's not. I don't think he's used to being around girls." Francine should talk, thought Emelie, the way she used to ogle Vincent. She couldn't explain to Francine what she most liked about Marcel. His attentions and adoration were genuine. The adoring way he saw her was exactly opposite to the sleazy way other boys did when they spoke about the LeClair sisters and it made Emelie feel good about herself again.

At the next dance Emelie approached Marcel and practically forced him to dance with her. She liked the sense of power over him that she had. She felt smug about how she managed the conversation and got him to ask her out. He was as naïve as someone who had just come into town on the back of a hay truck, but it didn't bother her. She liked the idea of being the more experienced one.

Emelie would have bragged to them, but neither her sister Annette, nor Annette's friends, thought much of Marcel, so she kept things to herself. That was nice too. She could be happy without someone trying to compete for him, or destroy what they had. By coming into her life Marcel had given her something of her own.

MARCEL AND EMELIE BEGAN to regularly attend the movies in Hartley on Saturday nights. Marcel favoured the westerns and Emelie liked anything with Bing Crosby, Judy Garland or Jimmy Stewart.

They developed a ritual of walking along the main street, holding hands, in the early evening before the movie began, when it was still light and there were people to see two people who were now a couple, if anyone cared to notice.

Emelie loved the looks from men as she wore her summer dresses. She imagined they wanted her, that they fantasized about being alone with her and touching her. The way she moved her hips when she walked was enhanced to drive them crazy.

One guy almost fell after tripping on his own feet, he was ogling her so hard.

"You know that guy?" Marcel asked, tight-lipped.

"Nope, I never saw him before," Emelie answered with coy innocence, aware this was jealousy, that she could name it, and she was pleased to see it. It showed he cared. She felt Marcel must know it was only him she was interested in.

What she liked even more than men looking at her was to see the attentive looks that Marcel got from other women. It was a sweet kind of jealousy. It made her aware of his manliness; he was a big strong man and he'd protect her if need be. He was more of a man than Vincent or any fella she'd ever known. In a short time, Marcel was transformed in her eyes from a stray dog generating sympathy to a virile trophy.

The next week, Marcel asked Emelie to go for a walk with him to the lake and then, afterwards, into town for a Coke at the restaurant. They did the same thing the next week, and every one that followed, until it became their ritual.

They sat on a rock one evening, on a small hill — there were no other kinds of hills around Wegebow — overlooking the lake.

"Did you notice we never go to the dances or movies anymore?" Emelie asked.

"I don't like people much," he said, "only you." Then he thought about it for a bit. "Do ya mind?"

"No, actually. It's nice to be off, just by ourselves, where we don't have to listen to all the stupid high school gossip. I lie in bed at night and listen to Annette talk about all the scandal. I hate it. I want to be away from there more than anything."

"It's good you feel that way. That you don't mind, I guess. I didn't mean to take you away from all your friends."

"You're my closest friend now," Emelie said. "It's just you and me."

Later, the two of them lay side by side in an alcove of soft grass and weeds. Emelie, let Marcel run his hands over her in a way she never had before. But she became scared. There was a sense of his immense passion. It felt somehow like the start of a fire. There were flames here and there and if she didn't stop them they'd burst out of control.

She jumped up and walked to the side of the opening. Reaching up she took hold of a leaf she could barely make out in the dark hanging from a tree.

"What sort of tree is this?"

On the walk back to town, Emelie listened as Marcel told her the story of his upbringing, of the way his family had treated him and excluded him, and of the way he'd been shunned at school. She suddenly knew, with absolute assuredness, they were destined to be together. They would create the family neither of them had ever known.

She became angry when she remembered Francine referring to Marcel as a 'retard'. He was no such thing. He was just shy and hadn't spent enough time around people. In time, she knew, the girls in Wegebow would come to see him as attractive as the girls in Hartley did, and as she did.

Emelie unashamedly told Marcel about her feelings. He listened and, although she couldn't see his face in the dark, she knew that he smiled. She was the first person to ever make him happy. And she thrived on this feeling; of looking after him. He came from circumstances worse than hers. When they were married, Emelie decided, and they had their own place, Marcel's life would be better than he had ever known. She would quit the hated high school and never associate with anyone there ever again. A respectable man wanted to marry her. It would show them all!

On her 18th birthday Marcel got her a card and signed it, 'Regards, Marcel'. He's never had anyone to teach him how to love, thought Emelie, and she knew she would be the one to lead him.

THEY WENT TO SEE Marcel's Aunt Estelle one day, shortly before the wedding. Estelle was a thin woman who looked fairly young. Dressed like a country and western music fan, she managed the town hall where they staged bingos and dances.

"You brought your young lady. Good." Estelle said, without explanation. She told them an incredible story of an old love affair Marcel's mother had once had. Marcel was the product of that union. As the aunt talked she looked continually at Emelie, perhaps trying to convey with her eyes that Marcel would need her help to get through this. Emelie took his hand.

When the story was finished, Estelle got up from her kitchen chair and walked up behind Marcel. She extended her arms as if to touch him. Her hands hovered above his shoulders but she stopped, obviously uncomfortable with the idea. She caught Emelie's eye and nodded towards Marcel.

In the next few days Emelie and Marcel would go over and over the story. He would bristle about it and say he hated his mother for her actions and how he had no desire to find out anything about his real father. Emelie understood. The man was just another person who had rejected him. She too had lost her family now that her sister had largely abandoned her.

"DO YOU THINK KIDS whose parents weren't married, who didn't have a real mother and father, get a hard time from other kids?"

Francine looked intently at Emelie. "You mean bastards?" she said.

Emelie hated the word. The cold ugliness of its sound alone cast moral judgement.

"Yes."

"Of course they do. Other kids will avoid them, pick on them, call them names. What do you expect?"

The brief conversation confirmed Emelie's worries.

Immediately after the revelations from Marcel's aunt, Emelie had been too wrapped up in comforting him to think much about them. She'd been shocked at first, then put it aside. But over the next few weeks she began to consider what had been said that day at Estelle's. Marcel's parents hadn't been married. He was the result of an extra-marital affair. If she married him, and they had kids, her own children would be forever in danger of being shunned and picked on by other kids if the story of their father's parentage ever came out.

School was out for the summer and Emelie began to avoid Marcel. She would visit Francine and stay nights at her place but didn't say anything of what was on her mind to Francine, who had never thought too highly of Marcel. It was obvious what sort of advice she'd get from that quarter. Her own counsel, though, told her that maybe it was time to back out of her relationship with Marcel before it went any further. It was already to the point of being very serious.

When he would eventually see Emelie, Marcel would complain a bit about having had time on his hands and no one to spend it with, but he didn't read anything into her absence.

Emelie was surprised when she realized how much she missed him and how happy she was to see him, so she resisted saying anything about her concerns or about ending the relationship. She would think, just leave it for another day.

But the inevitable began to happen up on the Row, as it always did when she spent time around her sister Annette and the Boucher girls. With the exception of Francine, they would exclude her from their conversations, slip off when she wasn't around or make sly comments not so subtly aimed at her. She was continually reminded of how much she wanted to get away from this life where she was perceived as a fallen woman whom no good man would ever want.

Marcel was a good man and marrying him would show them all. With him, she would never feel cast out or lonely. No one would ever know his history, she thought. She'd been worrying about nothing.

MARCEL NEVER ACTUALLY PROPOSED, not like they do in the movies, or brought her chocolates or flowers, or said anything romantic. He couldn't say he loved her. He was too much of a man's man for that, Emelie decided, but she knew how he felt. He just announced one day in September that they ought to get married immediately.

PART 2

They eloped a few weeks after Emelie's 18th birthday and she left high school, her family, and her few friends on the Row forever.

☙❧

# PART 3
## *Maddy & Emelie*

EMELIE ENTERED THE DOCTOR'S office, openly, through the front door of Maddy's house. For months she had snuck along the beach and anxiously approached the back door. All it would have taken was an innocent remark, like someone asking Marcel if his wife was okay because they'd seen her at the doctor's, for her husband to know of the visit and then violently retaliate for not being obeyed.

Emelie arrived with a new perm and in a short-sleeved summer dress; garishly bright and aggressive. There were no longer any bruises to conceal. The sleeves weren't really appropriate given the declining September temperatures but they had nothing to do with fashion. They were Emelie's way of proving to herself and announcing to the world her regained authority over her own body.

She smiled and laughed frequently when she talked. The sombre, damaged look was gone, replaced by something apparently friendlier but, to a discerning eye, more wary and practiced than in the past.

"How are you feeling?" Maddy asked.

"Fine. Healing. Making plans. Francine helps, looks after the kids sometimes and gives me a few hours to myself." She played with the hem of her dress. "It's funny. I don't think about Marcel at all," she added, as a quiet, confidential aside, looking pleased. "Not sure why. I don't look back, just forward, and the future looks good. I still got most of the money the town raised for the kids and I'm talking to Paul Desjardins about a job at the hotel working on the books. He says he'll do anything he can to help me. What a nice man. You know Gloria's retiring, she's gonna show me how to do them before she goes. I was always good at math."

"That's terrific!"

"I'll be lucky if I get the job. Since the fellas came back from overseas there aren't many jobs around here that women get."

"Don't count yourself out."

Maddy thought this positive enthusiasm was an astonishing transformation from the timid, broken woman of only a few weeks before.

"How're your kids handling things?" she said.

"René's a lot calmer, much happier than he was. He never asks about Marcel. Cecile doesn't look for him at all, but then her father never had anything to do with her because she's a girl, so she's not likely to miss him."

They talked casually, with the conversation straying here and there. Emelie said she was getting to know some of the local women and was even learning to play bridge.

The remark induced the same sudden anxiety Maddy associated with seeing Emelie out and about town with Francine; the intense vulnerability she had first felt on the night of Marcel's death after recognizing their lives relied on Emelie's ability to maintain the lie about her husband dying of a heart attack. To be caught was tantamount to them getting death sentences. When Emelie and Francine were in the presence of other women, standing on some street corner or sitting at Woolworth's lunch counter, Emelie's voice was uncharacteristically loud and she expressed herself with broad arm gestures. She was never like that. Who knows what she might be saying?

The two women avoided any direct reference to the night of Marcel's death until Dr. MacQuigau said abruptly, "Emelie, I need to ask you about the bottle of pills you took from me. It was a huge bottle. I need it back."

"Oh my God no! I don't have it. I didn't want it around in case…you know. I flushed the pills and threw the bottle away."

"Fine then," Maddy said, slowly exhaling the breath she didn't know she was holding and feeling intense relief, not just because the evidence of her collusion was gone, but because Emelie's actions told Maddy that she shared her sense of vulnerability.

As MADDY WALKED DOWNTOWN a short time later she thought of how, lately, the outline of the picture in her mind of her young friend was increasingly becoming blurred. Emelie had changed. For a long time she had always been ready to forgive Marcel and to blame herself and René for his violence. That's what made her behaviour in church, at the funeral, even more shocking. She had shown a capacity for anger that Maddy would never have believed possible a year ago. And it was still the talk of the town. For the folks of Wegebow it was unthinkable that a Catholic girl could act so. It was unforgivable. What kind of lesson was that for her kids, they would say?

Maddy worried this radical change in demeanour would start up gossip, leading to the police examining whether Emelie had killed her husband. In bed she practiced a speech for the police about how she'd given Emelie the pills to help her sleep; she had no intention of them being used to kill Marcel. It was only after the fact, knowing why Emelie did what she did, that she'd decided to help.

In Maddy's current placid mood, however, she was inclined to think only of the strength of Emelie's new personality. And she began to feel some sense of peace for the first time since the funeral. Perhaps, she thought, it would become easier as time went on to avoid the company of the guilt and fear which came to visit in the lonely hours of the night.

When Maddy turned on to Main Street she passed the stately Mrs. Tremblay. The Wegebow matriarch had never so much as acknowledged her before, but today she nodded imperially. On the heels of that, a woman coming out of the restaurant smiled and said 'lovely weather, eh?' and two others, just going into Woolworth's called 'hello'.

These weren't the first signs of a thaw in attitude towards her. In the past week Maddy had noticed an increase in general friendliness towards her when she took her daily walk to the market. The alteration wasn't pronounced—she wondered if perhaps it was all in her head—but things felt different. Some still ignored her, but other faces now appeared, through store windows and in passing cars, looking back at her instead of diverting their eyes, and many now smiled when their eyes met. The change seemed to be mostly with the women of the town. Males still ignored her for the most part, but the withering Jack LaPlante went so far as to tip his hat—albeit looking somewhat uncomfortable and nervous while doing so.

There'd been a couple of new patients over the past week—both women. It was ten patients if you counted Mrs. Daigle's eight kids whom she said she would bring to Maddy if they were ever sick. Two or ten wasn't exactly an outpouring of love from the town but it made her feel optimistic about things improving, given time. She speculated that the changes must be attributable to her presence in the Catholic church three weeks ago, for Marcel's funeral.

At the market Maddy wheeled her cart up one of the narrow aisles of the grocery store, heading for the check-out. A man stepped in front of her just as she got to the end of the aisle.

She smiled at him and waited, giving him a moment to move.

Immobile, he stared at her. The guy was small and his blue jeans were winched in at the waist by a big belt. They had six inches of rolled-up cuff. His head came to a sort of point at the top and his hair was oiled back into a ducktail. Three or four of his front teeth were missing. As short as he was, he was still too wide to pass by with the cart.

"Excuse me," said Maddy, smiling.

There was no response except for a glare.

"Oh hello there," said Paul Desjardins walking up behind her, as if her presence in the store was a great surprise. For many months Maddy had been going for her walks at different times of the day instead of the old regular schedule when she and Paul would arrive at the store at the same time, but there were still days when their schedules coincided.

The little guy blocking the way turned and walked towards the front doors.

Paul went into a spiel about how he hadn't seen Maddy in such a long time, but she wasn't paying attention.

"Do you know who that is?" she interrupted Paul. The stranger could be seen through the store window as he walked up the sidewalk with a woman while carrying a couple of bags of groceries.

"Sure, it's Guy Gagnon, Marcel's brother. Why?"

"No reason. Just thought he looked familiar. I must have seen him at the funeral."

What Maddy didn't know at the time was that this would be the last normal conversation she would ever have with Paul Desjardins. The next time she saw him, and mostly ever after, he would beetle away at the sight of her.

ON EXITING THE MARKET Maddy turned in the direction opposite to home. A light rain began to fall and she pulled a plastic kerchief out of her bag and wrapped it over her head. It would have to be a short walk, she decided, or the paper bag holding her few groceries would get wet and break.

Maddy liked to take longer walks these days. It burned off some of the nervous energy she still felt. Often she thought about Robert. Could she tell him how Marcel had really died? She wanted to talk to someone, but it was over now so likely best left alone and, anyway, her feeling was that he wouldn't understand or condone what she'd done. She normally felt certain of his support but he was from Wegebow and here family was everything. You stood by your family without question. Maddy worried her husband would reckon her actions had only been on behalf of someone else's family.

Who would understand the decision she'd needed to make? Nobody, likely. But the desire to share what had happened, she felt with some gratitude, was becoming less pressing.

# *Maddy*
# Late October

Emelie's second emergency call to Maddy came about the same time of night as the first, 1 a.m. or so. She sounded different this time; stronger, more forceful.

"Bernie's dead," she said efficiently. "He had a heart attack. Same as Marcel. I need you to come right away. I'm at Francine's."

Maddy woke Isabel to say she was leaving, grabbed her things and went out to the car. The autumn air felt like there would be frost that night. Wegebow was silent but nature was speaking softly, rustling, lapping, whispering, until a car went down the dirt road shattering stones in a tattoo against its underside, three times as loud as during the day.

Writing about it years later, Maddy said she immediately suspected that Emelie had killed Bernie. As she drove, she thought about the pills that had supposedly been destroyed; the pills she had given her. If Emelie had used them to murder Bernie then Maddy was also involved. It was too desperate a situation for her not to pray on the trip to Francine's that she was wrong. After all, why would Emelie murder Bernie? She avoided her own question. It simply couldn't be true.

As she drove, a sheet came detached from some clothesline where it had been left overnight, and danced across in front of her in the strong wind. It was a startling apparition fitting the feel of the night.

From the road, Francine's war-time bungalow looked asleep and Maddy wondered if there'd been a misunderstanding and Emelie had phoned from home; but when she drove up the driveway, a single light was visible in the kitchen.

She knocked several times at the back door before it opened a few inches, Emelie peeked around it to ascertain who was there and then let her into the kitchen. Francine was slumped forward on a chair, crying softly and holding her left arm as she rocked back and forth, apparently oblivious to Maddy's entry. Her face was colourless but marked by blood-red contusions.

"Oh my God!" Maddy said, immediately going to her and kneeling down. She carefully pushed Francine's hair back. "What happened?"

"Bernie did it," Francine said through clenched teeth. "He knocked me down the basement stairs."

The doctor gently examined Francine's arm. "It's broken, I think. We'll have to go to my office and temporarily set it, but first I need to see Bernie."

She looked around, not knowing where he was. In answer to the question, Emelie, casually leaning against the door frame, flicked up a thumb and pointed back over her shoulder to the darkened livingroom behind her.

Emelie made no effort to move so Maddy squeezed by her. The doctor turned on a livingroom lamp. The house didn't reek of poverty the way Emelie's did. It had decent furniture, but things were knocked about as if there'd been a big fight. Bernie slumped in an easy chair, his face resting on his chest, looked as if he were unconscious. There were three or four empty beer bottles on the end table beside him.

Emelie hovered behind Maddy, intently looking over her shoulder while the body was examined.

Francine stopped crying and wandered to the livingroom door to watch. As soon as she saw Bernie, Maddy knew. She stood up.

"What happened Emelie?" she said sternly, as if speaking to a recalcitrant child.

Emelie began repeating, almost word for word, the same outline of symptoms she and Maddy had rehearsed after Marcel's death.

"Look at this place. Looks like a hurricane went through," Francine said to no one in particular, disconnected, looking around with amazed eyes, as if seeing the room for the first time and finding it marvellous.

"What happened?" Maddy asked Emelie again, softly but with insistence.

"He had a heart attack."

"Alright. Our concern now is Francine. I'll call the police in Hartley. What you're describing sounds like a heart attack and if it was it'll be confirmed by the autopsy."

"An autopsy! Why an autopsy, you're a doctor, you can just issue a certificate."

"I hate this mess," Francine said to someone not there, still looking dazed.

"Oh will you please leave it Francie!" Emelie loudly interjected.

Tears welled again in Francine's eyes and she went back into the kitchen.

"Yes, I'm a doctor, meaning I have to notify the police when there's a death. I can't call Bernie, obviously, so it'll have to be the O.P.P. in Hartley. My guess is they'll go to Dr. Savard in Hartley and unless Bernie had a history of heart problems there'll be an autopsy."

Maddy returned to the kitchen, brushing past Emelie who stood in the doorway emotionless, and sat down beside Francine. Looking directly into her eyes and speaking gently she said, "I know you're in pain and it's hard to talk but I need to know what happened. All Emelie said was that Bernie had a heart attack."

"He did," Emelie interjected. "He was beating up Francine and his heart went."

In utter confusion, Francine looked back and forth between Emelie and Maddy.

"I thought you were going to help," she cried plaintively to the doctor.

"I'd like you to tell me what happened," said Maddy, authoritatively. "There'll be an autopsy. The cause of death will come out, so if you did something to Bernie there's no point covering it up. I think a court might understand."

"Not in this part of the world," said Emelie dryly.

Francine ignored her, looking intently at Maddy, absorbing what she'd said. "But Emelie said you'd help…" she whimpered.

"I need to know what happened!" Maddy emphasized, emphatically chopping the air with her hand. "What really happened. I'm not stupid and the police aren't either."

Francine propped her elbows on her knees and buried her face in her hands. The sobs began as Maddy watched her.

They waited.

"It started a few days ago…when Bernie's dad died," Francine eventually managed to get out through sobs. "We came home after the funeral…and for the last three days he's been drunk…He beat me up the first day…He did that before but not like this…I couldn't get away from him. Things didn't change until Emelie came over after dinner last night."

"I couldn't believe what the bastard did to her!" Emelie put in. "I told her what happened with Marcel."

"I was shocked at first, but I know why Em did it."

"Okay," said Maddy shaking her head, suddenly feeling very angry, but controlling it. "What happened here?"

"I told Em I'd do the same thing to Bernie if he didn't stop hurting me. I don't know. I didn't mean it, you know. You get fed up and say stupid things. It woulda just bin talk but Bernie started up again today. When he sent me flying down the stairs I knew my arm was broken but he wouldn't let me leave the house…so I just lay in bed crying. I took a bunch of Aspirin. I still can't believe he let me lay there in such pain, even threatened to break my other arm when I said I wanted to see you…I didn't call you when Bernie passed out though, I called Emelie. I wanted someone on my side…some help. When Em came over she brought the pills. We ground some up and I put them in the next beer I got for Bernie after he woke up. I don't know why I did it. I wasn't thinking. I was angry. Furious. I wanted to kill him…but not really."

"He woulda killed her," said Emelie flatly.

"Get out of here!" said Maddy in Emelie's direction with undisguised bitterness. "Go home," she added more calmly. "You were never here tonight. Do you understand? Francine and I'll decide what to do. If the police are involved, the best thing for all is that they make no connection between this and Marcel's death or they'll know something happened to both of them besides a heart attack and they'll exhume Marcel's body. So, go home."

"She's right Emelie," said Francine, having regained some composure. "Go home. I'll feel better knowing you're safe."

After a long pause to consider, Emelie agreed. She hugged and kissed Francine, then left.

Francine and Maddy drove to the doctor's office. Three times Maddy slammed down the brakes to avoid hitting something; a deer who ran across the road in front of them and two groups of staggering drunks wandering aimlessly home. It was another surreal element of a night she would always remember.

Her house was quiet when she opened the front door. It led directly into the office. They wouldn't wake Isabel or the baby if they stayed there.

AT A MUCH LATER date, Maddy would write in her diary:

> *When Emelie killed her husband I was acutely aware that she'd been left with no other option. She had nowhere to go and Marcel would have killed her eventually. I helped her because I understood. His death had likely prevented one or two others. But this was different. As much as I felt sympathy for Francine I didn't think Bernie would normally have acted as he had in the few days before he died, although, granted, I didn't know him well.*
>
> *I also didn't think that Francine was stuck, like Emelie, with nowhere else she could go. She had family in the area the same as he did. A brother probably. A father. They would have crippled Bernie if she said something to them. Testosterone is good for some things.*
>
> *This was murder and I wasn't planning to participate in covering it up! It was a terrifying moment of decision to rise above the unreality.*
>
> *I don't know how I transcended my panic, but I immediately understood the ramifications of my actions: if I didn't help to conceal what happened, if I told the police that Bernie died from sleeping pills, it would be the same as confessing to his murder because everything would have to come out. How else could Francine have gotten the pills? My own safety, and that of my family, depended on helping Emelie and Francine get away with murder.*

☙

AFTER A CAST WAS put on the arm, Maddy told Francine that she needed to travel into Hartley the next day for x-rays. "If the arm's not properly set, they'll have to do it again."

In less pain now that the cast was on, Francine was ready to talk.

"What'll I tell the police? I can't tell them the truth. They'll hang me, and Emelie too."

Maddy told Francine it was possible a jury wouldn't convict her if she told them the truth.

There was silence and Francine looked at the doctor as if waiting for something more credible.

"Here's one approach," Maddy said. "The only thing connecting Emelie to what happened is that she gave you the pills. We could say you came to see me because you hadn't been sleeping so I gave you some sleeping pills. That would at least get Emelie out of the picture. I could give you a bottle with one or two pills in it. It'll look like that's all that's left of them."

Francine watched the doctor, nodding, and didn't respond. Maddy didn't know if she was getting through. It was bloody self-serving. No wonder Francine was looking at her, she thought. Probably wondering where the part comes in that was going to help her.

"You can either choose to say you killed Bernie in self-defence or make something up. Say he killed himself with them. God knows he sounds like he was depressed enough. You could say he'd been threatening to do it for the last three days. He could've been overcome by remorse after beating you up."

"You can't hide the bruises. I think you should draw attention to them. One thing I will say though, is if you decide what your story is by the time I call the police I'll say it's the same thing you told me from the beginning."

Madeleine could hear recriminations from her own conscience even as she spoke. What she was advising was not about protecting a victim who had no choice. There was no altruism here. This was colluding in a murder to the extent of even writing an alibi. Her morals had deserted her and she knew why. This was simply about saving herself.

AT 3 A.M. MADDY put in the phone call to the O.P.P. office in Hartley but it was closed. She had to call again in the morning after they re-opened and report Bernie's death, of unknown cause, but an apparent suicide by sleeping pills. When the police finally examined Bernie's body they found an empty pill bottle in his hand, a couple of pills on the floor beside him, and a wife telling them a long rambling story of a husband who had been depressed about the death of his father, took it out on her and hurt her badly, cried after, and said he'd kill himself for what he did.

THE NEXT DAY REQUIRED re-scheduling her appointments. Maddy didn't want to see anyone. She felt like hell and had been up all night. The police left at eleven a.m. and after speaking to Isabel they took her home. Madeleine went to bed. In spite of extreme exhaustion, there was no way she was going to sleep.

She went over her rationalizations for helping Francine. Reviewing the events of the night before was like flailing around in Lake Wegebow, it was disorienting. Decisions had been made on the fly, and she needed to recover a solid footing. Maddy lied to herself, that she hadn't acted out of self-interest, but mostly she attempted to calm the overpowering sense of fatalistic dread telling her that every sound was the police coming. She knew she had to go through the police investigation, have the suicide story accepted, and a lot of time go by. Then maybe…Eventually the doctor dozed off.

At 7 p.m., after getting up and having something to eat, Maddy walked to Emelie's place. The resolution she arrived at, just before sleep came a few hours before, was to ensure there were no pills left. Having them destroyed would be the start to putting these inexplicable events in the past and to begin, maybe, to make sense of them. Killing wasn't in Emelie's nature, despite what she and Francine had done. The doctor simply didn't understand.

The thick grass was almost a foot high, giving the place a derelict look. It was desperate for attention after Marcel's neglect and Emelie's being trapped indoors.

She doesn't cut the grass because she's out 'running the roads', Maddy thought. Lately Emelie had been too busy to look after the place, getting her hair done, buying clothes and socializing every day. Fair enough.

Emelie's greeting—she was sooo pleased to see her—felt affected to Maddy, who let herself be led into the kitchen.

The kettle happened to be on. The kids could be seen in the backyard. Francine was there too, sitting at a new, sparkling chrome and pink arborite kitchen table. She looked drained and battered, lethargic from sedatives and aspirin, but still seemed happy to see Maddy.

"Can I speak to you, alone somewhere?" Maddy said stiffly.

Emelie stared steadily back, picking up on the tone. "Sure," she said, looking bemused. She followed Maddy into the livingroom.

It got to Maddy. The smirk, and the tone of condescension she'd heard. Her anger from the night before resurfaced. It was time to be direct and let Emelie know how she felt!

"You lied to me about the pills!" she accused Emelie as she spun around. "You told Francine how Marcel died! And when you did, you put me in the position of having to cover up a murder!"

She was loud, angry and wagging her finger in Emelie's face. And as soon as the words were out she knew this had been the wrong approach. It was bullying of the type men used. Emelie said nothing, but you could see the physical discomfort and sudden coldness of expression, and Maddy knew, assuredly, that if this went any further in this way that it would create a distance between them that could never be closed.

"Are there any pills left?" Maddy asked evenly, softening her voice.

"No."

"You have to give them to me Emelie." She was trying to sound reasonable, "It's important. They're the evidence of the connection between you and me, and you and Francine. If the police get suspicious about Bernie's or Marcel's deaths, come looking and find those, they'll end up knowing everything."

The two women stood just inside the livingroom staring at each other while Emelie pondered.

"There's none left."

"You told me the same thing once before. You…I know you wouldn't use them," Maddy struggled to find the words to explain, "but I need to know absolutely that they're gone. Do you still have the bottle?"

"No!"

There was a long silence. Was there something else in Emelie's response?

"Well, it's over then," pronounced Maddy. "End of discussion."

"I'm sorry," Emelie said contritely, sounding genuine, "there could be more."

"What? Pills?"

"I'm saying there could be more."

"Huh? You mean men? Killing men?"

"I don't know."

"You'd consider doing this again? Unbelievable!" Maddy threw up her arms.

"I didn't say we were considering doing this again. I'm just telling you, if some other woman is trapped like I was, I'll help her in the same way I helped Francine."

"That is utter…your situation was the extreme. Women aren't in your situation just because their husband does something…You can't do this again Em, you'll force me to go to the police and we'll all be hung…I can't let you do this. I won't let you! Marcel was one thing, he mighta killed you, but husbands who hit their wives…killing them?…that's too much!"

"No it's not! They hit you one time they figure they can do it over and over. It just gets worse. Men are such bastards. If a woman needs help, I'll help her."

"By killing every man who…"

"Maybe. And you're a part of this. Listen Maddy, you have to help us."

The statement hung there between the two women, still standing face to face. It was a question. A delusional fantasy of Emelie's, spoken with affectionate appeal.

"You know, I don't even care if people know what I did." Emelie added brusquely. "I sorta hope they do. It tells the guys, 'If you do this, you know what'll happen'."

"Oh that's really smart. I can't believe you mean that. Do you want to be found out? Do you want your kids to lose you too? You may have already made sure that'll happen by killing Bernie. The police are looking at this very closely…Can't you see you're not the law?"

"Well in this case, we are the law," said Francine who'd approached them from the kitchen. "There's a lotta brutal men out there since they came back from overseas." She was slurring her words, but was aware enough to have been following the discussion. "You must know what goes on in people's houses. You're a doctor."

"Listen, you talk about war. These guys came back damaged. Their nerves are shot. They saw so much. They're desensitized and they think the way to deal with everything is with violence. They're not the enemy! You need some compassion. Not to kill them!"

"Compassion?" said Emelie loudly. "Like the compassion they show women? And who are you to talk? How much compassion did you show Marcel? You helped me kill him!"

"Marcel was different. Maybe I was wrong. Maybe not. He probably would have killed you and your son. But I don't think Bernie was like that. You're lumping these guys together. Marcel was the exception."

"But you don't know that! None of us do, and we aren't gonna wait to find out," said Francine. "We're the ones who have to take the beatings."

"And by the way, it wasn't the war made 'em like that," said Emelie, "these guys were like this long before. Marcel was never even in the army! Men run everything and they run women, and they feel when they don't get what they want they have the right to do anything they like. They sit around on their fat asses and joke about it. Hardy, har har. Well we gotta fight back."

# *Emelie*

Two hours later, Emelie paced back and forth across her livingroom. It was dark outside but there were no lights on. The kids and Francine were asleep.

The doctor wouldn't say anything to the cops. She couldn't be that stupid. She had kids of her own. She'd be committing suicide to go to the police.

Marcel. Would she have killed him if the doctor hadn't pushed her in that direction? Probably not. But it was the right decision. Same with Bernie.

She recollected the first time Marcel had hit her. She'd wanted to get a reaction, not that she expected him to do what he did, but she knew she'd pushed him, so she forgave him and blamed herself. But over time, no provocation was needed. Marcel came to think he could do whatever he damned well pleased!

She tried everything she could to protect herself and the kids. She insisted Marcel leave her alone. She let him see her anger. But it just made things worse. He didn't even see her as a person after awhile. He did whatever he wanted and didn't worry about it. It was like she didn't have feelings. He would have killed her for sure, and thought nothing of it.

She had no choice. He deserved to be dead.

Men stick together. They protect each other. Bernie was too useless a cop to see he'd be protecting Marcel if he did his job and stop the guy from hurting his family. He couldn't figure it out. Thought he was smart and that men should stick together. Well, he'd found out different. And he was a bastard too after what he did to poor Francine who wouldn't hurt a fly.

Bernie was another one who deserved to die.

It was like the war hadn't been enough killing. Like they wanted to keep on going. Like women were the enemy now. Well, women had to fight back. Maddy would understand that in time. This was an undeclared war.

I hate them all, Emelie thought. They had never treated her in any way that was not domineering, or used her, or made her feel cheap. For a long time she forgave Marcel because she remembered the shy awkward guy she'd married, but it was a lie. He turned out to be just like the rest. The only people with any decency were women. It's like men and women are two different species. When you have to fight to survive you do whatever you have to and put decency aside.

## *Robert*

Robert backed out of the driveway in the Nash. It would have been a ten minute walk to Gus Vezina's hardware store but the hell with that, he was on his feet all day every day and had been for ten weeks. Now he was going to grab every opportunity to drive. It was odd though, the first time or two after an absence, being in a moving car was a little scary, even just doing twenty miles an hour. The speed seemed so much faster when you only ever went at a walking pace and never saw any cars going by.

He walked past a group of men loitering outside the store's entrance, talking about the inquest. It held little interest for him. Too bad about Bernie. Robert knew him of course, they'd gone to school together when they were really small, but had never been chums. It was understandable how depressed people could get about things, but to kill yourself, Jesus! They guy survives the war, comes home and kills himself. How do you make sense of something as pointless as that?

Looking for some nails, Robert squeezed his way up one of the crowded aisles of Vezina's. The shelves were jammed with everything imaginable. A pair of men walking up the other aisle stopped. Without meaning to, Robert could overhear their conversation.

"Those bitches killed their husbands. I don't believe for a sec that Bernie would kill hisself. He wouldn't hit his wife either."

"Marcel woulda though, he was a screwy one."

"Yeah, it's hard to even blame what's her name, Emelie LeClair, if she killed him."

"It's the doctor. She's gotta be in on it. She's tellin' the cops Marcel had a bad ticker. That's bullshit. Guy was strong as a horse."

"She probably gave those women some poison. Well, she won't get away with it for long if that inquest does anythin' worthwhile."

"Bloody gutless government never does anythin' worthwhile."

Robert silently appeared beside the men. He squared his shoulders and clinched his fists.

"You got something to say to me you son-of-a-bitch," he said to the bigger of the two.

Both men stepped back.

"Just talkin' Bobby," said one, his voice wavering. He started to rub the back of his neck for all he was worth.

"Yeah, I heard you *just talkin'*." Maybe you better keep your mouth shut. Talkin' shit's a good way to make a lot of trouble for yourself."

MOUTHY BASTARDS, HE THOUGHT later. He'd grown up in this town and people were willing to believe this sort of garbage about his wife? All they did in this dump was gossip about each other. Even the men. There was nothing else to do. It was time to get out of this shit hole.

The whole thing was so unbelievable. How could they even come up with a story like that? Maddy spent her life trying to care for people. That was just the way she was.

He never liked the idea of Maddy and his son being around Emelie and her brood. Now look what was happening because of it. He'd heard about the LeClairs. It was said that when they were young that they put on airs and ran with people from the Row. Emelie had been a tramp apparently, and the sister too.

Robert moved on in his thoughts. He didn't like to think about Emelie LeClair. Her name had bad associations since the day he tried to give Maddy hell about interfering in Marcel's and Emelie's business. For a long time after he thought about what Maddy had said. She figured he was a coward. It upset him. She didn't understand. He wasn't afraid. It was just 'live and let live.' You don't interfere in people's lives and they don't interfere in yours.

If he had to do it again, he decided after, he'd have gone to Marcel and straightened him out. The one thing that Maddy said that had been true enough was about Emelie having no family. He should have helped her.

The coroner's inquest would soon be over. That would clear things up and the gossipy old men would start thinking about some other dirt.

## *Maddy*

Maddy was always pleased to have Robert at home but never more so than now. She stood at the kitchen window watching him in the backyard pontificating to Lawrence about weeds. He cupped his hands and broadly gestured before starting to pull them up. Lawrence watched him gravely and then, looking back and forth between the weeds and his father, imitated his weed-pulling technique precisely.

Earlier in the year Maddy had been on top of the weed situation but hadn't paid attention to them in weeks. Now she wanted to think about weeds. She wanted to become engrossed with weeds. Completely and utterly spellbound by them. Weeds were inconsequential day-to-day life. They were the kind of thing that absorbed the thoughts and time of people who lived uneventful lives. Weeds were what she needed.

Longing for domestic normalcy was painful. It brought home the vulnerable feeling that this could all disappear so fast. Now, looking at the two of them in the yard, in matching knitted coats, brought tears to her eyes.

The floorboards in the house cracked as they settled. Maddy started. The police would be coming for her at any moment, of that she was certain. In her imagination they'd become a calculating, omniscient, and cold spectre. They would figure things out somehow, and she would be brutally torn away from her family.

It used to be that when Robert was home she felt safe, as if nothing bad could happen. But her problems were well beyond that now and there was no way she could talk to him about them. Their whole life had been put on the line by her actions. He would certainly condemn her. How could he not?

After Robert fell asleep she would go to Lawrence's room, look at him sleeping and make herself cry thinking how this could be one of the last nights she would spend with her family.

On Tuesday, she had driven to Hartley to testify at the coroner's inquest into Bernie's death. On the way down in the morning she'd rehearsed her lines for the drama to come. Could she stay calm enough to pull it off? Her manner must be professional, formal, yet it was important to make it sound matter-of-fact. Maybe routine was a better word. Yes it was a tragedy but there was no medical reason to suspect Bernie's death was anything other than a suicide.

The coroner asked just four questions and Maddy repeated what she'd said to the police. There appeared to be no suspicion her testimony lacked veracity. They were apparently only getting her words on the record.

Maddy hadn't stuck around for the rest of the proceedings. It was routine. Not something she wanted to appear unduly interested in. Francine would acquit herself well, she thought. She wasn't nervous the way she would have been if Emelie was testifying. Francine was more articulate and intelligent than Emelie. She had taught school and even spent a year in university.

Now it was just a matter of waiting.

Life would never return to normal.

Emelie said they would kill again. Stupid, stupid woman! Maddy thought she understood Emelie's feelings to some degree; as much as one could from the outside. She had been treated like an animal and backed into a corner with no escape. She had to fight for her life and now wanted to help other women who were in the same sort of hopeless situation. That was fine, as far as it went, but Emelie interpreted 'help' to mean dealing with all violent men exactly the way she did with Marcel, as if they were all irredeemable. There was no grey. She was generalizing to the point where she hated all men. And, after killing once, all her moral restraint seemed to be gone.

No moral person could stand back and let Emelie and Francine do what they promised. They would look at her as an ally if she did nothing. She couldn't let them think that, to feel confidence in her complicity, or even that she could be forced into helping them for her own survival. Not going to the police meant she would have to find another way to stop them.

The right thing to do would have been to have refused to help Francine create her lie in the first place. To let the truth come out and put an end to it. It was too late for that decision now, so Maddy resolved, as she had a dozen times before, to go to the police and tell them everything. Just get it over with. It was the only thing that could be done to protect potential victims and to end the fear.

When that was resolved it gave her a sense of finality. Then she thought about her son. Didn't Lawrence need a mother? What would his life be like if he had to go through it with the stigma of having a mother who was a known murderer? That's what would happen if she went to the police.

So, as she had a dozen times before, she resolved to do exactly the opposite of her earlier resolution. She would take no immediate action and hope that the pair didn't follow through on their threats.

But resolutions were short lived. They were just a way of returning to the beginning in order to go through the same cycle of logic all over again. So, for the fiftieth, and soon the one hundredth time, she weighed different scenarios around how she could protect her family by stopping Emelie. She remonstrated with herself about why she had taken the course of action she had in giving her the pills, then rationalized how she could have done nothing different. The thoughts looped over and over. She couldn't get away from them. Life wasn't about avoiding them but of finding places where she had the luxury to review them unbothered, which she did, until she wanted to scream in frustration.

Her obsession was the only way she knew to rise above the fear of the police as a menacing presence ready to pounce. It was a mechanism for the mind to try and find its way through a wild jungle of predators waiting to devour her. Obsession was a means to grapple with the stress, not the source of it. There was no way the police could find out what happened, she tried to convince herself. No way.

Most of the time Maddy struggled to not get lost in her thoughts while she was with patients or her family. One morning she saw Robert watching her and looking puzzled. He had been speaking to her, she was pretty sure, but she hadn't a clue what it was about. Maybe he'd asked a question and was waiting for an answer.

Robert had gone back up north by the time the news got to Maddy that the coroner's inquest had reached its conclusion: Bernie's death was deemed a suicide. It was no relief. The threats to Maddy's freedom and her family did not go away. She knew the coroner's verdict might actually make things worse by giving Emelie and Francine the boldness to kill again; the feeling that they were invincible.

The verdict should have ended her own terrors but it felt like they might just be beginning. The threat to her family would go on forever.

IN THE WEEKS FOLLOWING the inquest, Dr. MacQuigau added twelve new patients, all women. They came from throughout the region. Sometimes in pairs. Such and such told me about you. I've been meaning to make an appointment for ages. So happy you're here!

Finding the available time to squeeze in her daily outing was becoming increasingly difficult.

When she went for walks she noticed more evidence of a change in attitude towards her. The neighbour woman who ignored her in the past now nodded in her direction and said hello. A woman she didn't know, but who'd passed her maybe forty times with no acknowledgement, finally smiled.

The change in the men was striking too. Jacques, the big intimidating neighbour who used to scowl, now seemed oblivious to her when she went by his place. The few men who had been friendly to her no longer looked at her or said hello, not even Paul Desjardins. The last time she saw him at the market he'd beetled off looking nervous. It wasn't much but it sent her paranoia into high gear. Why would men be acting so strangely around her? They must be talking amongst themselves and speculating on Marcel's fate, she reckoned. That would explain the repugnance towards her she saw expressed in their behaviour.

After thinking about it a number of times, to the point where she was convinced she was right, she began to wonder if Emelie had let something spill. The girl had said she didn't care who knew what she'd done. Maddy was forever seeing her around town with her kids, and she was always yakking it up with someone or other. It kindled Maddy's paranoia.

God, she hated Emelie! The last couple of times she saw her coming down the street, Maddy had gone in a different direction. She couldn't face the possibility of a meeting. At the sight of her, Maddy would walk faster, wish she could hit something, scream, or find some other way to get rid of the energy surging through her. Emelie was going to be the cause of them all being hanged. It was like she was holding Maddy's hand to a flame; that flame being the terror of imminent disclosure.

Maddy tried to force herself to think more reasonably. Everyone in this town gossips constantly, she'd tell herself. Of course there'd be stories. Most people hadn't changed in their behaviour to her so most wouldn't have heard anything or believed it if they did. The reactions to her were just a coincidence.

But, she then wondered, if there were stories, and the new cop heard about them, how seriously would he take them?

Emelie had to be stopped from talking and from taking any further action! There was nothing else to do. But how?

Emelie had had gone from victim to enemy. From an abused and helpless mother to an aggressor making the doctor's own life a terror. Maddy hoped she'd wouldn't be inimical to reason when she approached her. It was what she had to do.

PART 3

# *Emelie & Maddy*

With wipers knocking around an opaque film of rain, Emelie could barely see the pavement as she wheeled the lumbering old Pontiac that Marcel had been so proud of off the highway and on to the slick paved road, pointing it towards Wegebow.

She had left the kids with Francine and driven to Hartley on her own to go shopping. There were bags on the back seat with dresses for Cecile, jeans for René and a few things for herself and Francine. It was the first time in months she'd done something on her own, and she wouldn't have gone except that Francine—who was thoughtful like that—had convinced her this morning she should take a break.

Emelie was happy with the direction of her life. In control for the first time, she was working evenings at the motel while Francine babysat. Most days Francine supply taught at St. Rita's Catholic School. The four of them were a family. Emelie had just put her house up for sale so they could all share a place. Between the assets from the sale of the house and the two part-time jobs, they would get by quite nicely.

Emelie wasn't going fast but it was still hard to navigate through the unexpected torrential downpour. The thick black vertical cumulonimbus clouds that had suddenly appeared, eclipsed the sun to make late afternoon look like late evening.

There's a small bridge at the outskirts of Wegebow running over the mouth of the river emptying into Lake Wegebow. Emelie was driving slowly as she hunched over the wheel and peering outside to try and see the road, still, she had no time to react when the oncoming car drifted into her lane. The two vehicles brushed against each other. When Emelie swerved right the Pontiac tore into a corner of the bridge. The passenger door heaved inward, its window shattered. Stupidly, the heavy car pivoted around the corner pillar and slid drunkenly down the hill. Emelie bounced about inside, as powerless as if the hand of some malevolent god was knocking her about. Her head walloped the roof. Then it hit the windshield.

The car almost came to a stop at the bottom of the hill before, in close to slow motion, as if impending death was something banal, it rolled over the edge of the bank and with a demure splash plopped delicately upside down into the river.

Emelie was unconscious. The water wasn't deep but it poured into the car through the broken window, submerging her. She was drowning.

The vehicle that collided with Emelie's was owned by a young couple on their honeymoon just driving into town hoping to find a restaurant and restrooms to escape the downpour. It slid to a stop against the other side of the bridge. The driver, looking in his rear view mirror, saw Emelie go over the embankment.

"Geez," the man yelled to his wife, "they've gone into the darn river!" He scrambled out of the car and ran back to the start of the bridge, his wife arriving seconds later.

"There! It's there!" she yelled, hopping up and down and pointing to the car in the water, "but I don't see anybody."

"I'll go down there! See if you can find some help!"

The husband started off. Turning, after a few feet, he pointed up the road and called, "Try that house! Try any house. Get a doctor too!"

He raced down the slope while trying to pull off his dark grey windbreaker. He skidded and slipped to his hands and knees on the wet scratch grass. At the water's edge, his momentum propelled him off the bank, splashing into the river.

As he stood up, the wheels of the car were the only thing that could be seen above the chest-high water.

Crouching down, he tried to look inside the vehicle. Nothing was visible through the murkiness. Blindly patting the door he found the handle and squeezed it. It was locked. Standing up, he waded his way to the driver's side of the car. Again he crouched and once more found a locked door. On this side of the car he could see enough in the black water to figure out the window was broken. He reached through and unlocked the door.

Bracing one foot against the side of the car, his muscles strained to move the door against the weight of the water. Twice he was forced to stand up and catch his breath. When the door was finally opened, he drew himself up, sucked in a deep breath, and dove down through the doorway. His searching hands found Emelie, grabbed a handful of clothes, hauled her across the front seat and out of the car. She was pulled to the surface unconscious. Keeping her head above water, the man dragged her to the bank of the lake and rolled her up on shore.

As he got there he could see his wife, with another woman, scrambling down the hill.

"This is the doctor! This is the doctor!" his wife was calling.

"Come with me!" he yelled back, "I don't know if there's anyone else in the car."

Together they plunged into the water.

Dr. MacQuigau knelt beside Emelie. She put her head to Emelie's chest to check for a heart beat and grasped her wrist looking for a pulse. Nothing. Maddy glanced at the couple in the river, too preoccupied with trying to find people inside the car to pay any attention to her. Somewhere in a house at the top of the hill was an old woman who knew about the accident. She was the one who had phoned Maddy to get over here as quickly as possible. But there was no way she could see the river's edge from any of her windows.

Maddy hesitated. It would be so easy to do nothing while creating the appearance of attempting to revive Emelie, just in case anyone was watching. And Emelie would die. It would fix everything, almost like the answer to a prayer.

The moment it took for Maddy to realize the implications of the situation she had come across took mere seconds. That was the extent of her hesitation.

She began in earnest to try and resuscitate Emelie. Maddy did her best but it was no use, Emelie still died.

# *Maddy*

The next morning, Maddy drove to see Francine.

*I assumed Emelie's kids would be there, and I hoped it's where they'd stay. I was sure it's what Emelie would have wanted too. The only ones who might have objected were Marcel's family but that didn't seem likely. As it turned out, after his death, his family showed they couldn't have cared less about the kids. They never even offered to take them for a day.*

*Francine grabbed me when I showed up at the door. 'Oh, Maddy,' she cried, and hugged me for a long time. Her eyes were rimmed red—I was sure she'd been up all night—yet her hair was immaculately coiffed. Over her shoulder I could see the kids in the backyard, digging in the snow, and they looked dressed for the weather, as they should be.*

*As for myself, there was no immediate sense of release from my worries because of Emelie's death. I had done everything I could to keep her alive. All I felt now was sadness at the tragedy and loss.*

*I walked Francine over to the table and had her sit. There was still a lingering fetid smell from Bernie's cigarette smoking, but it was dissipating, and the kitchen was much neater than the last time I'd been there; the night Bernie had died after rampaging around the place for days. But it was too neat. There were a couple of bowls and glasses in a drain board, which I assumed were from the kids' breakfast, but there was nothing else.*

'Have you eaten anything?'

'I'm not hungry?' she waved the idea away with a flick of her hand.

'When was the last time you ate?'

'I don't know. I'm not hungry.'

'I know you're not hungry but you have to eat something. Can I make you some toast?'

'No, really.'

Francine came over to me, took one of my hands, and pulled me along as she edged backwards towards the kitchen chair, like she couldn't bear to let go. I followed her and snagged one of the other chairs as I went past, dragging it behind me. I sat down directly in front of her.

She did the talking, saying the sort of things one would expect: how tough this was, how much she loved Emelie, how it was her fault because she'd urged her to go out that day. That made her cry again. We sat there for a long time.

"Em's in Hartley for the autopsy," Francine said eventually (not her first statement that made it sound as if Emelie were still alive) and told me how a couple of O.P.P. had been there earlier. One of them, a sergeant who'd known Bernie, said he would help arrange things afterwards.

'What happened?' she asked me.

'Well, I wasn't really there,' I began, and started to tell her what I'd heard at the scene from the people who found the accident. 'That man was incredible. He did everything he could to get her out. He was blue when I got there. Lucky he was in such good shape. I can only think it must have been the adrenaline that stopped him from getting hypothermia. It's amazing. The water was freezing cold and he was in there for a long time…'

'No, no. I've heard. That's not what I meant. I mean, what about Emelie? It must have been the same for her.'

'I don't think she was ever conscious Francine.' I said as soothingly as I could. I felt uncomfortable proceeding because anything else I said would be hard for her to hear.

'Why do you think that?'

'Well, she hit her head.'

'How do you know?'

'You could see the marks…you don't want to know about this Francine. Believe me I saw her.'

'The police say she probably drowned.'

'I think so.'

'I know you didn't like her,' she said, flipping her hand like she was batting the remark away, as if not liking Emelie was an irrelevancy. 'But she mattered more to me than my whole family.'

*'I know that. But don't say that about me not liking her, Francine. I didn't feel that way.'*

*'No, no, you did!'* It sounded like my denial had annoyed her. *'I saw you a couple of times coming down the street and you turned the corner when you saw us. You were angry with Emelie. Me too, I guess. It's okay. I understand.'*

*'It was just feeling awkward because of our last conversation.'*

She let go of my hand. I sat there with it in my lap, deciding to let things settle a bit.

*'Did you even try to save her?'* she said unpleasantly.

There was a hard edge to her voice. The idea was incredibly insulting.

*'Of course I did! How can you say that? It's ridiculous! You know I did.'*

*'Did you give her mouth to mouth? You didn't! I asked Sergeant Sullivan. He said you didn't.'* Now she was angry.

*'How would he know? He wasn't even there?'*

*'Well the police know…So did you?!'*

I sighed.

*'You coulda saved her!'* The latter statement was yelled so loud it verged on the hysterical and I wondered if the neighbours would hear. *'I'm sure you coulda. You wanted her dead. You were afraid people'd find out you killed Marcel. You wanted her to shut up. You said you'd stop her when she said we'd deal with any other man who treated his wife like Marcel treated her. I know, I was there when you said it, remember?'*

*'Francine! Stop it! Emelie was just talking. I knew that. But I wanted her to realize how it would hurt her more than anyone else if everything came out. I wouldn't have killed her! God! You weren't even there at the accident Francine. She was in the water for almost ten minutes by the time they got her out. Her heart had already stopped. The guy who pulled her out of the car was an ambulance driver. He told the police he never saw anybody try as hard as I did to revive someone.'*

*'Where's this guy?'*

*'How should I know? Gone I guess. They were American tourists. What's it matter?'*

*'Yeah. Gone. So I can't ask 'em.'*

*'Do you know how much I risked to stop Marcel from killing Emelie? My family. My life!'* I was getting pretty loud and angry with the injustice of it all. *'How can you think I'd turn around and do something to harm her?'*

Francine paused, she looked taken aback, but said with decisive clarity, *'I want you to leave my house and I never want you to come back.'*

☙

# *Maddy*

Maddy had pulled a chair up beside her, for Lawrence to stand on, while she worked at the kitchen counter.

They were making a cake, or, more accurately, Lawrence was perched at her elbow watching, waiting for the mixer to stop. When it did, Maddy poured the cake batter into a pan.

" Now I get to lick it," Lawrence said triumphantly. "Can I have the spoon too?"

"You think you can eat all that?" It was said as if the notion was a dubious one.

"Yeah." Said with determination.

"It's not 'yeah', it's 'yes'."

"Yes."

"Alright then."

He climbed off the chair, sat on the kitchen tiles, and spread his legs. Maddy put the bowl in front of him with the large spoon in it she'd used to stir the ingredients.

He dove in, practically submerging his head while he licked the bowl.

"You'll get batter in your hair."

He didn't seem to care and Maddy didn't stop him. She would have liked to have licked the spoon herself but was too happy that Lawrence enjoyed her cooking to not give in to him. What pleased her more was that this little boy liked to help her cook. She encouraged it by making it sound like a big adventure.

He enjoyed helping her clean, and she encouraged that too. Maddy vowed to herself that her son wasn't going to be a helpless male thinking some woman should be waiting hand and foot on him. He could get off his behind and look after himself. Each household task he learned how to do was a real accomplishment she told him, part of growing up, and like most kids, he took great pride in trying things he saw adults doing.

After the batter came the icing. A smaller bowl this time. Not only was there a spoon too, but the two pop-out arms of the electric blender.

"You're going to make yourself sick if you have all that sugar."

"No, no, I won't. I prom...Boom! Boom!" He had stopped in mid-sentence to accompany the recorded cannon fire at the end of Tchaikovsky's *1812*

*Overture* playing on the hi-fi. He had tucked his hands in his armpits and flapped his elbows in unison. His mother had tried with only modest success to interest him in those of her favourites that she thought would appeal to a little boy; Sibelius, Saint-Saëns' *Carnival of the Animals*, Prokofiev's *Peter and the Wolf*. It wasn't until she told him what the bangs were at the end of the *1812* that he'd gotten excited.

Maddy had spent more time with Lawrence in the weeks after Emelie died than she had in months. She could now pay attention to him without her thoughts constantly drifting off. It was her first measure of peace in over a year. Maddy still worried about being found out, but Francine's performance at the inquest had proven she understood what would happen if the truth came out and that she could think on her feet well enough to tell a convincing story. That was reassuring.

Emelie's funeral, three weeks earlier, had drawn only a modest crowd. Maddy thought there'd be more women given the number that Emelie looked to have befriended lately, but women didn't attend these things on their own, they came as part of family units, and the men weren't related to Emelie. The avian Father McNeil had been in his usual fine predatory form, only coming just short of saying his parishioner's death had been retribution for the way she stormed out of the church after Marcel's funeral. Her defiance left her cast adrift, a rudderless ship, and any number of other marine metaphors. What she did was to walk out of the safe harbour of the Lord and into the icy waters of Wegebow River.

Maddy stood at the back corner of the church that day so Francine couldn't see her. She would like to have asked her about the sleeping pills that had been in Emelie's possession but was too tired to trudge over to her house and hear again how much she was hated.

In any case, Maddy pushed away any idea that Francine might share Emelie's idea of murdering more men. That had been all Emelie's idea, Maddy felt. She easily convinced herself that there were no worries. She wanted to be convinced. She was too drained to feel any more tension.

"Is René coming over or is he still sad?" said Lawrence thoughtfully, looking up from where he remained sitting on the floor as he licked icing off a spoon.

"I think he'll be sad for awhile yet."

"How long?"

"I don't know honey."

Maddy hoped there'd be some way Lawrence and René could continue to be friends but she thought it more likely that nothing would change and Lawrence would eventually, with time, just forget…hopefully.

"Do you want to go outside and play?"
"Yeah!"
"Yes."
"Yes."

# *Maddy*
# November

Dr. MacQuigau drove home from a call on the other side of town. Mrs. Villeneuve's three kids had whooping cough. All the children in town were coming down with it, almost without exception. It was when the kids couldn't sleep in the quiet of the night, when their barking sounded most frightening to parents, that the doctor was called and Maddy would drive or trudge over to the house. Tonight's journey had been through the year's first snow flurries.

Nearing her own house she saw a police car in the driveway, and despite having met the new constable the day before, her first frightened impulse was to keep driving. Slowing down instead, she saw Isabel at the front door, holding it open and speaking to Constable Jessup.

Maddy parked on the side of the road in front of the house. Perhaps from unconscious guilt she looked around inside the car, as if making sure there was nothing incriminating on the floor or seats, then reached over, picked up her black bag, and took a long deep breath. Slowly, she climbed out of the car but then, once out, strode up the walk with an air of confidence to greet the pair.

"Here! Here she is! Here's the doctor," said Isabel to the policeman, beckoning Maddy forward with her hand.

"Dr. MacQuigau," Jessup said with his awkwardly formal, just-out-of-college manner. "You had a little trouble here."

"It was a boulder...a big boulder came through the picture window," gushed Isabel gasping for breath, "it smashed it! There's glass everywhere."

"Lawrence?" Maddy said with some alarm.

"He's sleeping! He never even woke up."

Poking her head through the open door Maddy could see numerous shards on the hallway floor. She stepped back outside to get a perspective of the front window.

"Oh my God!"

"I looked in the back yard and there's no one around," said the constable. "It was probably some kids. They do stupid things sometimes. There's some dandies around here. It's Friday night and they probably got some wine." His formality had quickly dissipated. It was too small a town to sustain long.

"I guess. I can't imagine anyone thinking that throwing rocks through windows is fun. Well, Isabel, it looks like we have some work to do cleaning this up."

"I'll get a shovel for the glass."

She bustled off.

Turning to Jessup, Maddy said, "I don't want to keep you Constable. Thanks for everything."

"Do you have some plywood to put over the window until you can get it repaired?" he asked, looking up. "I can put it up if you do. If you don't, I can get something for you."

"No, no thanks, but I appreciate the offer. I think it'll be okay for tonight."

Jessup looked doubtful.

"We'll rig something up to block out the cold. My husband'll be back tomorrow. He'll fix it. Give him something to do." She laughed.

When Robert came home the next day he swore about 'damn punks.' "These hillbillies love to hear a big crash. That's the mentality in this dump of a village. It's why nobody'll live here."

IMPATIENT FOR WINTER, THEY had already built a rink in Hartley, so that's where they took Lawrence skating for his first time. Robert held his hand while Lawrence's feet scrambled around in front of him like a cartoon character's, first in one direction and then another. Maddy's tears, from laughing, rolled down her cheeks. Driving home she thought about how happy she was. finally beginning to feel enough respite from her fear of being apprehended by the police at any time to enjoy her family again.

Nearing their house they could see the phosphorescent glow from the backyard, and when they went past, the tangled writhing flames in their back yard.

Robert accelerated, pulling the car into the driveway. He leapt out, as soon as he shoved the gear into park, and ran to the back of the house.

Maddy looked to the rear seat. Lawrence hadn't been awakened by the abrupt stop, so she too heaved opened her door and ran behind the house.

The back shed was burning. In a show of helplessness, Robert turned and raised his hands in the air when he saw her.

"There's nothing I can do," he called over the crackling fire. "The hose is in the shed." He pointed to the burning structure. It was a small shed holding their gardening tools, flower pots and lawn mower, not a lot, but it was completely enwrapped in flames and there wouldn't be much left after it was out.

"It won't touch the house. The wind's blowing the wrong way."
Smoke and sparks drifted harmlessly off over the trees into the blackness.
The two of them stood and watched the shed burn.

"Do you know anyone who might do this?" the constable asked, looking from one to the other.

The three were standing at the back door of the house assessing the charred and smouldering remains of the shed.

"This is the second problem you've had in a week," Jessup added. "It's almost like someone is targeting you."

"It's got to be the teenagers around here," said Robert. "This place is pretty isolated. There's nothing to do and too much inbreeding."

"I can't imagine anyone doing this deliberately," Maddy cut in, to give a more moderate impression. "There's nice people around here."

"No neighbours you had words with? No kids you told off for cutting across the lawn?"

She shook her head. "No one."

Maddy would write:

> *I thought about Jessup's question long after he left, and into the night, while the others slept.*
>
> *Was it possible we were being targeted?*
>
> *It was an incomprehensible and frightening idea, that there was some unknown person out there planning things against us.*
>
> *I wondered if these acts were directed to me and connected to the violence that had been visited on Marcel and Bernie.*
>
> *Because of that, I thought of Francine, although it was more like something a kid would do, but I couldn't think of anyone else. With Francine there was a motive if she really felt I'd let Emelie die. What purpose would targeting me serve though? I didn't understand. Did she think she was getting some kind of revenge by terrorizing us?*
>
> *I couldn't see it. It wasn't like her. She was from Wegebow and shared people's attitudes from what I could see, and she talked like the locals, but there was something about her that I could only define by calling it ladylike. It was incomprehensible that she would be going around setting fire to sheds and throwing boulders through windows.*
>
> *I dismissed the idea of her being involved. It had to be kids and it was only my paranoia that made it into something else. Like Rob had said, we were the last house in town, beyond us was the bush where teenagers went to drink*

*and spark. If they decided to make some mischief we were the nearest place at hand. It would be okay to pick on us wouldn't it? I was a doctor, someone in authority, and I was an outsider. Even Rob wasn't entrenched in the families here like most of the locals.*

*This way of thinking allowed me to get past the idea that someone nurtured a grievance about us, or was targeting us, as Jessup had suggested, and for a moment, at least, the neurosis and fear were kept caged.*

*I rolled over thinking sleep would come but my thoughts wouldn't shut off. It occurred to me that for the last couple of weeks there'd been other small things happening, but I hadn't paid much attention to them. Things in the line of harassment. I'd gotten some phone calls at the office and at home. When I answered, the caller hung up. Isabel got a hang up too, but since it was almost always me who answered the phone, she didn't realize it was a recurring problem.*

*The attacks on the house and the harassment had to be connected. There were too many things all at once. They had to be deliberate.*

*I hated to think it was Francine, but who else would it be? The phone calls, now that I thought about them, began after our falling out and following Emelie's funeral.*

*My nervous energy got me out of bed and I walked to the living room and sat down. I've had enough! I wanted to scream. This was even more disheartening because this was happening just when I was beginning to feel some relief from fear. I was sick of being dragged into the orbit of these women of Wegebow. I couldn't even spend one day enjoying being with my family because of the encroachment into my life and lack of respect for my things and my family. I wanted them to bloody well leave me alone.*

*I decided that I had to control my anger and speak to Francine despite her not wanting to see me. I wasn't about to accuse her of anything. I didn't much care what had happened. I just wanted it to stop. Repairing our relationship was the only way.*

*I thought back to my visit to see her the day after Emelie's death. She hadn't meant what she said, I felt, she was just upset. I reckoned she'd have thought about things and calmed down. Or at least I hoped.*

☙

WHEN SHE WENT TO Francine's house the next morning, and knocked on the door, Maddy received no answer.

The next door neighbour, a stout 50 or 60ish looking woman in a house dress with a heavy plaid jacket, who was sweeping snow off her front porch, called over that Francine wasn't home.

Dr. MacQuigau asked when she'd be back and the woman answered that Francine was with the kids at her sister's about two hundred miles away.

"Really! I thought I saw her last night."

The woman stopped sweeping. "Oh no, I phoned her in Port Arthur and talked to her last night."

"You called her?"

"Yes."

Maddy hoped the neighbour hadn't noticed her real question had not been whether the two of them had spoken but whether it was the neighbour who made the phone call. It's what confirmed that Francine was out of town, which meant that she couldn't have been at the doctor's the night before.

Someone else had it in for her or her family.

*I had to conclude that since it wasn't Francine who was responsible for the harassment that maybe my suspicions of a few weeks before were true; Emelie had been shooting her mouth off and now someone was blaming me for Marcel or Bernie's death. Maybe it was Marcel's creepy brother. What would he do, I wondered? I felt the old wave of stomach churning anxiety. I was coming to accept that it was still a long way from being behind me. Emelie's death hadn't ended the fear of exposure. I now felt even more vulnerable than when I thought it was Francine striking back at me. The possibilities of who might be targeting us were so vast that my imagination was working long hours speculating on who was responsible and what might have been said to have set them off.*

*There were no immediate ideas about what to do to stop the threatening behaviour, except pray that the harassment ended soon, whatever its purpose.*

☙

# *Maddy*
# Late November

Had she not been in a brightly lit room Maddy may have seen the figure with the rifle briefly emerge from the bush, by the corner of the lot, to be silhouetted against the lake before stepping back under cover to take up a shooting position.

It was right after dinner, the night before he was scheduled to return north, and Robert was playing with Lawrence on the livingroom floor. They were wrestling. They always wrestled until Lawrence banged into something, bloodied his nose or otherwise got hurt, cried and Robert would then lecture him about not acting like a baby.

Maddy hated these rules of manhood getting passed on to their son. She was standing at the sink doing the dishes, facing the small kitchen window above the sink.

The shooter's left hand, wrapped around the stock of the 30-30, was nestled in the crook of a tree to provide stability and accuracy. Through the rifle's sights Maddy's head was visible through the window. She was turning and talking, looking up, looking down. Aim for the middle.

Off in the distance, from somewhere on the peninsula, a teenage girl squealed with laughter and it carried across the water.

"Rob, you'll get him so excited he'll never sleep!" There was no answer. Oh well, it was Robert's last night here for awhile so may as well let them play together. As she turned her head to glance at the pair there was a distant crack from outside the house. Splinters of glass slapped against her face.

"Geez!" She stepped back and looked around. Her face stung and started to bleed.

Outside, the teenagers fell silent while the figure in the trees swore and reached down to feel for the spent shell on the ground.

Robert was at the kitchen door with a confused Lawrence under his arm. In two strides he crossed the room.

"That was a gunshot!" He looked at the window and at the wall behind in open-mouthed dismay. "Son of a bitch." He pulled Maddy away from the window. "Get back."

He handed Lawrence to his wife and purposefully strode out of the room.

She had no idea of what to do or how long to stay there. It felt like they were under siege. Robert could be heard opening the hall closet and rooting around, and she recalled that he kept a rifle and shells in there. When Maddy heard the front door open she yelled, "Robert don't go out there!" She hurried into the hall. "There's someone shooting a gun."

"Stay inside," he ordered as he walked out the front door.

She immediately called the police, but it was the last thing she wanted to do.

AT ONE POINT CONSTABLE Jessup used the MacQuigau phone and called his sergeant at home in Hartley.

"We're treating this very seriously," he said afterwards to Maddy and Robert. "It was a 30-30 and that can kill. It coulda been a hunter out on the peninsula. It wouldn't be the first time some clown hit a house with a bad shot. But with the other things happening to you we've got to figure it coulda been intentional. I'll start driving by your house as much as I can and do some asking around to see if I can figure out what's going on."

When the constable left, Robert walked him to the car and Maddy nervously watched through the window, wondering what they were talking about.

After Robert returned he wandered around, looking at the window and at Maddy cleaning up the glass. "Do you have any idea who could be doing this?" he asked, a puzzled expression on his face, perhaps not expecting an answer.

"No, of course not. Do you?"

"No," he said, still looking distracted, trying to sort things out.

Later that night, after Maddy was in bed, she heard Robert pacing about the house in the dark and pulling back curtains to look out the windows. Even after he'd come to bed, satisfied that things were fine, she lay there too anxious to sleep. It was if she was waiting for something to happen. Every creak from the house or noise outside put her on high alert. Was that someone trying to get into the house or coming through the nearby bush? Every sound was translated as to its cause, and undoubtedly translated incorrectly.

*The thing that kept going through my thoughts was that Lawrence could have been with me in the kitchen when the shot was fired.*

*I wanted out of this town. I'd had enough. The only sure way to protect us all was to leave. I was giving up. My nerves had had it.*

*What was compelling now, what made things worse than ever, was that both Robert and Lawrence were now also in danger. Could I say nothing, for one kind of self-protection, while knowing that it left not only me but my family in another sort of danger? If I knew who was responsible for the terror, I thought, maybe I could do something myself. But who was it? Again I came back to the idea that Emelie had said something to someone. It was a crazy idea. She stood as much to lose as me if word got out. I knew Francine wasn't behind the attacks. Was it possible that there was indeed a war and it was a group of men who were now attacking me? Or maybe Francine had told someone about her suspicions that I had withheld treatment for Emelie. But that couldn't upset anyone so severely since Emelie mattered to no one but Francine. The threat to my family, I concluded, could be coming from anywhere.*

*Emelie's death, for me, had meant that one impossible dilemma had been replaced with another. I wanted desperately to flee but was trapped here because leaving would require admitting what I'd done and telling Robert everything. If, by some remote chance he understood, he would see running as cowardice. If he didn't understand, I'd end up losing my family.*

PART 3

That the constable was going to investigate precipitated a further crisis. What if he found something out? I'd be arrested. Robert would be completely unprepared for what was happening. He'd reject me for not saying anything to him and wouldn't understand it was something I couldn't do. Even knowing this, I could still tell him nothing.

The best case scenario, if I said anything, was that Robert would insist on staying and try to stop the attacks. If he thought Francine was responsible—say she'd maybe gotten one of her brothers to help—he'd approach her. But then if she thought she was being threatened she might go to those brothers. Maybe she would figure I taken the first step in going public and then open her mouth. Telling Robert would almost definitely lead to violence in return. I knew him well enough to know he'd want to fight back and was too hot-headed to make sure he had the right person. I'd learned that violence perpetuates itself until someone says no.

In the week after Emelie's death, three women had cancelled appointments. There were two more cancellations the second week and more the third. Was it a coincidence or my imagination? People must be talking. Or was it just the women?

After Robert went back up north I felt so vulnerable at night I couldn't sleep. The muscles of my stomach were perpetually contracted as were those at the back of my neck. I imagined people in the bush. There were times I would get up and creep outside in the dark just to get a break. The dark offered safety. I would watch the house from the bush and that relieved the anxiety about someone possibly being outside targeting the place.

❦

# Isabel

Isabel Gagner, 41 years-old, was only 34 when her husband of sixteen years, Phillipe, had been killed trying to cross the beach at Dieppe.

They had no children, to Isabel's regret, and she knew from Dr. MacQuigau that she never would. To be a mother would have been the only reason for Isabel to remarry since she considered Phillipe to have been the great love of her life. Sometimes she missed the human contact, but Isabel had no wish for another husband.

Working as the live-in housekeeper for the MacQuigau's was, in many respects, the ideal job. It was a nice house and Isabel didn't have to be living at her parents' place. She loved kids and being constantly attached to little Lawrence was the next best thing to having one of her own. The boy was very fond of her. Sometimes, to his mother's great distress, when he was upset or lonely he would cling to Isabel instead of her.

Isabel loved country music and square dances at the town hall. Her job provided a credible excuse for escaping the single men who sometimes wanted to take her home afterwards. She had commitments. The doctor needed her in case she had to go out in the middle of the night on an emergency house call. Or, if it was a night when Isabel was staying at her folks' place she'd say she had to be at the doctor's early the next morning.

At 11:30 on Saturday night, Isabel left the dance and began to walk back to the doctor's house, five blocks away. The only people she saw were the usual cluster outside the hall, smoking and laughing, delaying the time until they too would walk home, usually staggering slightly. She saw a short thick stick that someone had left at the edge of a ditch and picked it up. People's loose dogs—many of them with wolf blood in them—would travel in packs and sometimes approach people out walking at night. Raising a stick and a couple of harsh words were enough to get them to leave you alone.

Isabel had gone three blocks and was walking past a parked pick-up truck, leaning to the right because its wheels were on the downward slope of the ditch, when a man stepped around the front and said, "Hello Isabel."

She started.

"Sacre main Jacques," she said, "you scared me." It was one of the Boudreaus, Bernie's family. Behind him his brother Luc stepped out from behind the truck. There was a noise behind her and Isabel turned and saw Guy Gagnon.

Isabel had bumped into the pick-up as she turned.

"You scared me, you bugger. What are you guys doing around here?" It sounded aggressive. Not what she intended, but they'd spooked her a bit. The stuff at the MacQuigau's lately was enough to unnerve anyone.

"Sorry. Just out for a little walk," said Jacques Boudreau, "can we walk you home?"

"Eh? Okay, if you want." It wasn't such an odd request in a town where nothing ever happened but she looked Jacques in the eye as she went past. He was handsome in a way, clean-cut and always employed. No one really understood why he chummed with his alcoholic brother Luc and the oily little Guy Gagnon. He had a pretty wife too. He should have been at home with her.

Jacques and Luc stepped apart and let Isabel past. Luc flicked his smoke into the road. Firefly sparks flew where it skipped across the gravel.

"I hear you had a little excitement," said Guy Gagnon hustling his little legs to slide up beside her. "Kids starting fires and shooting off rifles around the house. You'll be safer with us around."

He had leaned close to her, with would be intimacy, but the stench of tobacco and liquor made her draw back. Would Guy's presence provide comfort to anyone, she wondered?

"Can I ask you a question?" Guy said. "Whatdaya think about what some people are sayin', that your boss killed Marcel and Bernie 'cus they were slapping their wives around a little?"

Isabel stopped suddenly and was almost stepped on by the guys trailing behind.

"What? Who said such a thing?" She hadn't heard these rumours before. Living with the MacQuigaus cut her off from the town to a large extent. Some people would have considered her an outsider too because of who she lived with.

"No, nobody would say that! I don't believe anybody would. It's awful! The doctor wouldn't hurt a fly. Is someone really saying that?"

"Well, I heard it."

Isabel frowned, turned and resumed walking with her coterie in her wake.

"How do you know the doctor didn't help those women kill their husbands?" asked Luc. "She was there when they died."

"She's the doctor! What do you think she was doing there? Geez! It's who you call when people are sick. What's the matter with you?" And she added, imitating the voice of a very dim questioner, "Why was she there? Ha!" She was turning on the boys as if they were the ones spreading the stories. "Anyways, she wasn't even there when they died. People oughta get their stories right. Both times there was calls in the middle of the night and the doctor came and told me that she had to go out on emergency. It was the same as any other emergency. I'd a known if there was anything strange. The night Bernie died she went out and got Francine and came back and put her arm in a cast. Maddy knew nothing before then. It's a horrible thing to say anything different."

"Yeah, it's nonsense," Jacques said. "I said that when I heard it. Probably just one person talkin' eh?" They reached the house and the men continued walking.

"You take care of yourself Isabel."

# *Maddy*
# Early December

Maddy would always remember the next few weeks as some of the most difficult of her life. At every moment, when out of the house, her eyes went everywhere, scanning everything, looking for the invisible threat she knew was lurking. It would have been easier to have stayed at home but she would have her coat and boots on and be out walking without it having been a conscious decision. It overcame the feeling of being a sitting target. Anyway, it was better not to be at home and subject Lawrence to her sudden bursts of anger, she rationalized.

She took to slipping down by the beach. It was preferable there when the waves were choppy. If the water was still you could smell the dead fish at the shoreline, drawn out by a receding wave and then slapped back against the beach by the next. One time, east of home, she saw a sheltered little space under some trees. She crouched down and squeezed inside. Someone could pass by and not realize there was someone there. It was the first time in weeks she felt safe and at peace.

The one conclusion she always came to in the wild dervish of thoughts that wouldn't let her alone was that her family had to get out of Wegebow.

How would they ever be safe? Someone, or some group, was targeting her. It had to be connected to what they knew or suspected about recent events. And there was nothing she could do to prevent it because there was no way of knowing who or what the violence was about.

How could Robert be approached, with the idea of moving away, without solid reasons? It would be a big step. Wegebow was where he wanted to be. His job with Hydro would keep him here for now. And as a crew chief, he was doing well. Promotions were sure to follow.

Robert would understand the urgency of her desire to move if he felt her fear, but trying to convey that was out of the question.

WALKING THROUGH TOWN REMINDED Maddy of how much she hated the place. Everywhere you went the steeple of the church was visible and she heard it, saying with smug sanctity, that her actions had been immoral and she was on her way to hell.

As far as she was concerned the piety of anyone in this place was hypocritical and based on denial. The good citizens of Wegebow wanted one thing only, to appear to be moral. That meant hiding what went on. They pretended immigrants weren't beat-up. They closed their eyes to 13-year-old girls who were cut-off from the world by their fathers. And they didn't want to know what went on in families, ignoring the brutality inflicted on some women and kids by the man of the house.

Because she had done what the men of the town should have been doing she was under attack. Was she being threatened, warned to leave, or targeted for something she'd done? Back and forth, over and over, she covered the same emotionally swampy terrain.

She lost weight. She would begin to eat and then feel an intense distaste for whatever was in front of her. Her health was declining in general from the stress and insomnia. At night she took sleeping droughts but the next day could taste the chemicals and would struggle with grogginess. At times, alarmingly, she had chest pains. She wondered how long a body could withstand this. Obviously for a long time, she concluded. Consider the guys who'd been in the war. But, over time, it was going to make her sick and susceptible to all kinds of things.

At moments, Maddy would get caught up in something and forget her worries. She felt euphoric with the reprieve from so much pressure, like the effect of opening any infected wound and discharging the poison.

*Perhaps the biggest struggle I had then, and always, was the struggle with my own conscience. I worried about my soul and the morality of what I'd done. Of course, murder considered in isolation is immoral, and I didn't need God hanging over my head to tell me that, but I thought that protecting three people from being murdered was a graver moral obligation. I had to make a choice and I did.*

*Could murder ever be moral? No, I don't think ever (which is not the same as being justified). If killing Marcel had been a moral act it could never have grown into the malignancy it did, leading to more death, suspicion, gunshots, and a day-to-day life that was so racked with fear I wonder how I stood it at all.*

༄

"I was drunk," said Suzanne self-consciously, looking down at her lap, likely aware of her mother's censuring look, but just as likely, embarrassed by what she was talking about. I don't even remember it, honestly, I've been a little tipsy before," her voice dropped and so did her eyes, avoiding her mother's, "but never drunk. It was after the prom, we were drinking in his car, and next thing I remember is waking up in the back seat about 3 in the morning."

"Who is he?" Dr. MacQuigau asked. "Who's the father?"

"David Vezina. He's 18. He's the best hockey player in town," Suzanne said perking up. "I think he's gonna be in the NHL some day."

Maddy breathed deeply and suppressed a sigh. The girl in front of her, chewing a wad of gum, was 16 but looked 12. "Does he know you're pregnant?"

"No…I mean, I didn't know for sure until you just told us."

"Please help," the mother begged Maddy.

"Okay…so there's no chance of getting married?"

"No, no, she's too young," the mother curtly interjected again.

Suzanne looked to sag both physically and emotionally.

"The people in this place are ruthless," Suzanne's mother said. "There were women during the war, women who's husbands were overseas…and who got themselves into trouble…you know what I mean…or at least that's what people said, but nothing came of it." She stared at Maddy as if this were a question and she needed an answer.

"Well…" Maddy fumbled, looking for the right thing to say. She put her elbows on the desk in front of her, slowly rubbing her temples while watching the two women sitting across from her; the childish teen and the grim mother, who was in her thirties but looked old and matronly. Family life here did that to you it seemed. "I suppose, if you don't want people in town to know about this, you could go and live with a relative until the baby is born. But that only makes sense if you're putting the baby up for adoption. If you're not, then you may as well have the baby here since people are going to know about it before too long anyway."

She looked from mother to daughter.

"She can't keep the baby and ever hope to finish school," the mother said. "It'll be too hard being around other girls. They'll treat her like poison…I mean, even if I look after it. The other girls'll look down on her. Everyone will."

"If you're giving the baby up, you could stay with the church until it's born," Maddy said, referring to the Catholic home for unwed mothers in Prince Arthur.

The mother said to hell with that! Absolutely no way. Her cousin Anne went there. The nuns, she said, were "sanctimonious old witches" who did a moral number on her cousin.

"They told her she was evil and needed to repent. It was the same stuff she got at home. My uncle did this speech about how 'no Christian man will ever want you now' and I think it affected her for years."

"I don't want any of what happened to her to happen to my daughter. She'd have the shame of this forever," she said, frowning at Suzanne, letting her see how she characterized her daughter's actions. "She could never live here…and I don't want her father to find out. For God's sake no! He'll be furious and probably throw her out. Anne's father kicked her out. It ruined her life for sure." She finished her speech and stared at Maddy. "Please help her!"

Dr. MacQuigau looked blankly back although it was obvious what was being asked of her.

"I need to speak to Suzanne alone," she said.

"Is there any chance of David and you getting married if you had your way?" the doctor asked the girl after her mother had stepped out of the office.

"No. None. Well, if I told him about the baby he might marry me but my mother says it's crazy, we're both too young, you heard her, and, anyway, we broke up a week after the prom, and I don't know if I want to marry him now." She looked pouty and childish. "I love him but it's been coming to an end for awhile. He's too immature. All he wants to do is play hockey and hang out with his chums. And they like to buy booze and get drunk up in the bush. My mother's right. It'd be crazy to have a baby with someone who's just a kid himself."

"Do you understand that you're mother is asking me to perform a procedure that would terminate the pregnancy?"

"Yes, an abortion. I understand. It's what I want too. Mom said we're so lucky to have a woman doctor here; someone who might understand. She said you'd probably say no, but she knew you were a person we could at least ask."

Maddy sighed. "And do you understand this is an illegal procedure and that I would no longer be able to practice medicine and could even go to jail if someone was to ever find out?"

"No, I didn't know that," the girl said, her eyes wide. "I understand then if you say no."

"So what will you do if I say no and you're forced to have this baby. Have you and your mother talked about that?"

"Yes, a bunch" said Suzanne. "But I'm not having the baby," she replied slowly and decisively, "one way or another."

Maddy exhaled slowly, in frustration. She understood the import of the statement.

Maddy asked Suzanne and her mother to think about what they were asking and to come back the next day. Part of her reasoning was to give herself a chance to think about what she would do.

THAT NIGHT, MADDY REMEMBERED Ruth for the first time in ages.

Ruth lived in the flat beside her while Maddy was in school. She was another woman who also lived by herself, but in Ruth's case it was because she had no family.

Ruth was really pretty, Madeleine remembered. She liked to wear smart dresses with bold patterns and get her hair done, and walk on Sunnyside boardwalk with her fiancé Arthur on Saturday nights, and go to the dances there.

In 1944, on Arthur's last night of freedom before he went overseas, the two spent the night together.

Over the next several weeks, Maddy and Ruth's other friends saw less and less of her. On the two occasions when Maddy saw her, she remembered her looking haggard. Ruth was coming in from work, and hadn't stopped to talk, just said 'hi' and looked like she had to rush off. It was unusual behaviour, since she was normally so out-going and friendly, but people do get caught up in life and Maddy had too much on the go herself between work and school to pay attention to Ruth's behaviour.

It was a shock then when Katherine came to Maddy's apartment one night to tell her that Ruth had died. She didn't know how, some mysterious illness maybe, or an accident. But after two hours of tearful commiserating over Maddy's kitchen table, and self-chastisement about not having paid Ruth more attention, Katherine eventually confessed that what happened was that Ruth had bled to death during an abortion attempt.

# *Maddy*
# January — 1953

Maddy began by telling Robert she had something to tell him and for him to sit down in the kitchen.

He looked uncomfortable. Looked like he could get angry at any time depending on what was coming. Or maybe he didn't like the feeling of not being in control. The kitchen wasn't his realm.

She'd performed an abortion, she told him directly. She told him the facts. The girl and her mother were going to end the pregnancy one way or another so the father wouldn't find out. What choice did she have? To not help this girl would have been to stand by while she destroyed her life.

Maddy paused, waiting for his reaction. It wasn't like the deaths of Marcel and Bernie. She felt certain he'd understand. They had talked in the past about Ruth, about girls dying because they had no other option. One time, she remembered, someone on the radio had commented on the terrible scourge of abortions. "Bloody asshole," Robert said, "I wonder what he'd think if it was his daughter getting butchered in some back alley."

Robert shook his head. "It's good you did what you did. It maybe saved her life. But it's risky for you. When was this?" he asked.

"A while back," Maddy said vaguely, immediately aware that Robert might jump to the conclusion that the abortion Maddy had done was the reason for the attacks on their home.

He nodded his head and looked thoughtful.

# Part 3

AFTER THAT DAY ROBERT no longer phoned the local cop to see if he was any closer to finding out who was behind the harassment, and only part of his reason was that the attacks had stopped.

Over the next three months of winter, Maddy slowly came to realize that the fear she'd been living under, of exposure and violence, was slowly dissipating. It was no longer a continual presence, forcing itself upon her no matter where she was or what she was thinking. She slept late on occasion, without sleeping pills, and her muscles no longer ached from the perpetual tension.

Much of the time, when she had struggled to guess who could be behind the attacks on her, the speculation was that they were the acts of an anonymous coward who'd heard rumours about her involvement in one or more of the recent deaths. She knew it wasn't simply paranoia on her part, that rumours and gossip spread, and could be pernicious in a small town. What was happening to her practice vindicated this view. A few weeks after the first procedure she was approached by an older woman with thirteen kids who begged her for an abortion. She'd had enough she said. She was only 35 years-old and wanted to have a bit of a life.

Shortly after that there was another abortion request, and then another. Women, at least, were talking.

Her female patients returned and the males of the town still avoided her. Maddy reasoned that there had to be a connection, although it didn't make sense in a way. She thought that Catholic women would be opposed to abortions and shun her if word got around she was involved in such things, but Maddy had noted before that people will act in their own best interest, they might lie or cheat if it served their purpose, while simultaneously being an obedient Christian on the surface. It calmed Maddy when she thought that word of this type of thing would not likely reach the constable. It was more along the lines of private information that would pass between women. Even if word did get around, how would the police prove such a thing if no one provided them with information?

It occurred to her, with desperate hope, that there'd been no attacks on her since the gunshot through her kitchen window. Did that mean the attacks had stopped because they were only ever a co-incidence, that the person suddenly decided they'd gone too far, or was it because something had changed? That would mean that she was doing something now that the attacker approved of. If it was the fact of performing abortions then it suggested the person was a woman and that led back to Francine. She thought about their encounters in the last several months. Nothing had changed. When they passed, Francine would still look the other way.

# *Robert*
# Spring

The camp was a miserable place to stay. It smelled of sweat, smoke and flatulence. Without women around some men didn't bathe at all. Or maybe they were just being sensible. The perfume from soap attracted mosquitoes. With the spring blackflies it was a place where you could almost, literally, be eaten alive.

Outside wasn't much nicer, even without the bugs. It was an ugly part of the world, just flat swampy land dotted with short evergreens mostly and scrub brush around the base of the trunks that made walking anywhere next to impossible. The sole outdoor recreation was fishing for speckled trout. The diehard went up a creek leaping from rock to rock looking for pools where they'd fish for awhile until the bugs caught up with them and then move on.

Others preferred to stay inside and play poker; which meant enduring the smell. But with a family to think about, Robert couldn't afford gambling. He preferred sitting in a lawn chair outside the prefab hut, swapping stories with the other young guys, trusting a fire and cigarette smoke to deter the bugs.

He was tired of the north. Other guys liked to hunt and fish but Robert had seen enough killing in the war and wasn't interested in seeing any more. Increasingly, his only rationale for sticking around was a financial one. Maddy had been telling him more and more lately to forget the money, a boy needs his father. Maybe she was right, but what could he teach him that his wife couldn't. Well, he'd taken the boy into the bathroom with him so that he could see that boys stood up, so there were a few things he supposed.

Last time he was there Maddy said, "I'm so happy I could scream." How could he not miss that?

Robert had put in for promotion to manager. There were vacant positions in two districts. He hadn't spoken to Maddy yet. Both jobs meant moving to another town or city. That was all to the good. Robert wanted nothing more than to get his family out of Wegebow, especially after the recent troubles. It was dangerous.

When he thought of the abortions Maddy was doing he knew that wherever they went she was likely to find trouble. This was a portent of the future. He'd read in the newspaper once about a doctor being charged because he'd given some drugs, that he had as part of an experimental study, to someone whose life he figured depended on it. It was an illegal thing to do and the doc was charged.

Robert had never heard what happened after. You couldn't trust the courts to get it right so it probably wasn't good. Maddy was like that, always wanting to help someone. It was just the sort of thing she'd do.

Maddy had only pooh-poohed his concern when he said he worried about her and she pointed out there'd been no vandalism for months. He didn't say it but he knew there'd be more trouble ahead. Maybe he should lie to her. 'I want to take this job,' he could say, 'and I want you to quit your job and stay at home.' Would she do that? Would she believe that after all he'd said that he really was like most men and couldn't handle his wife working? Truth was, he'd rather she didn't work, it was a point of pride that he could support his own family, but he'd long since gotten used to the idea of his wife's career. He was actually proud of telling people he was married to a doctor. It said something special about him.

He thought about what he'd heard that day in the hardware store; people gossiping that Maddy had helped those women to kill their husbands. It was impossible she did anything to hurt Bernie, the guy wasn't that bad and Maddy wasn't his wife's doctor. But Marcel, that was different. Maddy had been Emelie's friend and was on Marcel's case.

But killing him? Could Maddy do that if she thought she was saving a life? Robert wondered and he hated himself for it.

# *Maddy*

Maddy became pregnant.

For the first couple of months she and Robert had this sort of dialogue:

Robert: "I think, after the baby is born, you might stay home. You don't need to work."

Maddy: "I spent a lot of years in school. I want to be a doctor very much."

Robert: "And you can if you want. I'm just saying that you don't need to. A man should be able to take care of his family and I can."

This was the attitude she always guarded against. It made her angry to hear it now. But Robert wasn't pressing it, he was leaving the choice to her.

She was surprised he would take a job away from Wegebow because he'd wanted so much to come home, but she felt maybe that his ego needed this. Maybe he wanted to take the job because it showed he could support his family. Her attitude softened. Who understood the male mind? Perhaps her working as a doctor was emasculating.

What was most shocking to Maddy, when she thought about it, was that after everything that had gone on here, that she was no longer anxious to leave. She thought of how much she'd wanted to go. And now here was her opportunity. She began to remember the stresses of the past year. They could start up again. Maybe leaving would turn out to be a blessing. Take a break and then start fresh in a new town. Being a doctor was work that could be gratifying and important. It wasn't as if she would give it up. She could continue with it after taking a short time off to have the baby.

When they offered Robert the job in Sudbury, he was noticeably very keen to take it. He was a crew chief in one of the smallest districts and this was a promotion to manager of one of the largest. It was a good step for someone on the way up and there was more pay. It made sense.

Arrangements were made. A house was found. Since the new baby was only a few weeks away, Maddy made no effort to jump into a new practice. She'd return to work in time.

The car was packed. Before they got inside to follow the moving van, there was a long lingering look over the house. Her house. The place she had built from her own design. The car backed out of the driveway and, as they pulled away, Maddy saw Denise, the young girl who lived alone with her father, across the road at the edge of the bush, watching, half-hidden behind a tree. Maddy waved and Denise raised a hand in acknowledgement. As they drove off down the road Maddy began to cry.

༄༅

# PART 4
*Lawrence*
1972

A ROUND THE TIME I read my mother Maddy's journal, we were living on the second floor of another old house, this one in Toronto. We had use of the backyard and our 1-year-old daughter, Beatrice, would play there sometimes. A week before her birth I had read the story of Beatrice Cenci and it gave me second thoughts about using the name but the decision of name had been made and we stuck with it. Bea's name had actually from another famous Beatrice — Dante's unrequited love interest and muse.

It was the seventies, a new decade, but nothing much had changed since my mother's time. The Americans were still telling us who was the enemy and they were still at war in someone else's country.

A year after I started university as a mature student — the reason we had returned home from Vancouver — Dee did the same. She had turned 21. We lived on student loans and petty theft, stealing toilet paper from the school washrooms and the like.

I was giving up on being a hippy, I think. With university, Eastern religion and astrology were giving way to psychology, sociology and philosophy.

THE JOURNAL CAME FROM my father.

"Lawrence. This is your father. Come over. I wanna give you something," he said on the phone, in his disjointed and direct way. The call itself told me this was important to him. He never phoned. The receiver was a foreign, awkward thing he'd hold at a distance from his ear, and you'd hear him trying to wind up whatever conversation he was having so that, as soon as possible, he could get rid of the bloody thing that was forcing him into being sociable. "It's a journal your mother started writing a couple of months before she died. I want you to read it. I think she wanted to get down the story of her life."

"What is it? A diary?"

"I don't know. She called it a journal."

"It's gotta be pretty short right?"

"No, no it's a big book and it's full of writing. She put a lot into it."

"Huh? Sounds more like an autobiography. Was she writing her life story? Did you read it?"

"No. My eyes have been bothering me. I was hoping you'd give me the run down."

"Sure."

His eyes had been bothering him? I hadn't heard that one before. He read all the time.

I said, sure, of course. My mother had wanted someone to read her story. As I hung up I wondered if he was afraid to read it. Maybe scared it would shatter some of his illusions about her and he wanted me to screen it first. I could live with that. I was flattered he had asked me and not my brother Martin.

It was a Saturday night and I told my father I'd head up in the morning. Dee was out. She hadn't been home from her class that afternoon. It was typical. I figured I'd wait up and tell her I was leaving early.

THE BACK DOOR OF the apartment opened on to a wide balcony that hung over the backyard. I kept the door propped open through the summer and into the early fall, and a breeze would blow through.

I remember the breeze wafting the smell of oil paint through the apartment after we painted the kitchen cupboards bright red. A small print of Breughel's *Children's Games* was thumb-tacked to one of the upper doors. After my mother's death I added a photo of myself as a baby, with my parents, and knew then that I would write a poem about it some day.

I used to play with Bea in the morning, mostly inside. She wasn't the most co-ordinated girl as a result of not getting the chance to run around, and she'd only just started walking. She liked it when I read Dr. Seuss in stirring, Shakespearian, over the top tones. "I DO NOT LIKE THEM Sam-I-am!" I would thunder, waving my arms and shaking my finger.

The idea was that I would baby-sit during the day while Dee was in school and that she would take over on those evenings when I had my classes. But I was spending all my time with my daughter.

Dee was almost never at home. In only three months her life had come to revolve around school. She liked the company of academics and was carrying on some sort of affair with one of her instructors. It wasn't shocking to me, not for the time period and who we were, but we didn't talk about it. In any case, I never would have said I objected. That would have gone against everything

I espoused at the time. When I felt jealous, I had intense, recriminatory conversations with myself, arguing that jealousy was the result of indoctrination by society and the church. It was the jealousy, not Dee's infidelity, that was the issue I needed to work on.

When we'd gotten married two years before it wasn't due to the new baby or a belief in the institution of marriage but because it opened up a bunch of possibilities for bursaries, grants and scholarships. We went into marriage agreeing it didn't bind us to anything. But the odd thing was, I was starting to feel like I wanted us to act like a married couple, meaning I wanted monogamy. And I felt guilty about it, like I was giving into societal expectations and losing the battle to my own jealousy.

I watched the hockey game on a tiny black and white TV in the livingroom while laying on the mattress that served as a couch. It was covered with a bedspread and pillows, and small toys that had found their way between or under them. And I fell asleep.

I don't know what time Dee came in but it woke me. I sat up, felt a definite sense of relief she was home, rubbed my face, and looked at the Indian head logo on the TV telling me the station was off the air. I got up to turn off it off and kill the high-pitched drone.

Dee's face poked around the door frame, and grinned.

"Good show?" She laughed, drunkenly. "What are you doing?"

"Waking up. What time is it?"

"Three, I guess." She laughed again. She was always laughing and it had an endearing quality. Men took it as personal, assuming it reflected on them, showed their charm, and said they were sharing something unique and intimate. They became romantically attracted to Dee — at least temporarily, after they'd had a few drinks — which pleased her immensely. She loved to tell me of all the men who were in love with her. I normally liked her laugh but at this moment it was pissing me off because what I wanted to hear was contrition.

Jealousy had slipped into the room behind Dee and slouched towards a shadowy corner, trying to be inconspicuous. I did my best to pretend he wasn't there but I knew he badly wanted to be fed.

"You're late," I said to Dee, and was distressed about the way it sounded. There'd been judgment there. A provocation.

"Yeah, I was visiting friends." She grinned and giggled, as if the memory was a charming one.

I threw jealousy some table scraps, perhaps to calm him.

"'Till 3 in the morning? You could have at least called." There was now a definite edge. My annoyance was announcing itself. Fuck, I thought. I didn't want to approach the subject of her behaviour.

"Why would I do that?" She walked, staggering a bit, into the livingroom and picked up my cigarettes. Pretending to smile she said sarcastically, "I didn't know I had to report in."

"It's not about reporting in." Funny how all paths led back to the same disagreement from whichever direction we approached. "It's only that I thought you were gonna be home earlier. It's just courtesy. Maybe I had plans myself. It'd be nice to be asked if I mind giving up another Saturday night so you can stay out half the night."

I heard myself. Shut up Lawrence!

"It's not 'half the night', it's maybe 3 o'clock, you sound like my father. Was there something you wanted to do?" she said this as if she was really concerned I might have been inconvenienced. "You didn't say anything when I left." She was rooting around, searching for a match and not looking at me.

"I didn't have anything in mind. But if you'd come home, if you spent some time with your daughter, for once, I might have gone out just to get a break." Fuck it, jealousy had taken over and was voraciously ripping into a chunk of meat.

"What-do-you-mean?" she said slowly, enunciating every word as if speaking to an idiot. "I spend lots of time with her." Her voice was rising now as she dug around the end table like a terrier, tipping the overflowing ashtray, cursing and interjecting loudly that I smoked too much. "I'm here everyday! Maybe I need a break myself…Where's the damn matches!"

For some reason I'd been holding them in my hand while I slept. I pitched them at her.

"A break! From what? I do the cleaning, cooking, baby-sit, pay the bills."

I got up and grabbed the pack of cigarettes as a way to quiet down—Bea was stirring—pulled out a smoke and fired the pack on to the mattress, with extra gusto for dramatic effect. It was hard to argue reasonably when you were so pissed off. I had to go through this type of thing, this histrionic excising of energy, before I would be calm enough to talk. This was what all our arguments were really about lately; displaced and unacknowledged jealousy. I'd been telling Dee how I needed a partner. I needed help with our daughter. That I can't do this alone and she had to be home more. I felt consoled when I took this approach. I was venting some of my frustrations but talking about real things, real issues with real situations, and not about jealousy.

"You don't do bugger all!" I added.

"I do! Yeah, you're such a wonderful parent making Bea suck in your tobacco smoke non-stop."

"Well at least I'm here."

"You and I both know that what you're pissed off about has nothing to do with that. It's about me being with other men!"

"Bullshit."

"I'm not your mother! You're a hypocrite who suddenly wants a marriage like your parents. I didn't have this cozy, middle-class mommy and daddy growing up where my father went off to work and my mother stayed home. My father treated me like I was his wife! It was sick and I got the hell out of there as soon as I could. The kind of relationship you and I have was what we agreed to. We weren't going to be your parents with the furniture you're not allowed to sit on and the 2.5 kids. You said all those things, about how open-minded you were and yet you act like you own me!"

"Fuck it! I'm leaving." I said with mock, phoney laughter. I'd made this threat before. It was losing its melodramatic impact. "You gotta take some responsibility for Bea, and me getting the hell out of here is what it's gonna take." I calmly added. "I'll take her with me but…"

"You think you're taking Bea? Like hell you are! She's staying with me." The loss of control had now switched sides.

WHILE LIVING IN YORKVILLE — I lived there on and off during my teens — I developed an interest in poetry after discovering Leonard Cohen. I first heard him playing in a dinky little coffee shop (as most were). His music led me to check out his poetry and from there, being the sixties, it was no surprise that I moved on to the Romantic poets. Artistically, and in their ideas, they reinforced my preoccupations and those of my peers: radical politics, ecstatic experience and drug use, vegetarianism, pacifism, atheism, feminism, utopian societies, and open love. They were the radicals, counter-culture sages and rock stars of their age.

I began to read the radical poet Shelley. Shelley met 16 year-old Mary Godwin while visiting her father William, the anarchist philosopher. Her mother was the deceased feminist Mary Wollstonecraft. Though Shelley was married, he and Mary were perfectly paired and they ran off together, much to Godwin's disapproval.

I espoused Shelley's written views on open marriage and the reactionary quality of monogamous relationships. The ideas had at first been shocking and somehow upsetting, disturbing the sense of innocence I'd grown up with that life was one big Disney movie, but the security of received ideas dwindled and I liked the feeling of being a radical.

Shelley advocated a panoply of extreme ideas, but those around free love appealed to me most. They seemed to capture what was natural and important to me. I loved being with different women, the passionate sex and romantic intensity of new relationships. Even when I was in a steady relationship I wanted to sleep with lots of other women, and often did. In the months before I met Dee I'd sometimes sleep with three or four different women in a week.

It seemed hard to reconcile sexual attraction to a lot of different women, and the standards of traditional monogamy. I shared my views with Dee and we decided to have an open relationship. Monogamy and marriage were about the power of the state and the church to control people and passion, and were also about patriarchy; to ensure a man he was the father of any offspring and that his economic heir would be of his seed. We saw our position on the subject reflected in the emerging women's movement. Sexual freedom, we thought, was political freedom.

The double standard between what I wanted for myself, and how I wanted Dee to act, had always been there from the first. It was ages before I acknowledged it to myself but there was no way I would ever have done so openly. I knew, in some damnable way, that this was the same old shit I'd grown up with; guys could sleep with whoever they wanted and that was cool, but girls who did the same thing were sluts. The double standard fully remained, even after I endorsed the concept of an open relationship.

I first became aware of the double standard when we were living at a dilapidated B.C. farm. We used to hang out with a couple named Dennis and Rachel. Dennis was a skinny American draft dodger in his late twenties with waist-length blonde hair and a scraggly blonde wisp of something like a beard. He spoke in this professorial tone as he pontificated on American foreign policy. I assumed he was correct. I was versed in anti-war rhetoric and knew all the slogans, but I really didn't know much about the specifics of the Vietnam war. It was different for Americans I'm sure. They stood to be drafted and then sent out as cannon fodder to sustain a puppet government and kill civilians on its behalf.

Dennis also liked to expostulate on literature and philosophy, things I knew more about. Dogmatic was just his style. I started to realize he was a pompous, annoying asshole.

Rachel was younger than Dennis, maybe 19 or 20. She didn't look much different than many women her age and was probably attractive mainly because of her youth. When you start to fall in love with one of these young women, with all the impassioned intensity of a youthful crush, she becomes the most beautiful thing you've ever seen. I became insanely attracted to her.

The farm was a commune of sorts, near Nelson. We lived in an old farmhouse with several other hippies having gone there from Vancouver with vague notions of a utopian lifestyle and the chance to, not exactly commune with nature in a quasi-religious way (although some people spewed that nonsense), but to appreciate it more. We talked about self-sufficiency, the rejection of a consumer lifestyle, and anti-industrialization. I remember painting the wooden floors and walls using what was left from a bunch of cans of different coloured oil paint found in a shed.

In the end, we almost froze during our first (and last) winter there after the power got turned off. And we nearly starved as we subsisted on a diet of potatoes. But at the time I met Rachel we still believed we could grow all our own food. The two of us worked in the garden together, kneeling side by side, brushing against each other; every touch painfully arousing. Our tomatoes and potatoes started to grow and flower, from love, I assumed.

More and more we hung around each other, laughing at our inside jokes as if they were the most adorable things ever said. Since there was never a word of disagreement spoken, the dreamlike state never give way to reality.

We began to listen to records in Rachel's room, when Dennis wasn't there, absorbing ourselves in her folk music. Love and intense lust reverberated in the air with Dylan, Donovan, Eric Anderson, and Bert Jansch, creating an intensity that was unbearable. It had to be satisfied and it was apparent that we both felt the same. I was uncertain though, about going any further, because it would have been the first test of the open relationship agreement I had with Dee.

I began to expostulate on poetry and the Romantics one night with Dennis and Rachel. We were all drinking wine and laying around the bedroom I shared with Dee. The only light was a candle. Some sort of folk music was on the stereo. To my surprise Dennis said something about Shelley being a social visionary and Rachel said how she agreed with him as well. That was enough of a test for me of their views. In fact, I think that what was to come was people trying to live those views; to show each other we were radicals.

Shortly after that Dennis went to his room and returned with a new bottle of wine. He sat on the far side of the bed beside Dee. Rachel sat cross-legged on some cushions on the floor. After we drank some more, I slid down on to the pillows beside her. Soon, I started to play with her foot and Dee and Dennis laid down together. No one spoke. Incense burned in the near dark and the music was loud and consuming. I would have said the feeling of wanting to be with Rachel was as intense as anything I had ever felt (although I've felt the same many times since). Nothing else mattered, not Dee nor Dennis. We began to pull off our each other's clothes.

As we groped, I listened acutely to Dee and Dennis. At least, in part, the noises we all made were likely to show each other how relaxed we were and how natural this was to us. Incredibly though, I suddenly began to feel intensely jealous of Dee and Dennis because I could hear them getting to the same spot as Rachel and I. Should I stop? I wanted them to stop but I wanted Rachel too much to stop myself. I struggled with the contradictory feelings. Rachel and I continued.

It has been the same dilemma ever since. I don't like Dee fooling around but sleeping with other women is a drug I can't forgo.

So what Dee was doing now wasn't anything we hadn't agreed to. And she wasn't acting any differently than me. The previous summer I'd been offered a job at a daycare in Montreal by a guy from school who worked there. I went and stayed at the house of the woman who ran the daycare. I soon moved into her room…except when Dee was there. When Dee came to visit, she asked if I was sleeping with the woman. I admitted it, matter-of-factly. She frowned but said nothing. So now, even if I had given in to my jealousy and not continued to fight on against it as a perversion, I was aware of what a hypocrite I'd look like if I admitted it.

# *Lawrence*
# Sunday

I left Bea at home, and took the subway uptown.

I don't know what it was about me that had always pissed off my old man. It started well before the long hair and becoming a hippy. He just never liked me much. Well, maybe he did when I was a baby.

I was forever being accused of having a bad attitude and of being something less than macho, and I hoped both were true. I speculated that my lack of bowing to his authority on all subjects was a challenge to his manhood; that stupid authoritarianism of his generation, especially among men who grew up in strict families. I think my rebelliousness when I got older pissed him off. He wanted to be lord and master over his kids. And I wonder too if he was jealous of having to share my mother. She and I were real close when I was young.

As I began up the walk in front of the house my stomach tensed in a Pavlovian reflex. I was afraid of the old man, like the proverbial dog that's been smacked too many times and now cowers when he sees a hand coming his way. I can't say that I liked him and hoped to hell that I wasn't a bit like him. In my view, I was always my mother's son.

When I was 16 years-old, my curfew was 10 p.m., which likely made sense to worried parents from Wegebow but was way out of line for Toronto. I pleaded with them to no avail to lighten up.

I came home one Saturday night at midnight because I was still a little drunk at 10 p.m., and even staggering a bit at eleven. I was more worried about coming home drunk than late, I guess.

Where you come in the side door at my parent's house there's a landing. It's a typical suburban place near the edge of the city. There are three stairs up to the kitchen and about twelve stairs down to the basement. When I finally got home, my father emerged out of nowhere at the top of the stairs and came down them with his arm raised, the elbow cocked up behind his head. He pounded me twice in the face sending me flying down the stairs. I landed on the basement floor. Maybe it scared him or maybe he'd gotten it out of his system but he left me there laying on the floor, semi-conscious and moaning. I think I was unconscious on the way down. I just remember being on the landing one second watching a blur coming at me, too quick to react to, and then being on the floor of the basement. I figured when I woke up I'd just lay there awhile since I really didn't feel like moving anyway, or feel well enough to.

He'd do things like that sometimes — extreme things. He'd just lose it and strike out at his kids because we were near at hand and he could do it. Maybe his nerves were shot from the war because it didn't take much to set him off. Lots of people hit their kids, their dog, their wife, whoever or whatever they can, and they get away with it because the other loves them and will forgive them, but with kids it could be justified with bullshit axioms like "spare the rod." The excessiveness was never acknowledged. He'd later hold forth about discipline and having done what he did for my own good, to make a man of me and teach me discipline, but that was just his rationalization to avoid self-recrimination. The validations are close to hand when you come from a strict family.

The result was that I was always terrified of him, was careful about everything I said, and figured I probably would be afraid for life, even in thirty years or so when he would become an ineffectual tiny octogenarian who couldn't hurt a fly.

I found him painting the livingroom. All the furniture was pushed into the middle of the room and there were drop cloths on the floor around the walls.

I stood awkwardly, watching him, after we said hi.

"Painting, eh?" I added. Because I couldn't relax enough to speak normally to him and he was socially dysfunctional, our conversations tended to be fairly simple and absurd.

"Yeah, your mother planned it before she passed away. I don't know why. It doesn't look like it needs it," he said, frowning at the inconvenience of conversation or of having to be pleasant.

A long awkward and baffling pause ensued during which I watched him paint.

If he hadn't been pre-programmed with stuff my mother had planned for him to do he'd be sitting around lost, having always left the decisions to her.

She had died in a car accident three months before. I wish she could have lived to see her grandkids grow up. All of the people who the world could spare, who never acted except for themselves, and it was the people that did for others, like my mother, who died young.

"Maybe your mother thought I needed something to keep me busy."

"Um. Who picked the colour?"

"The grey? I did. It suits the room don't cha think?"

"Yeah…For sure."

It was an ugly colour, even for the inside of a factory, but it wasn't like it affected me one way or the other and trouble always followed when I spoke honestly.

I watched him paint through another long break in the conversation.

"How's Martin?"

"I don't know." But the old man perked up at mention of his youngest. "He's never here much. He's working tonight. He got a job at some little pub at school. You probably see him as much as I do. He tries to be here only when you're around. Otherwise when he's here, he's sleeping…Grab yourself a beer if you want."

"You want one?"

"Naw."

I wandered out to the kitchen. There was a few beers on the bottom shelf of the fridge and lots of food that looked like it had seen better days. Two guys living like students; both emotionally that age. I grabbed a bottle and opened it at the counter, looking out the back window. The grass was cut but the hedges spilled over in an unruly tangle and the flower gardens were scattered with weeds. I turned and scanned the kitchen. On the face of it, things were neat enough, but you could see dirt collecting on the floor tiles in the corner. No matter what he thought, he couldn't keep house the way my mother had.

I took my beer, got my bag from inside the front door, and went upstairs to my room.

Once, when I was 18, after moving back home, I took down everything I had up on the walls; all the posters and the pictures clipped from magazines. I embraced an anti-decoration aesthetic. Even though I moved back out shortly afterwards, I still thought of the room as mine, and always would. Following her usual penchant though, my mother had re-decorated 'my room.' There were now large art prints on the walls. Her version of who I was. And even though I was never so organized and neat, I liked the restorative feel of it because it told me I was home.

I walked past my parents' room but ignored it. I didn't want to stir up any ghosts. I didn't want to get angry.

I wandered into Martin's room to check on the latest. He had added some posters since my last visit — Mao, Ché Guevara — the latest revolutionary poster boys. Martin spent his free time at peace marches and protests of one kind or another, and these guys were his rock stars.

My younger brother was 19 and just starting at York University. He was a good student and could've gone to whatever school he wanted. I didn't understand why he wouldn't get out of town and away from the old man. Who wouldn't have?

Martin and I got fairly close after I got busted and had to move back home at 17. I was working at a factory to pay off my lawyer and feeling trapped. My life was avoiding old haunts, waiting out my probation and watching my ass. In any case, I'd lost the taste for doing anything illegal so I hung out at home and worked; that was about it. Martin began to imitate the way I dressed, spoke and acted, as well as my opinions. He borrowed my Hesse and Castaneda books — and likely those by some other people you never hear of any more — and my folk and rock records.

I liked to look through the books on his shelves and flip through his records that rested in a milk crate. It was a way of checking up on his development. Since I came back from Vancouver, I noticed he had gone off on his own direction. Among his records there was stuff by the likes of John Mayall, Johnny Winter and Jean-Luc Ponty. His books were mostly on radical politics.

It wasn't until I was about to leave that evening that I was given the journal. "It'll maybe tell you a lot about your mother." And perhaps, as an added inducement, "There may even be stuff about you in there."

I didn't read it on the way home. I had some reading for school the next day that I had to get through.

## *Lawrence* Monday

June was at the bus stop, as usual, on Monday. We were neighbours and in a couple of the same classes, so on the days we rode to school together we hung out with each other while we were there. She wasn't overly straight-laced and was divorced with a young kid, but she was way more mainstream than I was used to. I tried to keep my embarrassing opinions to myself because I liked her and didn't want her to scurry away. I marvelled that she didn't see through me; that what I had internalized was not visible to the external world. I always felt fraudulent when someone treated me as normal.

It was a drizzly October day with that first chill in the air and the distinctive melancholic smell of fall approaching. A boy in school, when I was in grade 3, died on a day with a feel like this—it was the first time I'd ever encountered death first hand so it's not something that leaves you—and to this day those early autumn smells always bring back memories of that numbing and confusing time.

I leaned on the newspaper box beside the stop. The paper's headline undoubtedly contained the word Vietnam or Soviets.

An old couple huddled under an umbrella on the other side of the box.

Our conversation drifted aimlessly around school topics. June leaned in with her head close to mine and shifted her umbrella to cover me as well. Her voice dropped to something usually reserved for plotters.

"Didn't see you at the wine and cheese." she said.

"No…I stayed home with Bea…Dee went."

"Yeah, I think I saw her," she said casually, but flicked a glance up at me.

Yes, I felt like saying, I know about Dee's boyfriend. I was sure June would have found the idea quite bizarre if I told her I knew and didn't object, so I let her sympathize with the unknowing cuckold.

"I didn't do anything else all weekend…" she added, lingering over the gratuitous personal information, "but I was there on Saturday."

That garnered no response. We remained silent, watching for the bus.

"Did Dee have a good time?" June asked with studied casualness, still looking down the rain-soaked street for the bus, but obviously wanting to get something more out of the subject.

"Don't know."

"She seemed to be enjoying herself."

"Pardon?"

"Dee seemed to be enjoying herself."

"Uh huh."

The conversation turned to details of the wine and cheese. June was warming up. Her focus was the largely uninteresting Luc, a French Ontarian with a heavy accent and a throwback from the fifties, with shiny black shoes and gelled hair.

"He was following me around all night. God, he's like a shadow, for whatever reason."

At the end of the night he had spun some story for June of having been dragged into a classroom and ravaged by a beautiful young thing who left soon after.

"Really?" I became suddenly interested.

"It's bullshit!" Her voice rose. "Women don't act like that except in men's daydreams."

I could have told her about one wine and cheese the year before when I slept with Sharon—it wasn't so much different from Luc's drunken fantasy—but I chose not to.

June's umbrella had drifted off to one side and I was developing a dark wet stripe on the left side of my body. I reached across for the stem, repositioned it and glanced down at her to take in those things only noticeable when your face is a few inches away from someone's: the texture of their skin, their smell, the pleasure of proximity. She was small with undulating rosé hair and tiny freckles—the summer skin colour had drained away already. She smelled well-scrubbed, like one of the commercial hand soaps, but suddenly there was that irresistible magnetic pull I'd been feeling around her lately.

I psychologically and literally backed up a bit. I was trying to change my ways.

The bus pulled in eventually and as we were getting on the old codger said to his partner, nodding in my direction, "Did you notice that guy there looks like Charles Manson?"

"Hey June, did you notice that old fucker looks like Al Capone?" I said, loud enough to make her blush. I noted to myself to be more careful about not revealing to June the type of person I was.

THE FACULTY OFFICES WERE small, windowless closets down a cramped hallway running off a common area in the middle of the squat brick building. One of the offices belonged to Bryce, an English professor, my friend, who frequently invited me and Dee and other students over to his apartment. Bryce had snow white hair, a small chin and pink skin, but he was something of a Lothario. Being a professor obviously overcame the fact of looking like a snow monkey. Actually, his reputation for having slept with so many attractive female students seemed to be the impetus for many others to sleep with him themselves. Like the urge to try Coke because it's so popular, I suppose.

I deserted June, veering down the faculty hall to talk to Bryce. His office was typically overflowing with papers skewed over his desk, books laid everywhere, jammed in various directions in the bookshelves, but the room was now devoid of Bryce's things, except for one box sitting on the desk. He was going through the open desk drawers and putting stuff into the box.

I sat down without an invitation and fell into conversation about the sabbatical he was ready to leave on and school in general. Students walked by the inner sanctum offices, quietly whispering to each other, from courtesy or reverence.

The conversation turned to Lynch, a philosophy professor of mine, in whose class I'd been waging a war of words with several students about Nietzsche in the ardent way that only students can; with intense passion and the intellectual promiscuity of youth where we pillage and personalize any ideas we come across. I used to say that I liked Nietzsche's emphasis on individualism, the attack on conventional morality, and his idea of the Superman, to fill in the void of a dead God and provide a basis for morality.

Bryce had stopped doing his packing and sat down at his desk.

"How did you know about it?" I asked after his referring to a nasty letter I'd written to Lynch.

"He told a few of us in the faculty lounge. He was pretty shocked. Said you got really aggressive in his class about some remarks."

"Well... sure. This old man was talking as if there was some intellectual similarity between what Nietzsche was saying and fascism, the old chestnuts, and Lynch didn't challenge it at all."

"I don't know much about Nietzsche. He talked about the will to power though right?"

"Yeah but with the will to power he was talking about stuff like the urge to be creative and to become ourselves; to have power over ourselves, not others. He admired saints, even though he hated Christianity, because they had the ability to overcome sexual urges and live a life of chastity."

Bryce looked out the door, as some female voices went by, ignoring the will to power.

"Well, Lawrence. You know, you get busy with life and things get said and no one can always be all over everything. Who knows, maybe he was thinking about his kid's earache or something his wife did and not what some guy in class said. You never know. Maybe he just wants his students to make up their own minds. He's a smart guy."

"But this was Nietzsche!" I said, as if that explained everything, that the whole world was as turned on by him as I was. "A good teacher should always challenge his student's thinking."

"Okay ... so what are you up to these days that I can challenge you about?"

"I'm looking for a lawyer," I said, running my finger along the spine of a hardcover book on his desk. I got right to the point because I'd badly wanted to talk about this for a couple of days knowing Bryce would be a sympathetic audience. "A cheap one. I want to know if I leave Dee, if I have a chance of getting custody of Bea."

"Well I can answer that one. You don't. Not unless your wife was a criminal and drug addict," he said bitterly, speaking from experience, I knew. "But check that. Get a lawyer and ask them. Don't take my word for it, it's too important." He looked at me quizzically. "So you're seriously thinking of leaving? Things have become too much to deal with?" Bryce knew about the type of relationship I had with Dee. I suspected he'd slept with her, but this wasn't something that I thought worth disturbing a friendship over.

"No, er, no. I mean I am planning to leave but it's not that, it's not a problem; we act the way we want. I like her to have her own thing but I need to get some time to myself and my leaving will force her to spend more time with Bea."

Bryce looked as if he was trying to see the sense in this.

"Have you talked about leaving?"

"Yeah."

He watched more girls go by the door and they all looked in and smiled at him. "Er, you said you talked about leaving?"

"Yeah."

"Did you say you wanted custody?"

"Yeah, I did, and I do."

"And…?"

"She said no way and I assumed it was like you were saying, that the law will always give the mother custody…Fuck it pisses me off!…She's a crummy mother."

"I understand your feelings; you look after your daughter and you're really attached to each other. I went through this. I wasn't close like you but I found it emotionally really tough. Like my daughter had some terminal illness and I was losing her. I held it against my wife. I started to hate her."

"Yeah, every day I think about what it will feel like to be away from Bea. I look at her, you know, and I feel like crying or something. She's the one thing that holds me back from leaving. To leave means leaving her."

"So, you're looking for a place to stay I take it. Or do you have one?"

"Yeah. No. I'm looking…or will be."

"Well, you know that I'm leaving next week for six months of my sabbatical. Do you want to stay at my place?"

"You're keeping it?"

"Yeah, sure, six months isn't a long time. It's easier to just pay the rent than try and put stuff in storage. I'll be back around the time the school year ends and you can move out then if you haven't found something permanent before that."

"I don't know if I can afford the rent."

He looked at me and smiled as if I was dense. "I don't need any money. I was going to pay the rent anyway. You'd be doing me a favour; house-sitting."

"Sure," I said, shaking my head . "Yeah of course. Far out. Thanks." I was thrilled.

He smiled. "If you come by tomorrow I'll give you the key and we can talk about it."

# *Lawrence*
# Tuesday

Like most afternoons, I sat in a cheapo broken lawn chair on the back balcony, with feet up on the railing, smoking and reading for school while Bea slept.

There was an old lady in a two-storey house behind us who showed up at her upstairs window in a bra and stared at me. She was trying to look provocative I suppose. I don't know. She could have been 40 or 60, but the difference was lost on me at the time. I don't know why I recall that — or mention it.

Sometimes I wrote poetry there instead of doing schoolwork — but not as much as I would have liked. I had a sense of fatalism, that I wasn't long for this world, so I always scolded myself for not writing enough and used my imminent demise to justify writing instead of doing schoolwork.

```
The photograph shows three people
     surrounded by a colourful surfeit.
             She was a simpler woman at the time.
     There is no prophetic sense in him.
     Not discernible in this image is the black
     but the viewer knows of it is presence
     shadowing the young couple
     like a gathering hurricane.

     I barely mark out the lump
     of the baby's shape,
             formless,
                     and recall the durable gaze,
     present, distributing the covert equilibrium
     of that curious, wide-eyed stare
     awash in the colours of the garden.
     It will be his future,
             his destiny;
                     the gluttony of his future conduct.
```

```
Surely I know that we are bound
                    by pretence of the intellect.
Sculpted from the hoary clay,
The brilliantly greying shaving,
                    heart of the blackened start.
I live with this,
        forever,
                    the irrefutable,
unable to produce another offspring
ahead of it.
                    Ahead of what?
My meditation is absolute.
```

## *Lawrence*
# Wednesday

I had very few memories of Wegebow. Although I always knew my mother had once been a doctor — that much was family lore and a bragging point of my father's — the only mother that I had known had been a housewife who channelled an apparent desire to help others towards volunteer work for charities, church events and drives for causes. At some point when I was older, and thought that being a housewife was a wasted life, I asked her if she was ever going to go back to medicine and was told she'd always intended to but had now been away from it for too long; she hadn't kept up with the science.

I have this memory — one of those things where you're not sure if it was a dream or if it really happened — of my father and mother discussing, maybe arguing, about her going back to work. I have the impression my father didn't like the idea of his wife working. And I think, as I got older, my hoping she'd go back into medicine, was partly about wanting her to challenge her husband's narrowness.

Bea was asleep when I remembered my mother's journal and retrieved it from my rucksack. I was expecting something like a diary, but that's not what it appeared to be. It was a narrative, beginning with a summary of how she'd become a doctor and moved to Wegebow after getting married. The whole of that only took about five pages. I ruffled through the remaining pages of the journal. There looked to be about two hundred of them and she'd filled every one. I assumed this was going to be an autobiography.

I went into the bedroom, reclined on the bed (like the couch it was just a mattress on the floor with a blanket on top), turned on the small lamp sitting on a wooden crate beside the bed, and began to read the story of how my mother met Emelie Gagnon one day, came to realize she was being abused, and began to try and help her put an end to it.

I lived in Wegebow for the first five years of my life, even went to kindergarten there, so I had some specific memories from the time, but not enough to characterize the town. Being a small and isolated place it didn't strike me as odd it would be such a closed-minded backwater. I was intrigued though. As a city child, I tended to romanticize small and rural towns. Reading the journal I became disabused of the notion. The picture my mother tried to draw was of a place that could have been in the southern US during slavery; an area of isolation and darkness. The terrible happened and no one knew. It was covered up and secret, while the hypocritical townsfolk spoke of their adherence to family values and Catholic morality.

I heard Dee and jealousy come in around 1 a.m. She was giggling and talking to someone. It sounded like a couple of men, and then she said the name Sid. I'd heard that one before. He was a gay man from Toronto who she hung with sometimes.

I lit up a smoke, sat up on the bed, and continued to read without following the words. I was going over my story. Dee came in to the bedroom and said hi, in a very friendly and tipsy way. I put the journal on the bedside crate.

"Sid and Bart are here."

"Bart?"

"Sid's new lover." She dropped her voice. "They're sleeping in the livingroom. They painted their place today and the smell is pretty bad. We were just there."

It explained, I imagined, why she hadn't gone back to her lover's place. He would have had to take in her friends too. Or maybe she'd been there and then come here. Who the hell knew.

In a chatty mood, Dee proceeded to tell me about Bart. "He's from a small town. I find it interesting he got together with Sid. To Bart, being gay is natural and easy. Sid's from Toronto and he dresses in leather and is hardcore."

I put out that I found it hard to believe anyone from a small northern Ontario town would find being gay easy.

"No." She didn't disagree. "You have to keep your sexuality pretty quiet."

"There's probably no visible gay scene up north to speak of because it has to be hidden."

"Sure."

"So none of the flamboyance you get here."

While we talked, Dee got undressed and walking around the bedroom. She lit some incense, a smoke and opened the window a crack.

I debated whether to give her my speech or not. She looked pretty good and I realized that what I had to say would definitely put a chill in the air. Still…

"I want to tell you something," I began.

"Oh?"

"Yeah. I found a place for myself. I'll be moving out soon."

"Moving out?" She sounded shocked, like it was the first she'd ever heard of the idea.

"Yeah."

"You're serious?" She froze in the act of getting undressed, flamingo-like on one leg, with the other pulled up in front. Her right hand held the toe of a sock, stretched to twice its length, but only half off her foot.

"Yeah, I've been telling you for a month."

"But I didn't think you'd do it." There was an angry edge to her voice as she dropped her foot to the ground; the sock still half on. "I thought it was one of those stupidly reactionary and jealous things you say sometimes."

Her accusation of jealousy annoyed. "I think it's for the best. Like I said…"

"So you're leaving?" Said hollowly, while staring off, formulating her thoughts.

"Yeah."

"Why?" She knelt on the bed, facing me, now looking serious and concerned, as if I was sick.

"We've been through this. I think we'll like each other better if we don't live together and we can enjoy ourselves more when we do get together. Besides we'll have more freedom to pursue relationships with other people."

She snorted and shook her head. "You want more freedom? What's stopping you?"

"Bea. Babysitting."

"What do you want from me? You want me to spend more time with Bea. Would that do it?" She had started talking in a plaintive, little girl way, which was shocking me. I felt pleased, and then guilty. My resolve started to weaken a little bit.

"No. I'm leaving. You should live your life the way you want to."

There was a long quiet.

"When are you leaving?"

"The day after tomorrow."

"Christ? So soon. Where? You're not taking Bea there to visit, you're not taking her to no dump," she added forcefully.

The comment about Bea coming for a visit — that attitude of Dee's that she was in control and her assumption that Bea would continue to live with her and only visit me — pissed me off, even though I knew that's what would happen. It killed any doubts about leaving that I'd been developing. "It's near the university," I said coolly. "Bryce is leaving on sabbatical tomorrow and I'm going to housesit; look after the place in exchange for free rent. It's a nice place… I'll keep putting in money here."

Dee was silent. It was hard to dispute that this was a good deal. She lay down on top of the covers, facing me.

"So this is the end?" she said to no one in particular.

"No, not at all. I'm just getting my own place. We always said we weren't really married, that we just did it for the student loan money and we were free to come and go as we pleased. It doesn't mean we can't continue a relationship." I reached out and rubbed her cheek. "This gives us more freedom." I liked the way my speech had gone. I would have seen it as a failure to say I wanted something reactionary, like a monogamous relationship. I was aware this was hurting her the way her affair with the instructor prick was hurting me. I started stroking her hair and at some point I'm not sure if I any longer felt sympathy or was just using her distress to initiate intimacy. I had almost convinced myself that everything I said was real. That my bitterness wasn't driving me away and that it wouldn't kill any chance of a relationship once I was gone.

After we made love I am sure neither of us believed we liked each other any more or that we would really want to continue to see each other once I was gone. It had just been the last attempt to reverse what was happening, or maybe to cling to someone you can be close to when life is swirling around and taking you somewhere you aren't prepared for.

# *Lawrence*
# Thursday

After I got beat up by my old man, when I was 16, I took off for Yorkville. I couldn't get away from him fast enough. Developers were swooping in and Yorkville was becoming gentrified, but at that time it was still, for the most part, an old, decrepit and inexpensive neighbourhood where kids from dysfunctional families went. It had a cachet as the place where it was 'happening', but we also had a stake in believing in the romanticized image since many of us were coming from the same violent backgrounds with the same fucked up parents. You don't hear many people mention it — we were supposedly just a generation of rebels — but there were a lot of damaged kids out there who'd been kicked out of the house, or were trying to escape being knocked around at home or at school.

PART 4

It was a brutal time to be young and it was no wonder so many gravitated to the iconography of being hippies (yet who ended up, when older, espousing the same prejudices as their parents). It gave them a sense of belonging and acceptance that was absent at home.

I was luckier than the many kids who spent their nights sleeping on the streets or getting beat up by greasers. (They were tough cookies when they came upon a skinny 16 year-old hippy, alone in the dark.) Most nights I stayed at a friend's near the Village (as they called Yorkville). Paul had an apartment on the second floor of an old house that cost him ten bucks a week. The landlord was cool, and didn't care how many kids crashed there. I remember we once had twenty people sleeping on the living room floor. I tried to give Paul a couple of dollars every week, as a matter of pride, and he appreciated it. A few others did too but there wasn't much money floating around. Paul never kicked anyone out of his place unless they were unruly.

In Yorkville, kids had a variety of ways of making money; odd jobs, prostitution, but mostly panhandling and pushing dope. I'd buy pot and sell it up at the suburban high school I'd dropped out of. So, all in all, I didn't have it so bad.

Dee and I met in 1967 when I was 19 and spending most of my time in the Village after leaving home a second time. She was 16 and was both running away from something and towards something else. Her mother had died years before and left her with her father and six brothers in a small house in Orillia. As the oldest, and only girl, she'd been expected to be the mother. She cooked, cleaned and babysat. There was nothing in the arrangement at home that she wanted.

Dee wasn't like a lot of those you met in Yorkville; pretty, weekend hippies in miniskirts or paisley shirts. Dee was tall and awkward with wiry, crinkled, long black hair and she dressed in a way that's a cliché now but took guts and a rebellious spirit at the time; sandals, patterned pyjama bottoms, no bra, and tie-dyed t-shirts. I can't imagine she ever wore a dress in her life. She had few inhibitions, slept with who she wanted to, turned the occasional trick for money, posed nude for artists, and stole anything that wasn't tied down. She was a survivor who did what she had to, to get by, and ended up in Yorkville hoping to find people who were like-minded. I was exhilarated by the thought and sight of such an independent spirit, and was intensely proud to be seen with her.

I SOMETIMES WONDERED IF Dee's current affair was just retaliation for the relationship I'd had with the woman at the daycare the year before. Maybe it hurt her self-esteem. But then again, I guessed that any minor jealousy she felt wasn't the thing driving her. And she didn't act the way she did just to live up to some image of herself. I was coming to the opinion that Dee just loved doing dope, getting drunk and having sexual liaisons. The freedom I aspired to was just the way that she was naturally. And that meant she would probably never change.

I aimlessly wandered around the apartment, surveying my domain, looking through cupboards and closets, and satisfying my curiosity. I felt good about landing the place. Sometimes I just get lucky, like the stars align, not often, not like some people who are perennially fortunate, where things will always seem to fall in their lap, but sometimes things do just work out.

Bryce lived in a non-descript middle-class part of the city, a little west of downtown. It was a high-rise, something I hated on aesthetic principle, but it was on the subway line and I was hardly in a position to refuse it. Before he left for the airport, Bryce had taken me on a tour of the place. I lingered over the high-end stereo. "Don't hesitate to use it," he said, "or anything else for that matter."

I have since discovered that most of these types of apartments have pretty similar layouts and all the windows are along the same side of the building. This apartment was unusual because it wrapped around the front corner. From the balcony you could look at the apartment building next door or, from another angle, you could watch the road. Bryce's unit was only on the second floor though, so the view was limited.

I looked at the forlorn suitcase sitting in the corner of the livingroom. In the box I had brought with me, sitting beside it, were some books (poetry and school texts) and LPs (Dylan, Cream, Tim Hardin, the Mothers) and a few of Bea's toys.

I stared out the bedroom window that faced the front and scanned the park on the other side of the street. I'd once gone to an aquarium and saw the killer whales with their bent dorsal fins. All killer whales in captivity are apparently like that. I thought that this was a nice image for myself, here, looking through the glass at all the other captive killer whales on the other side (because we were all behind glass depending on the other's perspective). We were all deformed by our day-to-day experiences, and separated from each other.

I'VE FOUND THAT THE end of any intense relationship is always a time of self-criticism and despair, and this occasion was no different. I was a failure. I'd invested a lot of emotional energy into a relationship that had come to nothing. It only became a legal marriage for financial gain, by two people who didn't believe in the institution, but that didn't make any difference, I still felt I'd failed and was depressed.

I wondered why, after such a negative experience, that all of my attention when I looked around was still focused on women. Maybe I was looking for something to divert myself. I was forever moving from one woman to another, feeling the intensity of a new relationship for awhile, feeling totally alive, and then completely losing interest. I used to imagine, looking out the window of that apartment, that if I was making a film I would capture the mood and nature of a character by having the camera replicate what his eyes were doing. It would show a lot about someone by seeing the things that they stopped to dwell on as they looked around. Gazing out the window, I looked at the street traffic, the park, various people, attractive people, lots of them. My eyes went from one woman to the next.

I'd been thinking of Wegebow since reading about it in my mother's journal. She talked about how people stuck together. It was easy to criticize, when they closed ranks to protect some scumbag, but I was thinking about there being a positive side. They were a community and that was something positive. I'd never experienced that. We left the place when I was small and lived first in Sudbury and then in four different houses in Toronto, always moving further out into the wasteland of the suburbs where everyone's isolated from their neighbours and there's no sense of neighbourhood or uniqueness of place. It occurred to me that maybe this was why I went from woman to woman; I was trying to overcome my lack of a home, as Heidegger may have put it.

## *Lawrence* Friday

Cut. New scene, next day, following an establishing shot that pans across the outside of a 19th century brick college with ivy covered walls.

I am sitting in a common area between the cafeteria, library and classrooms. The walls are some sort of dark grey plastic panelling and the furniture is purple, the regal colour, but instead of appearing royal the room looks clownish, as if begging for attention. It's hugely inappropriate decoration for an old building and a disturbing experience to sit there…but I often do anyway.

I am talking with June who sits beside me. She asks about not seeing me on the bus the day before.

"I moved."

This surprised her, of course.

"Bryce let me have his place while he's on sabbatical so I went there…It was time to go…"

"You mean you moved out? On your own?"

"Uh-huh." I reflected on how subtly I'd led her to the fact that it was also a break up.

"Oh. Sorry…" she said, like she genuinely felt bad for me.

My ego was injured. I would rather she was thrilled.

"Did you decide suddenly," she asked hesitantly, "or was it building up to that? No! No! Sorry! It's none of my business."

"That's okay. It's fine. It was coming for a long time. Dee knew."

I told her a certain amount about what had happened. I had never confided in her before with the intimacy of friendship, and I didn't know if the intense way she was looking at me was because I was a strange specimen in a jar or was simple curiosity at the revelations of my character.

A continual stream of people wandered by. June's back was to them but I nodded and said hello to various ones.

"Hi Liz," I said in response to a woman passing by.

June looked over her shoulder and watched Liz until she had rounded the corner into a hallway.

"I'd suggest you let it sit for awhile," she said. "Don't be negative. It's not going to do your daughter any good to see you fight. Sounds like Dee could just be being miserable; using your daughter to get back at you. You know Lawrence, maybe she needs time to get used to the idea of not having Bea under the same roof as herself every night. Mother's do find that separation difficult." She seemed a little hesitant about proceeding, "Dee's a bit of a party girl." She intently watched my face, to see if she'd transgressed some limit I guess. "After a period of being home every night she may want time to herself. It may not be any consolation now but time is your best ally."

I thought about the perversity of this. I had left, on the one hand because I didn't want to be in a self-image destroying relationship, but on the other hand (only half-acknowledged) because it would force Dee to stay at home. Yet here I was complaining about how Dee's future plans were to stay at home with Bea. If I was to see my daughter more it would be because Dee had to pursue her social life; so now I would be cheering for that.

"My ex-husband wanted all kinds of time with his son after he left, but now he almost never takes advantage of it anymore. He doesn't see him for weeks at a time. You're not like him. You're a good father. Dee'll figure it out."

I thought about it. "I guess not having a built-in babysitter will make it harder for Dee to have it all; motherhood when it suits her, school and a social life."

"What a way to define 'all.' I don't understand someone like her. Sorry. I don't see how anyone could be in such a close relationship and not try to make it work."

We were back to that familiar point in our conversations where I was aware of how odd I would strike her if she knew more about me; if she knew Dee and I had an open marriage. I felt fraudulent, like every human relationship was dependent on some sort of con job.

"I mean, why bother getting married if you don't want it?" Jane added.

I nodded to another passerby, Karen, who'd said hi.

June briefly frowned with territoriality, but then smiled and said, "We'll have to have you and Bea over some day."

# *Lawrence*
# Week 2

Over the next few days I went back and forth to Dee's to baby-sit.

If it dragged into the evening, Bea was beginning to realize when I put her into bed that I wasn't going to be there in the morning and she would hang on to me, crying, and refuse to let go. Each night I went through the same assurances of telling her I'd be back the next day, without knowing how much she understood. I would lay beside her on her mattress until she fell asleep. She was resistant to the idea and would make a fuss when I tried to get up, so I'd stay there, feeling too guilty to move and, inevitably, angry with Dee that our daughter was so bloody miserable because of her parents' inability to maintain a relationship.

Most nights Dee would come in earlier than she had when we were together, and uncharacteristically sober. She was generally friendly but sometimes, coming through the door, would make comments along the lines of, "Oh look, the negligent mother is home. How shocking."

Every night, on leaving, I would stuff some things into my rucksack to take back to Bryce's; books and records mostly. I didn't want to root around and inadvertently find evidence of an overnight visitor, or to look for things in cupboards, closets and boxes. It was the first time I'd split up with someone I'd lived with and had quickly discovered the archaeology of past romances. You dig around a place and you come up with artefacts, like a picture or gift, and all of the old guilt and failure inducing history comes back. It was easier to be away from the old place as much as possible.

On Saturday afternoon, alone at home, I sat on the balcony, reclining in a lawn chair with my feet up on the railing, and read my mother's journal.

Looking back now I can see that the presentation was well thought out and served a purpose. It had one story to tell; to detail this particular episode in my mother's life. The journal didn't explain its intentions but began in Wegebow when a young doctor met up with an abused woman who was to become her friend and patient. My mother detailed all the steps she went through to try and prevent Emelie Gagnon from being murdered: going to the police, the priest, my father, Emelie's husband, trying to get Emelie to go to the police, or leave, and how none of them worked.

Two-thirds of the way through the journal my mother counselled Emelie to kill her husband.

"Christ!" I thought, dropping my feet down off the railing, suddenly very attentive. It was unbelievable. Shocking.

As I read through the events that followed I didn't recognize my mother. She was angry. She was active. She was violent.

And then Marcel was murdered. I put the journal down and walked back and forth around the apartment. How do I explain what you feel when you read that your mother was a murderer? That's what it was. She precipitated the murder. Emelie administered the drugs but my mother gave them to her.

I went across the road to the park. It's big, with a wooded area and ravines, and I started walking because I had to move and soon lost myself wandering in some bush.

Thinking about it now, the extremeness of my reaction to reading about my mother's actions, still doesn't surprise me. I was frustrated first, and then, after I began to internally editorialize on her actions, I became furious. I felt like she had tried to manipulate my reaction, to condone or gain sympathy for her behaviour. She had gone through what was obviously a difficult time and had not known how to act. Understandable. She detailed a story of growing abuse and frustration. She had to do something to protect this woman. I got it. But murder? That was a step that no one in their right mind contemplated.

I thought I should step back and look at this a little less emotionally. I debated the rationale of what my mother had done, but for me, there was no black and white. Her actions went flatly against my beliefs in non-violence. I suppose one could argue that this was a sign of youth; to grant an ideological stance precedence over the real decisions that affect flesh and blood people, but my convictions meant something to me. There was no provocation that justified violence! I thought of Shelley's introduction to *The Cenci*. Murder is never moral, he argued. When you resort to violence you are no different than the Marcel Gagnons of the world.

But it wasn't just that. What my mother did was a betrayal of who she was; the one who healed people. As I walked, she took on the qualities of an enemy. I decided that the betrayal was more personal. She had risked our family without a thought. Her actions were an absolute rejection of me and the rest of our family!

On Monday I discovered the local grocery store, which was essential, but then gratuitously kept walking and explored the neighbourhood. That was partly about avoiding being at home with schoolwork that I couldn't concentrate on because I was thinking about my mother.

I also enjoyed the sense of freedom when walking. I had missed Bea enormously at first, but was beginning to get used to being on my own. I thought about how I'd been neglecting my friends; absorbed with school, babysitting and a marriage that was falling apart. I could use those friends now to confide in.

I thought about June. Maybe I should speak more openly to her. I resolved that I wouldn't get myself entangled in a relationship until I could see whether things with June went anywhere.

I sat on the balcony that night, in the dark, smoking, trying not to ponder my mother's journal. I hoped that time would temper my reaction a bit and wondered if I was being too harsh on her. It must have been stressful and confusing to watch Emelie being brutalized. But I had decided, in a less emotional time, when I wasn't thinking of my mother, that I would be categorically opposed to violence. It would be self-serving to abandon my principles. When you resort to murder, I thought, you feel you have the right to kill someone and you have made a momentous decision. You are playing God even though the circumstances seem to justify it. Where will it stop? You have started the ball rolling. Violence precipitates more violence. Ironically, I was about to read my mother's words saying the same thing after watching her friend commit a second murder.

Feeling like Jimmy Stewart in *Rear Window*, I watched the show in the building beside mine, in an apartment across a strip of lawn maybe fifteen yards wide. I seemed to be looking through a lot of windows at other people lately instead of living my own life.

Several people came and went from the apartment. For some reason the couple who lived there made no effort to keep the curtains closed and it became evident the guy was selling dope. I watched various hippies and greasers come and go, and several transactions were made. A very attractive young woman I'd noticed before, who appeared to also live there, didn't seem to be present on this night.

I decamped to my bed and again picked up the journal. I felt like this was going to be painful, but the lure of it was irresistible.

I read about Bernie's startling murder and swore out loud at the stupidity and inevitability of the act. The violence had spread. It's what I would have predicted. But I didn't feel smug about being proved correct. What happened in Wegebow after Marcel's murder refined the idea I'd had, of just how this would occur. Once you accepted the premise that it was acceptable and moral to kill another human being for some reason, then more killings will inevitably occur for increasingly more dubious reasons. All of my mother's moral arguments seemed self-serving as I went through them. There was no way you could ever make killing someone moral. You maybe felt justified, but it was never moral.

As I MADE THE long bus ride home from the university, the next night, I thought, for the first time in ages, of the time that I got busted.

When I was 17, while living in the Village trying to survive, I went to my grandparent's in Sudbury. This was a place where I could stay for free and, of course, there was a girl. It looked to be a prime market for pot so I started dealing. I'd take the train to Toronto, buy up some dope and sell it in Sudbury. One night when I got off of the train in Sudbury I was met by several RCMP officers who had been tipped off and were waiting for me.

It was big news — dope was still a new thing — and I was all over the media. I was a gangster apparently and I was scared. I thought I'd be looking at major jail time.

Despite being angry, and not having seen him since the night he'd knocked me down the stairs and I'd left home, my one phone call after being busted was to my father in Toronto. Thinking about it now, as I rode the bus, it struck me as an amazing thing that I called my old man, of all people.

He jumped in his car and drove all the way to Sudbury to bail me out. I had called him because I knew somehow that he was the one to phone. There was trouble and then there was serious trouble, and when that came along he'd be there. He didn't reprimand, scold or berate me after he picked me up. He was most concerned with how I'd gotten caught. Someone squealed, I told him.

"Got to be 'the mob'," he said, "this place is loaded with wops."

It was a territorial battle for the drug market, in his mind.

"Don't worry about those bastards," he said. "I can deal with them. I grew up with Sudbury wops. They know better than to touch someone in my family."

I'd become the victim. He still had that insular attitude that you see in small northern towns. The sort that my mother had attacked in her journal. People protected each other when one or the other of them did something illegal, and then they stuck together. It was easy to criticize from a distance, and justifiably so in some cases, but it was much appreciated by me.

When I got home from Sudbury my mother's disappointment showed on her face. It was her way of making a point without saying anything. In retrospect, after reading her journal, I wonder if this was calculated. Maybe she felt she'd suffered from her previous actions and that if I stayed on the straight and narrow I could spare myself some grief. At the time though, it just felt like she was coldly moral and unsupportive of her family. I knew that my father, if pressed, would be critical too. But he understood that it just wasn't the right time.

I had always thought I was like my mother but I wondered if this was right. Maybe I was more like my father. Family above everything. Wasn't that a moral position, I thought? You protect your kids because they need their parents to be there. As right as it was for my mother to feel sympathy for the plight of Emelie Gagnon, and even though she truly thought she was doing the moral thing to protect her, she'd made a choice. You chose violence or you don't. You chose family or you don't. And you do these consistently. She'd put a stranger ahead of family. I wouldn't have wanted her to act like the townspeople who defended the violent husband; she spoke out and raised shit, and that was good. Emelie was in trouble and needed to be defended. But to jeopardize your family in the way my mother had was a moral failure, not as bad as the decision to kill another human, but as serious.

I took Bea back to Bryce's apartment one evening, mid-week, while her mother was at school. I didn't tell Dee. We just went. It was always a bit of an adventure for Bea to go on the subway. Old ladies and women smiled at her and she spent her time smiling back and just looking generally pleased with herself. She was curious about the new place, of course, and inspected everything, walking around while holding on to things as a 1-year-old will. I hoped that it would make it easier for her to accept my leaving in the evenings if she knew where I was going and my place became an extension of her world. She most liked staring through the rails on the balcony, fascinated by the park because there were other kids and playground equipment.

"Did you finish your mother's journal?" June asked me on Friday in the cafeteria, a small noisy room, in the basement of one of the colleges, that I liked anyway because of the smells and the perennial sunshine slanting in from the windows high up on the walls. This was where we met up these days since we no longer took the same bus.

We'd been bonding the last few days it seemed to me, smiling stupidly at each other, expectantly and possessively.

I answered yes, but the question felt alarming, because it would be an awkward subject to discuss.

"Guess it brings a lot back?"

"No, not really, unless she zips forward to present day. I've read most of it and it's all about life in this town called Wegebow up north where we lived when I was really small."

"Wegebow? Doesn't ring any bells."

"It's a rough kinda railroad town. My mom was the only doctor so she was always on duty, she'd go in the middle of the night if someone was sick. Lots of times she'd end up working for free because there was no public healthcare."

"I still think that's incredible, a woman doctor back then."

"Yeah, it's true. She didn't have a lot of patients because of the attitude. It was all…are you Catholic?" I asked her.

"No."

"It was all Catholics and they didn't approve of women working. Women were supposed to be churning out kids, making more and more Catholics. The Pope doesn't like birth control or abortion or anything that would interfere with the production of little papists; interfering with the seed of Catholic men. Women didn't own their own bodies. Men ruled."

"Not much has changed."

"And the men were pretty aggressive… violent, you know… my mother did… everything…" I slowed the word for emphasis, "she could…"

"I'm sure she did from what I've heard of her. I think we need people to talk about violence against women. It's been covered up too long." June stared at me intently, I assumed for affirmation but I wondered if she questioned what I'd meant.

It was tempting to tell her what had happened. What would she think of the lengths to which my mother went? I wanted to tell her. Share it. But didn't dare. Instead I just said, "Absolutely."

"My father came from there," I added, "but I never saw him violent with my mother. He was with his kids though, and he still has that troglodyte machismo."

"It's everywhere. It's the generation. My father's like that with my brothers. He's always telling them, 'act like a man.' They must get frustrated hearing that."

"Ah! Yes, I know it well. That's pretty much how my father always put it." It led me to think that I had to fight and be aggressive. I would scrap sometimes just to 'be a man', but I never liked it. Usually, when it came to fighting, I was on the wrong end of a fist or a boot for stealing someone's girlfriend or object of affection. It was pretty primitive; the struggle for women.

"Maybe…I wonder…I don't know." My comment slipped away into silence. What I'd been about to speculate on was the question that had suddenly occurred to me of whether my conquest of so many women was my own way of acting 'like a man.'

"What?"

"Well, I used to think I was like my mother, you know, the education, the interest in the arts and stuff like that, but I've been wondering if I'm not much more like my father."

"Oh, no, I don't see that. Not if he's at all like my father and your description makes him sound like he's pretty much the same. You're not violent or macho. Are you?"

"No, but there are things about my father. He took off for the war to get out in the world. I couldn't wait to leave home, and I went to Vancouver."

"Your mother might have felt like getting away too, but it was harder for girls."

"And then there's family. That's the most important thing to him and it is to me too."

"It seems to me you've completely rejected your father's way of looking at the world. You're your mother's son. Look at the kind of father you are. You're mother and father to Bea. Very nurturing. You're like — and there are other guys are like this now too — the product of men who were damaged by the war and women who were strengthened by it, who went out and worked and ran things. Boys have different views of women because of who they are, and see them more as role models than your father's generation did — you especially."

# *Lawrence*
# Friday

Martin came to visit on Friday night. It was Indian summer; a last gasp of summer temperatures. I had finished the journal a couple nights before and soon after called Martin to invite him over for a talk.

We pulled out a bottle of Blue Nun, a couple of glasses, and took up positions on the balcony. Neither of us knew anything about wine but the buzz around university at the time was that this was pretty great stuff.

I smoked. Martin didn't.

Across from us, on the balcony of the apparent small-time greaser drug dealer, people were gathering and loud rock music was pulsing across the divide.

"My guess is that Dad hasn't read the journal," I said.

I had been intensely worried about what to do with Martin and the journal. Should I give it to him to read? He had as much of a right to it as I did. But it was my father's decision and he had entrusted it to me only. In the end, my sense of equality won out. When I phoned my brother and started out by asking him if he knew about the journal he said, "Oh yeah, I read it a few weeks ago. Told Dad you should look at it too." My sense of pride was diminished, but I was glad I wasn't divulging any secrets.

"You're probably right," Martin replied to my question, sipping tentatively at his glass of wine, his body repulsing slightly from the taste. I don't think he did much in the way of drinking.

"I couldn't believe Dad'd be so sanguine about giving it to me if he knew what was in it. If he read it, it would shatter all of his conceptions about her," I said seriously.

"I wonder…He was there, in Wegebow. I asked him if he'd read it he said, 'No, I know all that stuff. I was there remember?'"

"But Mom said she never told him about things that happened."

"Yeah, but people kinda clue into stuff over time. And you never know, she might have told him stuff later."

"Might have. I was surprised you'd read it too. I thought when Dad gave it to me it was so I'd read it and tell him what was in it."

"Maybe it was," Martin replied, swishing his wine about his glass. "I was drinking some Mateus the other day, it's a rosé. Oh I'm sure you know it right?"

"Yeah."

"It's great. Greek, I think…"

"Portuguese… You know Martin, speaking of conceptions being shattered…" I leaned forward and looked at him directly in the eye. "I'm having a hard time forgiving Mom for what she did. If she was caught we would have spent our whole life being known as the kids of a murderer, with no mother to boot. That can't be the right thing…Killing someone never is!" I said emphatically. I'd been wanting to talk about this. "At first, I think I just felt a kinda categorical opposition to murder, but the more I think about it the more pissed off I get."

"So you don't think there was any justification for what she did?"

"No, there never is for murder! It's always immoral."

"That sounds a bit like a religious commandment. Pretty absolute. The world's a violent place. Sometimes violence is just about survival."

I was feeling a little pissed off by the characterization of my views.

"Survival? No one was hunting her," I said. "Not that that would have made any difference."

"I think circumstances matter. Mom figured she had to protect the woman and her kids or they'd be dead."

"Protecting them was one thing. Murdering someone to do it is another. Don't you see?"

"You know what's odd to me in what you're saying? You're pissed off at Mom for not protecting her family and then you're critical of that Emelie woman for doing the same thing. Murder just happened to be the only way she could do it."

"You always have a choice. She could have left."

"But those kids didn't have a choice. They couldn't pack up and leave or choose passive resistance or whatever. Mom was trying to protect them, and from their mother as much as their father."

We both sipped more wine and let the tone settle a bit. Martin asked for a cigarette. I didn't know he smoked, I said, and he told me it was just when he drank. The hero worship that had been there when we were younger had diminished over time and he'd developed his own tastes to the point where it always felt a little odd to me when he did something that I did, like smoke.

"So, any idea who was trying to intimidate Mom?" I asked. "Any theories about who was attacking her?"

"Nope," Martin replied, sounding a bit drunk. It was around 11:30 p.m. The music from the apartment across the way had continually increased as had the number of people inside. It looked like a major party. "Well, maybe. You know what kind of intrigues me about what happened?" He didn't wait for an answer. "Was that there was a sort of class violence to what happened. Emelie and her friend generalized their attention to all men and I'm guessing they shot their mouths off to women of the town. When Mom supported them, or seemed to, by covering up the murders or performing abortions, she was popular. When she challenged the women there were attacks on her."

"So, what are you saying? Some men were attacking her?"

"Maybe. But it coulda been women. When she turned her back on them."

"But it was the men who had power," I said. "They were the ones being murdered. Maybe they decided to fight back…Well, I guess that's not quite true of the abortions. They weren't under attack from them."

"Well… It is the same though. It's defiance of their authority. I remember there was a woman in Germany in the 19th century I read about. She was an abortionist and the men were terrified of her. She had power over life and death. I think that's why the Catholic opposition to abortion — these guys want power. Not that abortion and murder are alike, but they're both about who controls who lives and who dies. It sounded like the men in Wegebow were afraid of Mom. Did that make them weak? Too ineffectual to attack her? Or did they resent her power and attack her in a sneaky, gutless kinda way? Could be, but I still think it was the women."

"That's interesting," I said, drifting off in a thought. "My friend June thinks Mom was a feminist. Maybe what happened was a piece of feminist history. It was more than just Mom making the men cringe. It was all the women in town. Maybe I should write about it."

"You should probably ask Dad about that first." Martin kind of winced. "He may not want to have this made public."

The music coming at us from across the way suddenly blasted louder when the balcony door was flung open and dimmed again as the door slowly swung shut. Two young women had stumbled outside, arm and arm and now slowly zig-zagged across the balcony. They stood at the railing and talked for a minute before one of them took hold of the top bar, heaved one leg over it, then the other leg, and jumped down to the ground. The second woman just stood there—I assumed she was about to vault over the rail too—but she then began to sway sensually to the music and swing her long black hair behind her. It was the chick who lived in the place and in this light she was beautiful, not ethereally but in a sensual and earthly way. I could worship beauty like that and in an instant was aware of exactly why I succumbed to so many liaisons and to Romantic ideals.

"C'mon! C'mon!" said the woman on the ground in a loud whisper, but the beautiful woman on the balcony continued to dance, not seeming to hear, lost in her stoned dance. She started to sway in circles, back across the balcony, and through the apartment door.

The girl on the ground cursed and went away. So did we.

A DRUNKEN MARTIN, FIGHTING to stay awake, was finally succumbing and had laid down on the couch with a blanket and a pillow. I stood, leaning against the bedroom door frame chatting on about something or other.

The screen door to my balcony was suddenly flung open and the beauty from the apartment opposite walked in, appearing no more sober than an hour before. She looked between my brother, myself, and then around the room with a bemused look.

"Sorry guys," she said drunkenly, but with urgency. "Turn out the light." She held out a very large bag of grass. "I have to hide, just for a bit, or he'll kick the hell out of me again." She giggled, walked over and flicked off the end table lamp, the only source of illumination in the apartment.

"Shit," said Martin, miraculously sobering up. He got up and closed the balcony door, but there were many vestiges of light seeping through the thin curtains.

Outside some very loud asshole yelled, "Iris, where the hell are you, you bitch! When I find you, you're dead!"

"Should we call the cops?" whispered Martin.

"Naw," giggled Iris, "I got all his dope."

"Then why don't you just go out the front door of the building?" Martin asked, looking displeased. He edged towards the kitchen door like he was more than willing to help her find her way out.

"They'll be outside," I answered for her, with no evidence at all that there was a 'they' or without suggesting how they could be at both the front and back of the building. So far we'd just heard the voice of one guy.

"Just stay here and keep the lights out." I said to Martin and Iris, and then added, "Have a seat."

Outside the same yahoo could be heard yelling, "I seen her go into that apartment." Shortly after, there was banging on the balcony door. Iris and Martin both got up and moved across the room and into the kitchen.

"Iris! Iris!" an angry male voice called. "Let me in right now and I won't kill you."

"We've got to do something," Martin whispered, annoyed and a little tremulous.

"Let him try and come in," I said with genuine anger. "This is my home. We don't have to fuckin' do anything!"

Martin shook his head, disapproving of the bravado. "This guy's a dealer. He probably has weapons. Knives, maybe a gun. This isn't something you can deal with."

"It's true," said Iris. "He has some kind of revolver or whatever you call it. We need to get outta here."

"And you need to give him the dope back," Martin said.

"Stay calm," I said brusquely. "I'm not gonna take this shit; smashing on the door."

"Okay, you don't like it," said Martin, "but don't get too macho. Let's go outside so we don't get shot. Go through the hall and out the back door. We can call him over and give him the dope. Maybe with three of us he'll settle for the dope."

Iris said nothing, like she was acquiescing, which was odd in a way since she'd just stolen his grass, but now she was apparently going to give it back. Yet she wore this fantastically attractive, perpetual half smile of cynicism, which made you wonder.

Fuck it, I thought. I was inwardly furious at the idea of conceding my family turf to some Neanderthal but figured that I'd take the civilized approach. Go outside and give the guy his dope. It was his anyway and I didn't want it.

The three of us left through the kitchen and went out the apartment's back door. We went in shadow around the perimeter of the building. Stopping at the corner, still hidden, we peeked and saw the greaser on my balcony.

"At the count of three, I'm coming in!" he shouted. "One!"

We were thirty feet away from him.

"Give me the dope," Martin whispered, "I'll throw it towards him and tell him to take it and screw off."

"Two!" The guy bellowed.

The girl suddenly bounced past Martin and I, and into the space between the two buildings where she stopped and yelled, "Roy! You want your pot asshole, come and get it." She held the baggie up in front of her face, waved it teasingly, then tore off across the rest of the grassy space between the two apartment buildings and into the parking lot behind her own building.

The guy roared, leapt the balcony railing and came screaming after her.

Martin and I stood dumbly, watching Iris run. It looked as though she ducked behind one of the first cars she came to. The building was blocking the greaser's view so he thankfully couldn't see.

Martin took my arm to pull me back into the shadows.

I resisted, feeling embarrassed at the idea of hiding. I thought I should help her; protect her. It was a compelling instinct.

The drug dealer didn't look in our direction as he rounded the corner of the building opposite, on a dead run. He was a fast sonofabitch and silent. He stopped when he hit the parking lot. Iris was nowhere to be seen.

"Damn," he slammed his fist against the trunk of a parked car. Almost immediately, the doors opened and three or four guys began to climb out along with a cloud of marijuana smoke. It was too perfect.

Martin and I retreated to the back door of our apartment building rather than watch the carnage.

"We have to go over there," I said, catching myself, "and find the girl?"

"Let's go back inside," said Martin, holding my arm. "The guy's dead meat and if she has even the slightest bit of a brain she'll be long gone while he's getting his ass kicked."

I hemmed and hawed, but eventually gave in and went back inside.

MARTIN AND I SAT at the kitchen table, fairly subdued given recent events, but too jumped up to contemplate sleep for some time to come. We were in the dark, neither of us feeling the need for light. Martin, especially, was startled when the buzzer from the downstairs door went off. I went to the intercom to answer.

"Can I come back in?" we heard Iris whisper. I let her in.

"Oh Jesus, here we go again," Martin said waving his hands in the air in frustration.

I was exultant and went into the hall to watch for her approach. Her face was flushed with triumph and she smiled broadly at me when she stepped off the elevator, the bag of pot still in her hand.

Iris brushed against me as she went past to get into the apartment, and I half hugged her.

With a deep sigh, Martin made it known he wasn't pleased with her presence. He peeked nervously and clandestinely through the curtains, as if the boyfriend was going to sense her presence.

Iris tossed the baggie on the coffee table and went to look through the window.

"It looks pretty dead over there," Martin said. "The lights are on but I can't see anyone."

"Yeah, I hope the fucker is dead." Iris laughed. She left Martin to keep watch and sprawled on the couch, going into her story of how she had used the commotion between the guys in the car and her boyfriend to slip away, circle the block and approach my building from the opposite direction.

The pace of the conversation slowed as we all calmed down. Martin had reclaimed a spot at one end of the couch and his head now began to sag forward. Soon he was asleep, slouching over.

WE SAT ON THE edge of the bed, where we'd gone to smoke a joint. I lit a candle on the dresser.

"Are you going back there in the daytime?" I asked, not wanting her to, despite the recently demonstrated evidence of her ability to look after herself.

"Yeah, I'll wait until he goes to work and get my stuff. I need to get away from here. Roy's gonna be really pissed off that I took his shit and he's got lots of friends."

"Where you gonna go?"

"I don't know. Vancouver maybe. You ever been there?"

I told her I had and, as I related a bit about my experiences, in that close proximity, almost face to face, I felt the irresistible urge to reach out (such beauty was overwhelming and impossible to not want to give in to). As our voices softened and became intimate the refusal to reach out (to honour a promise to myself about June and a new direction I'd rationally decided on) felt even more painful and unbearable to resist. I wondered how I was going to stand this and then I wondered whether life wasn't, really, about succumbing to joy and beauty; a constant on-going radical acceptance of it.

# *Lawrence*
# Saturday

Martin left in the morning before we got up. Iris went later, when I did. We had stayed in bed together until the very last minute, until I absolutely had to leave to get Bea.

We stood outside Iris's building debating whether she should go in and retrieve some stuff.

"Fuck it," she said.

We took the subway downtown. She was headed for the railway station having decided to go to her grandmother's. Get out of town for awhile. Hopefully, the boyfriend, would head back to Montreal.

"I'll stay for a few weeks and when I can't stand it I'll go to Vancouver, sell some pot to get set up."

I wondered if she would or even could come back to Toronto. We had skulked away from the apartment that morning looking over our shoulders for her boyfriend. I didn't like the feel of that, but maybe in time, if she came back, it would be okay. I'd be living somewhere else and Roy would be back in Montreal.

As we bumped along, snuggling and cooing, we talked about her immediate plans. She told me that her grandmother lived in a place called Harris and that's where she was headed. Twelve hours by a milk-run train and forty-eight dollars away. That would take almost every cent she had.

"That's funny," I said. "I've heard of Harris. It's pretty close to Hartley and Wegebow."

"You know those dumps?" With a look of bemused curiosity she drew her head back to take me in.

"Don't go all sentimental on me, missing home. I lived in Wegebow when I was a kid."

"No shit. The place is a hole."

"You think it's any worse than other towns?"

"Not up there anyway."

"I'm curious though, because of the association, what its like. Is it really that bad?"

"Naw, not really. It's tiny. Just a backwater. The houses are crappy. There's nothing to do. All those towns all boring as hell, that's why I left. They don't appreciate people like me."

"I wanna go there sometime," I said.

She laughed. "Siding with them eh? Enticed by the glamour? Sorry, I know it's your home town and all that but I still don't know why anyone would go there who didn't have to. Maybe if you're really into hunting and fishing, but I doubt that's your style."

"Actually," I replied, a little more aggressively than I would have liked, feeling like she was implying some sort of wimpishness, "I am like that. I spent a lot of time visiting my grandparents in Sudbury. I go out fishing and hunting with the relatives all the time."

She looked a little less than thrilled with me for being a pissed-off guy who loved to hunt. So different than the people she'd fled from in Harris and now Toronto. Shit.

As the subway pulled into the Union Station stop and we got to our feet, I said, trying to sound very serious, "What it is, really, is that I've been reading a journal my mother wrote about when we lived there. I'm curious to see it; to see if it's changed."

We said good-bye on the subway platform and I caught the next train.

As I headed for Dee's I thought more about Wegebow. There was something intriguing about what had happened there that I wanted to follow up on. I remembered Martin's comments about my mother taking control of the life of the town; of the women supporting her and the men being afraid. I wondered if it had any lasting effect. If I had the time and a spare hundred dollars, neither of which was likely, I decided I would visit. I could write my mother's story maybe; a chapter of feminist history; a town where women subverted the normal social order and men were terrified.

But was my mother really a feminist, I wondered? I could understand she wanted to get the hell away from Wegebow and the on-going hostility and tension, but still, it struck me as odd given her independence of mind, that she would have acceded to my father's wish to settle into a typical middle-class marriage of the time back in Sudbury. It made no sense. How she could have done that, after all she'd gone through to go through medical school, was hard to understand. Maybe, in the end, she too was just a product of the period when she grew up. Or maybe — I thought of another possibility — she just knew the rules and knew which ones she could get away with.

The thought didn't reconcile the contradictions. For example, I remember she had very advanced attitudes about men and women that she wanted to instil in her sons: we had to do our share of the housework, we weren't to listen to stupid comments about women being 'used goods' and the like. She lectured against such nonsense. Yet, at the same time, she stood by while my father smacked me around and she said nothing, at least in front of me. Pretty hypocritical given all that happened.

DEE ASKED IF I would take Bea back to my place for the night. She didn't say why and I was too pleased to be getting my daughter to ask. I did wonder though, whether Dee was looking forward to the time alone—maybe she had some plans to have someone over—or had just reconciled herself to the situation. In spite of it having been her idea, she looked uncomfortable when we left; uncertain and shaken.

On the other hand, Bea was thrilled. She understood where we were going; the place that, except for one time, was off limits—my place.

Back home we spent some time at the park across the street. Bea played in the sandbox mostly and watched the other kids, which she liked to do. She awkwardly tried to imitate them run and squeal. I had a compelling tendency to walk around behind her. Because she was only 1-year-old she pitched over a lot and I was undoubtedly over-protective. That was okay, I justified, parents should be like that.

I was calmer being in the park than in the apartment itself; not that I would acknowledge it. When we were inside, while Bea was taking a nap, I was half expecting the greaser from across the way to come over. I told myself I could handle it, but mostly that he had no reason to come looking for me. As far as he knew, his buddy was mistaken when he saw Iris coming into my place the night before since she showed up outside a few minutes later. I was rehearsing speeches to convince him, if need be, that I hadn't interacted with Iris at all (as if I would be able to rationally discuss this with him if he showed up at my door). Several times I looked through my window at the apartment across from me and saw that the drapes remained closed. I hated my cowardice and was happy that no one was there to witness it.

I was getting used to the frowns from some of the residents when they saw me—long-haired, with a goatee and sandals—but it pissed me off when a few of the parents at the park, with horrified looks, steered their little 2 or 3-year-old beneficiaries to the monkey bars or slides as Bea approached; like she was going to contaminate their child. This was not protecting your kids but a disgraceful chauvinism, believing you could stop your family from being infected by other kids, like the Paul Desjardins of the world. Wegebow and Toronto weren't that different. I wondered if you could really keep your kids so chaste anywhere. To see their kids run to Bea, without thinking, was the most satisfaction I would get at the moment. It's too bad they would learn their parents' fear and snobbery over time.

PART 4

# *Robert*
# Sunday

Looking out the kitchen window, Robert watched his son sitting by himself on a lawn chair, reading a book. Lawrence and his daughter had come over for the afternoon. Martin had gone off to school and Bea was sleeping.

When he thought back, Robert always remembered Lawrence doing things with his mother; like standing on a chair to help her bake or trying to make the beds. He used to tell Maddy that this would make the boy effeminate, so tried to show him things a boy needed to know. He was maybe too tough on him, but had only wanted to make him more of a man.

It was time to talk, so he went outside.

"Did you read the journal?" he asked, pulling up a lawn chair.

"Yes," Lawrence said, watching closely for a reaction.

"And?"

"Well…it's interesting. I don't remember Wegebow or what it was like."

"Uh-huh," Robert agreed.

"Lots about Mom's early cases and a good picture of life in Wegebow. It's pretty candid. Pretty shocking, some of the stuff that went on."

"Yeah, it was a strange time. I wanted you and your brother to understand, that's why I gave you the journal. She was good like that, your mother, she'd always help someone. If a girl was in trouble she knew your mother would help her. I heard lots of people say that. I heard a woman at her funeral say that, that no one would do more to help you than Maddy."

There was a long interlude while they both considered the fact.

Lawrence knew a moral debate about his mother's actions would be out of the question. And, actually, his father hadn't even acknowledged some of his mother's deeds.

"Have you read the journals?" he asked tentatively.

"I don't need to. I was there." Rough and annoyed.

"I am taking a course in Sociology next term," Lawrence said. "I think that Mom's story might be something I could write about. I think other people would find it fascinating. What would you think if I did that?"

"No. Don't do that! I didn't give you the journal to use in school. Let them learn their lessons some other way. It's your mother's story not yours!" The reply had been pretty harsh. Softening, Robert added, "Maybe some day, long into the future...I don't know. Not now. I don't want your mother's reputation affected. Maybe after a number of years have gone by."

"I HAVE SOME LETTERS of your mother's," Robert told his son before he left for home.

With one hand he took up a small pile of three or four letters wrapped in an elastic band that was sitting on the dining-room table. "Take them. If you found the journal interesting you'll find these the same. I read them."

When Lawrence put the letters into his bag he took out the journal and tried to hand it to his father.

With his one free hand Robert waved it away. "No, you keep that for your daughter." He nodded down at Bea whom he held in his other arm. He loved babies in general, her especially, and she loved him. They would play together for whole afternoons.

Robert's good-byes were surprisingly earnest. "Always be happy. Have a good life. Look after your daughter. That's what matters in life. And remember," he added, "no matter what happens, please keep what you know about your mother to yourself."

## *Lawrence*

On the subway ride back home, after dropping off Bea, I remembered the letters that my father had given me and pulled them out of my bag. I'd indulge him and take a look. One was from a childhood friend of my mother's. I'd known her and her family for years. I saw them more than many of my own aunts and uncles. The letter was mostly about family events.

The second letter was very different. I noticed it was postmarked from Wegebow. Was this a coda to my mother's story? I hastened to open it. The letter was brief and unsigned.

It went, "Hello Dolly: Do you remember who called you that? I do. I was young but I remember and I also remember the stories that were told and discussed by my family at nights when they thought I was sleeping and couldn't hear. I know what my mother did to my father. It took a long time but I forgave her when I realized she wouldn't and couldn't have done it without you. You killed my father and I know you killed my mother to shut her up. You destroyed the lives of my sister and me by killing our parents. I've planned this for a long time. Someday soon I will be coming for you. As my mother should have said: Goodbye Dolly."

I sat forward, my body reacting wildly, as if I'd been attacked. I knew who'd sent this letter. My mother had written in her journal how Emelie had called her Dolly the day she took the drugs to kill her husband Marcel. Emelie's 4 year-old son René was there and would have heard. He was old enough to remember that day, if aided by hearing the family discuss it in an adjoining room, in whispers, conveying that something unusual had transpired.

I turned over the envelope and checked the postmark. The letter had been sent two weeks before my mother died when her car had gone off the road.

There was no reason the car should have driven into the bush except it was late and she might have fallen asleep. I'd told the police how she had once started to doze off on a late night when she was driving us home. The bastard had killed her and I'd provided the confirmation!

I got up and squeezed hard on one of the poles beside the nearest subway door. I stared out the window, not focusing on my reflection, and waited to get off, although I had four stops before mine. C'mon, c'mon, c'mon, I said under my breath when the train slowed. When it stopped altogether, between two stations, I shook the pole and swore loudly, "Fuck!" I was aware that people looked in my direction—there were lots in the train car—but I didn't give a shit what they thought. I had to get off. I had no idea of what to do next but something was waiting for me.

A SHORT TIME LATER, having gotten off the train, I walked and smoked at a savage pace. I had to go to the police, of course. I would call when I got home. I walked and smoked even more rapidly.

Why hadn't my mother gone to them herself? She knew who was threatening her, and why. Of course I realized why she'd kept quiet; it would have been confessing to murder to explain to the cops about the threat even though to not say anything was risking her own life. She couldn't even tell my father because she didn't want him to know about Marcel's murder. Well, I would go to the police and that would be the end of René.

As I walked I remembered my father's adamant words to me of not more than an hour earlier. He knew I'd be reading the letters soon and wanted to make sure that I maintained my mother's reputation and said nothing. Why? It was an incredible thought; to know someone killed her yet do nothing in order to preserve her reputation! The feelings that welled up must have been something similar to the immense frustration over the situations my mother found herself in several times when she was trapped into maintaining her secret.

I walked and attacked the contradictions from different perspectives but, in the end, realized that I must be silent. Protecting my mother's privacy and dignity was the only thing left I could do to defend her.

But, I wondered, could I really stand by and do nothing? There was no justice from sitting on my hands and accepting that someone could come into my life and kill my mother! Yet that was exactly what I had to do, and apparently what my father was doing.

I arrived at my building and, instead of going inside, walked around the back, right to the far end of the parking lot behind the building. I sat on the edge of the grass, just beyond the tarmac and, with just enough light left in the day, looked out over a large ravine.

Why had my mother told us the story? Why now? It didn't make any difference to her life like it would have years earlier. If she said something then she wouldn't have been trapped in silence or felt helpless. She could have gotten some support and protection. Yet now, when it didn't matter, she wanted us to know.

Did she feel that what was about to happen was justice? Did she just want her children to know who she was? Or—and the thought of this was compelling—did she want justice? Now, when she no longer had to be silent, did she want us to go to the police and end this?

I felt convinced that this was it. This letter from Marcel's insane kid would hang him. He'd convicted himself by writing it. What an incredibly stupid asshole. I got up, dizzy after smoking half a dozen cigarettes in succession, and thought something along the lines of, "Yeah, you sonofabitch. We're coming for you."

Back inside, sitting at the kitchen table, the receiver was in my hand when I began to think of how pissed off my old man would be. He'd hate me; see it as a betrayal of family. I put the receiver down because he'd be right; that's what it would be. After all I'd been telling myself the last week about the importance of supporting your family. I'd be a hypocrite to not stand up for my mother, even in death.

I made a whole new resolution at that point, one that flew in the face of everything I believed, or rather, had chosen to believe. Couldn't one, just as easily, choose not to believe those very same things? This resolution was based on anger, and my desire for justice or revenge, but I didn't care in the least. I was going to Wegebow.

I PHONED DEE, SPOKE to her quite calmly and rationally, told her I had a family emergency and needed to be away for a few days. She let me know what an inconvenience this was and grilled me until I got impatient and hung up. I wasn't worried about what she thought; it wasn't like it was going to change anything. This had just been a courtesy call to say she'd be looking after Bea the next few days. Work it out Dee.

It so happened that I was flush with money at that moment. I'd received the first instalment of my student loan which was meant to be enough income to get me through a meagre existence for the next four months. It was certainly enough to buy a ticket for Wegebow.

I called the train station. The Trans-Canada would be leaving Toronto the next morning at 9 a.m. It would go all day and night and get into Wegebow the following morning.

My immediate frustration at the idea of waiting all night before catching a train soon gave way to acceptance. This would give me a chance to think things out a bit; to make a plan.

THE PRIMARY PLANK OF the plan was to not get caught. I needed this to go smoothly; a way to get into town, find who I was looking for, do what I came to do, and then leave. I wanted the prick to know who I was, but only him. This wasn't suicide. It was important to approach the whole thing sanely, not crazily like the night before. This had to be approached as a challenge.

I wondered about my hair, beard, look. I'd stand out. So what! There was no one who would know me. No one who would connect such a person with me, a student in Toronto. To be on the safe side, after the killing, I'd go west to Winnipeg. Put the cops on the wrong trail. At that point I would get a haircut and some new clothes, and head back to Toronto. If the cops traced me from Wegebow to Winnipeg they wouldn't know that the same person that had come into town had also taken a train out of town.

# *Lawrence*
# Tuesday

The dawdling train dragged its sorry ass into Wegebow in the morning after an all night trip. I'd spent a sleepless night and was now standing on the platform between two cars, smoking and smelling the morning dew, hypnotized by the wall of trees passing in front of me. As we hit the town, people looked up and waved as we crawled by with the whistle blasting.

At the station I was directed northwards to a nearby motel.

Wegebow looked to be mostly paved residential streets of smallish, wooden houses with no sidewalks. There were only ditches at the sides of the roads. Impossible to miss was the cathedral in the centre of town which looked high enough to be visible from everywhere.

I walked down the main drag, past the sorts of businesses you'd expect to see there, and thought of my mother's journal. Not much had changed. On the train we had passed a few north-south streets with businesses on them, so the main street wasn't the only business area anymore.

The motel that I checked-in — maybe the only one in town — was north of the main street. There was a decent sized window in the back wall, facing the lake. Standing at the window, I could also see the town dock next door, to the west of me. A few motor boats were tied to it — probably belonging to people in the marina. It wasn't so different a set up to what you might find on many lakes in northern Ontario.

A couple of bush planes, bobbing in the water, looked to be the only things moored there. A sandwich board on the dock read: Desjardins' Tours.

Throwing my bag on to the bed, I took in the room. There was a damp, musty smell. The walls were covered with cheap wood paneling, bulging over insulation, with bits of it protruding around the window frame. The floor looked to be tilted slightly.

On the walls were two faded framed prints of fly fisherman in a river — the sort of cardboard prints sometimes sold in grocery stores back then. And there was a landscape that I spent a good deal of time looking at over the next hour because it was made from natural materials glued to a watercolour background; a strip of birch bark was a birch tree, a piece of poplar bark was a poplar tree, twigs were the branches and bushes, dried moss was underbrush and leaves.

I HAD DECIDED TO lay low to try and minimize the number of people who could identify me, so was counting on being able to locate René Gagnon by checking the phonebook.

I would kill him in the morning and then get out of Wegebow on the same train I'd come in on today. My objectives were to find a weapon and a place to hide the body to give me some time. These hadn't sounded difficult on the train but were a little more daunting now that the fierce emotions driving me had calmed somewhat.

The descriptions in my mother's journal served as a guide to get to the one gratuitous stop in town that I wanted to make, figuring I could do this without drawing any attention to myself.

I walked east, along the beach. The houses facing the lake were well back from the public beach. It felt creepy thinking that one of these places had belonged to the Gagnons; and maybe still did.

Peace and quiet are very stressful. I always find being in the country like that, at first. Not the idyllic pastoral for me. I think my central nervous system adjusts itself to the constant barrage of noise in the city and my body's defences, or whatever they are, continue in high gear even after the stimulus is gone. This day was no different and, if anything, the sensations were heightened. My heart pounded and my pulse raced as I walked along, almost hyper-ventilating.

Eventually I went past the place that I presumed was the house where we'd lived. Much smaller than I thought it would be, of course. It surprised me that it roused no new memories at all. To get a closer look I would have to walk by it until I came to some bush where I could cut around the house and approach the place from the road. I knew from my mother's journal that twenty years before this had been the last house on the road, but now I had to go by three more houses before I reached forest that wasn't part of someone's yard.

Through years of seeing houses in Toronto that were built in the same style, it didn't stand out as interesting, just incongruously suburban looking for Wegebow. The office space at the front had no sign and looked like it was now incorporated into the house. The whole place had a shabby, sad and unkempt look. I wondered what my mother would have thought.

I backtracked, returning the clandestine way I'd come, although I would have preferred to walk through town and ask questions. I wondered in a perhaps unrealistic way if my mother's actions had any lasting effect. Were the men still as violent as they'd been? Had the balance of power changed? I quickly reconciled myself to the fact that these were questions I would never have answers to. It was time to find my mother's murderer and remember why I was there.

I WENT INTO THE office of the motel determined to find a phonebook and start looking for René Gagnon. For all I knew Francine had adopted him and he'd be listed under her name. If neither of those worked, I reckoned that, given the size of Wegebow, I could probably go through every last name in it until I saw one that looked right.

I went to the motel office to look for a pay phone or phonebook but saw neither. The woman from earlier wasn't around so I snuck a look behind the counter. Nothing there either, but they at least had a phone.

There was a closed door, about six feet behind the high counter, which I figured might lead to some living quarters. I waited, thinking the slam of the cheap screen door behind me would rouse someone's attention, but nothing. I rang the bell on the counter. Still nothing. I just stood staring at the door wondering if the room behind it was where Marcel Gagnon had been conceived in lonely lust.

I went back to my room to wait, thinking I'd return in a half hour or so, turned on the TV and flicked it around the channels. Nothing on any of them, just snowy hissing. I went back to the office. Still nothing.

I should have waited. Not that in the final scheme of things it made any difference but I rationalized that since I would be heading to Winnipeg tomorrow what did it matter if someone saw me. In fact, there was something to be said for it. Not a lot of people mind you, and especially no one who would spend enough time with me to be able to provide much of a physical description after I was gone, but just enough circulating to get in a few conversations and mention how I was on my way home to Winnipeg. If the cops came looking for me the next day that's what they'd hear but if things went well there was no reason to think they'd come looking for me at all. All the same though, I thought, when I was done with René I should take his wallet so that the murder would look like it had been the outcome of a theft by some punk traveller.

ON THE TOWN DOCK, a skinny old man in a plaid shirt sat on a lawn chair. A roll-your-own smoke hung in the corner of his mouth. A line running from a fishing rod dangled in the water. He looked at me, curiously, slightly bewildered, but it didn't feel judgmental.

"What sort of tours do they offer?" I asked pointing at the Desjardins' sign.

"Whatever you want," he said with a surprisingly heavy French accent. "Go to the office dere."

"Thanks." But I knelt down on one knee beside him instead. "Do you catch much here?"

"Oh yeah, but I'd get more somewheres else. I like sitting here 'cus you meet all kinds a people." He pulled the skinny rollie from his mouth with bent, nicotine stained fingers, dark blue and red veins visible through the thin skin, and whipped the pathetic butt into the lake.

I wondered if he was senile and would remember me.

Disconcertingly, the old codger stared intently.

"You take long to grow your hair like that?"

"Not long no. Grows pretty fast."

"Some don't like that but I don't care. My grandfather, my mother's father, was Ojibway. He had longer hair than yours."

"Have you lived here long?"

"My 'ole life. Where you from?"

"Winnipeg. On my way home. Thought I get off and maybe do a little fishing."

"Well, yeah, like I say. Check the office." He swivelled in his chair and switched his attention to Desjardins' Tours. "Chester's always around."

"I will, thanks…" I said wondering who Chester was, because he didn't sound like a Desjardins. "…right after lunch. I saw a restaurant on my way in, from the train."

PART 4

"You eat your dinner pretty darn early."

I looked at my watch. I hadn't realized it was only about 10 a.m.

"I'm pretty hungry. I was on the train all day yesterday and all night, so didn't have much to eat."

"Me, I don't travel much," he said. "My legs get sore sitting in the car, you know, even to Hartley. I never bin to Winnipeg."

I continued to try and make small talk but finally made noises about heading off for the restaurant.

As I was leaving, I turned and as an afterthought said, "Desjardins' Tours. Is that the family who runs the business?"

"Oh yeah," he said. "They been here a long time. The whole family lives in town. Guess they like it here. It's a good place for families."

As I MADE MY way downtown, people looked at me quizzically — I was a hippy oddity — but they didn't stare aggressively the way many in the city did.

This was way too much exposure. I was regretting my decision not to wait it out at the motel but kept on going since I was almost at my destination.

Inside the door of the restaurant was a pay phone and on a shelf below was a phonebook. You had to go right inside the place to use the phone and I was glad I didn't need to call anyone because the whole place quieted down and watched me.

The residents of about ten different towns were listed in the book and it was still only the thickness of a Time magazine.

I angled myself so that my back was towards the crowd. Not like they cared, the noise had started up again, but I suppose I psychologically wanted this to be private. I felt exposed and vulnerable.

I discovered something about Wegebow at that moment that I hadn't known before. I didn't see it in my mother's journal and my parents hadn't mentioned it, but almost everyone there was speaking French.

One section of the phonebook had the word Wegebow in bold type across the top of the page. I flipped through a few pages to the G's, ran my finger down the column and there it was: René Gagnon! It had been as simple finding him as that. 53 Third Avenue. That, I thought on exiting the restaurant would be a breeze to locate. The east-west roads were Streets while the north-south ones were Avenues. Except for Main Street, both Streets and Avenues were named First and Second and so on.

THE NAME ON THE sign said Gagnon's Garage. The business was close to the road and there was a house on the back part of the lot. The large front garage door was open and a young man, with his back to me, was at work under the hood of a car.

I crossed the street, slowed as I approached and said, "Excuse me."

The guy who turned around was about my age, muscular, with a short brush cut. He looked me up and down with mild distaste.

"I'm in town for a bit of fishing and was walking around to have a look at things." I said, which drew no reaction. "I lived here when I was small. I'm looking at your sign and assume Gagnon is your name. Is that right?"

He withdrew from the car and looked me over. "That's right." It sounded like he was pissed off.

"I remember the name but I don't know why. I heard it somewhere back then."

"What's 'yer name?"

"Frank Cenci," I said and he looked at me a little bewildered. His manner relaxed. I preferred the nervous look.

"Hmm," he said, as if he was pondering far back into the recesses of his memory to try and dig up some recollection of me. "Did you go to the Catholic school?" he asked.

"Oh, no." My voice shook slightly. It wasn't fear, not of René, but of knowing what was to come.

"Ah," he said. Apparently understanding why he didn't remember me.

"You got a nice little shop here," I said, looking around at a large clean garage with a lift and three organized and well-stocked benches of tools. My life would have been so different if I had grown up here, I thought.

"Well, it's alright, I suppose. I've had it for a couple years. Business is pretty good."

His tone had softened but he went back to work.

Standing and watching him for a minute I was surprised that I felt no anger; just nervousness.

"See ya," I said, leaving, thinking that René was soon to find out that attacking someone in my family had been a fatal mistake.

I WENT BACK BY the lake, wandered east again, and found a secluded spot. It was time to complete my plans. The train would pull into town at about 9 in the morning. I would kill René, hide his body in the trunk of the car he was working on, so it would take awhile to find, and get to the train. Winnipeg was too far away. If they found the body the cops could be waiting there. I'd buy a ticket to Winnipeg but my destination would be the next decent sized town. I would buy some scissors and a razor today. Right before getting to the town I'd find a bathroom on the train, cut my hair, shave and get off. I'd board a bus heading for Toronto. This was all extra precaution I told myself, even if they did find the body quickly there would be no reason to connect me to it.

I went through some possible methods of killing the prick and decided I would buy a hunting knife.

I was pretty sure that if René saw me approach he would have no idea of why. If I was lucky I would catch him under the hood of a car or truck and could approach him from behind. I'd have to drag him inside the garage, stash the body and get rid of the knife.

I went over to Main Street and picked up a pair of scissors, a razor and a knife without anyone raising an eyebrow, except for my appearance. After that I went back to my motel room for the long wait.

# *Robert*

It would only have been a matter of time—back when they were under siege in Wegebow—before someone did something to hurt Maddy or Lawrence. Robert thought about it as he stood at the back door having a last look at the vegetable garden, which was done for the year. Being away so much, he wouldn't have been able to protect his family from attacks, so his power play to get Maddy to move to Sudbury was something that had to be done.

That aunt of Francine's who lived next door to her was a vicious old bat. When he was a kid him and his friends once went into her yard to retrieve an errant ball and she had chased them down the road running after them while swinging a hockey stick. She knew how to shoot a gun too. If he had to make a bet as to who it was had shot through their window that night, it would've been that crazy old witch.

The men of the town would have been too gutless to do anything to Maddy. He knew it from the time he heard those guys talking in the hardware store. If they were going to do something they would have done it already. They were afraid of him, knew he'd been overseas and wouldn't take any of their crap. Probably afraid to piss off Maddy too. Afraid she'd pass their wives some pills. She should have done it too.

It was the boy that got back at Maddy. The kid was brazen and trying to be heroic, which was just another word for stupid, as he'd learned in the war. Too stupid to know that whatever he did to Robert's family would be visited on his own. All he could see was getting his idea of justice. Probably spent too much time around Francine and her bitch aunt. He hated that old lady.

The yard looked good, not picture perfect good, but cared for and lived in. Maddy would have been pleased. She would have liked to have seen her granddaughter playing there the other day.

Robert knew what he had to do. It had taken him a while to get to the point where he could bring himself to act, not because he was afraid, he wasn't. He was angry but he didn't want this to be about that. This was about making people respect his family and knowing that they couldn't be tampered with.

Robert also knew that his hesitation was because what he was about to do was the end, and he wasn't ready for it. Well maybe he was now, he figured, after living with the idea for several weeks. What the hell, he was just putting in time working at the same crappy job until retirement and then death.

The kids had now read the journal and letter. He had wanted them to understand what he was about to do even if it meant them knowing about their mother. But he knew that was her call and she'd made it by writing the journal, so he had no business objecting.

He had read the journal in a single night. It surprised him that Maddy wouldn't have trusted him to understand the stuff she'd done. Of course he would have, and did so when he read about it. If you have to act to save a life then you act. Maybe if she'd told him at the time he would have looked after things himself. At any rate, it was too late now to speculate.

It was time to head for the train station and catch the overnighter for Wegebow.

He was sorry he wouldn't see his sons and granddaughter grow old. That's the only thing he regretted. But they would do okay. If he had worries it was about Lawrence. He always had a funny disposition. He wasn't strong. Things would get him down and he would brood about them. Hopefully, the family would support him. That's what it was all about. Family was the only thing that mattered.

Robert got his jacket from the hall closet. Stood at the livingroom doorway and took a final look around. His will was on the dining room table.

He locked the door on his way out.

ON THE TRAIN RIDE north Robert thought about that summer night, soon after the war.

How bad had he hurt that kid? It didn't matter he told himself, what he'd done was about justice and it was satisfying for that reason.

He had been at college taking one of the government offered training programmes to learn a trade; good for guys like him that had dropped out of school to go overseas. He was renting a room in Toronto, on the top floor of one of the skinny British immigrant houses near Rogers Road.

## PART 4

One tepid evening, an eternity from the Front, he was sitting in the backyard, smoking and having a beer with a couple of other former soldiers, Wallace MacPherson and Tony Lemon. Robert wasn't a tall man but was solidly built. He had his short sleeves rolled up to reveal bristling reddish-blonde hair on his forearms and an ex-soldier's tattoos. Like the other two boys he had a fatigued look in his eyes. They'd seen too much the last couple of years. They were laughing about one of Tony's jokes when the woman who owned the house came stumbling into the yard. She was crying and calling the name of her 7 year-old daughter in a desperate, pleading wail as if the kid was hiding and this would bring her out. "Did you see a little girl?" she begged of the guys, but they hadn't.

"Her name's Mira. She was here…she was here not ten minutes ago! I was upstairs and I looked out the window and seen her sittin' with her doll on the front steps, you know, just sittin there singin' to herself. Just five minutes ago! Now she doesn't answer. Would ya please help me look…please."

The three men started to search. They started up an alley but couldn't see anything behind the tightly packed garages so they retreated and headed up the street, and alternated nipping down the tiny walkways between the tightly situated houses to have a look into the backyard worlds of vegetable gardens and spindly trees.

In the yard behind the tenth or eleventh house a man who couldn't have been more than 18 or 19 was sitting on the grass against a huge, sprawling lilac hedge, talking sweetly and holding the girl on his knee while she struggled to get free. She looked scared and was saying something about wanting to go home.

"Here! Here!" Wallace shouted to his pals when he saw the guy with the girl. "What the hell you doing?" he said, as he walked towards the man on the grass, a chubby fellow with acne and slicked back hair. "That girl's ma is petrified!"

As he got near him, the guy let go of the girl and she ran to the soldier.

"Go home," Wallace told her and she raced off.

By then, Robert and Tony had arrived and gotten the gist of what was happening.

"Why you got that girl here?" Tony said. "You a pervert?"

"No… no," the kid stuttered. "I… I was just talking to her."

"With her sitting on your lap?" Robert strode towards him. "You lousy sonofabitch." Dropping to his knees Robert punched him square between the eyes. The pervert went down on the ground, and stayed there, pulling up his knees into a fetal position and rolling over on to his stomach. Robert straddled him, arms swinging. Over and over he pummelled the guy's head and side with blows that, deadened by sinking into the fleshy gut, sounded like the soft slap of a fish slopped down on a cutting board. He let loose, exhilarated. When the beating finally stopped, Robert's hands were red, bruised and hurt like hell.

His buddies had stood and watched placidly with no intention of stopping the attack. They'd seen this kind of violence before and each took a kick at the creep before they left.

None of the three ex-soldiers ever saw the young man again or found out who he was. When they talked about it later, they all took the view that they'd acted justly. "The law's on the side of punks," Tony said. It was slow and useless, a waste of time. Dishing out justice on your own gave you the kind of satisfaction that you couldn't get by going to the cops. If someone ever interfered with his family, Robert said, he'd do the same thing again but he wouldn't be so lenient.

"No one values family like Bobby," Tony informed no one in particular, nodding his head.

"Geez, too bad I didn't have my 30-30," said Wallace, "I'd a shot the bastard."

## *Lawrence*

On my way back to the motel from the restaurant I walked beneath the moving, unbelievable cacophony from an enormous flock of Canada Geese heading south.

In my room, I put on the TV for company, found that one channel was now up and running, and with the sound down low, sat in the chair beside an old table and picked at a piece of loose veneer.

I thought about *The Cenci* by Shelley. In the preface he'd written:

"Undoubtedly, no person can be truly dishonoured by the act of another; and the fit return to make to the most enormous injuries is kindness and forbearance, and a resolution to convert the injurer from his dark passions by peace and love. Revenge, retaliation, atonement, are pernicious mistakes."

I didn't remember the wording exactly, at the time, but recalled the gist of it.

I had been wondering why my mother had written her journal. Did she want us to retaliate? That's what I'd thought, but suddenly understood that the answer was, no. She wanted us to understand and forgive. She had stood in Francine's kitchen and argued with her and Emelie. She had helped to take a life in order to save others she said, rightly or wrongly, but to kill for this other reason, because a distraught man had struck his wife, was obviously wrong. What they had to do was to move beyond reprisal, punishment or confrontation, and instead, demonstrate compassion and understanding.

My mother's story showed that if I killed René the cycle of violence would continue. What she wanted me to know, I was sure, was that if I acted in anger and retribution, that in time, the violence would visit my daughter. To keep her safe I would have to say no to killing René.

I still marvel that I didn't want to accept that logic. At the time, I had come to feel, without hesitation, the determination to take action. Walking away would be to say, 'yes, you killed my mother and I can't go to the police, but I will do nothing; you can get away scot-free.' But this was what my convictions said to do. This was the real test of strength. In a perverse way, it would be harder to do nothing than it would be to kill someone.

What blew me away, after it occurred to me, was that my mother had actually allowed René to do what he did! She had told no one about the threat, although doing so would have likely stopped it. She had sacrificed herself to end the violence and to protect us. If I acted against René Gagnon then I undid that sacrifice. She had shown great faith in her family, that we would understand and let things alone.

I sat in that crappy hotel room for a long time that day going over my reasons to act or not act.

At something like 2:30 in the afternoon I pulled my mother's journal out of my backpack and headed for the motel office. This time, when I went into the office, I found someone there, who in response to my request managed to scrape up a large envelope and a blank piece of paper. I returned to my room and wrote a note on the paper, put it and the journal into the envelope and headed out.

I took the same route as earlier in the day and walked back to René's garage. I had nothing to say to him, the note said it all. It told him what the journal was and that I hoped he'd read it to understand the past about his father.

I was following Shelley's proscription "to convert the injurer from his dark passions by peace and love. Revenge, retaliation, atonement, are pernicious mistakes." If he read the journal perhaps he'd understand what his father had done and how my mother had acted from compassion to try and save him.

This time I wasn't nervous when I got to the shop. I felt I was on more familiar moral territory here. The garage door was up but no one was around. Despite having no planned speech I was slightly disappointed, I wanted him to see that I was at peace. My act would tell him something about my mother because I was her son. I wrote René's name on the front of the envelope and left it on his workbench where he'd find it at some point. At 10:40 a.m. the next morning, I'd decided, I would get on the eastbound train and go back to Toronto. Hopefully, René would understand in time.

WITH MY MOST IMPORTANT issue resolved, before I went to sleep that night I debated whether or not to get off the train in Harris and look up Iris at her grandmother's. I wondered what her reaction would be, assuming I could even find the place. I'd get off and call her, tell her I'd come north to visit family (so she didn't think I was obsessed with her after one night), and see if she wanted company. I somehow knew she'd say yes.

## *Robert & René*

René was tired. His head ached and his eyes were dry and burning. He'd been up almost the entire night reading Madeleine MacQuigau's journal.

What he'd felt, after first finding the thing, was intense panic. The note said that the journal made it clear who was the one that killed Dr. MacQuigau. But the note writer, after explaining who he was, said that he wasn't going to go to the cops and wasn't going to take any action on his own. Gutless. There was a bunch of shit in the note about peace and love—just what you'd expect from some skinny hippy. Still…

Why read this thing, he thought later? The murdering bitch was dead, got what she deserved, so what did he care what she thought. But in the evening, after his family was asleep, he'd gotten up, drawn to the book out of intense curiosity about a father he'd never really known, and started to go through it.

It didn't convince him that he shouldn't have retaliated against the doctor the way that Lawrence MacQuigau had hoped it would. Even if René had been convinced of the truth of what was said in the journal, it would have been impossible, in one night, to reverse the effects of so many years of idealizing a dead parent. Accepting that new perspective would have also meant taking on the self-recrimination that must follow if you became convinced you'd killed someone who didn't deserve it. But the journal had instilled in him the first feelings of self doubt. Predictably, he'd immediately reassured himself that he'd done nothing wrong.

The journal was written by the doctor so he knew that everything was from her point of view. The way she told it, she was perfect and his father was pure evil. That was bullshit, he knew. He didn't understand why the doctor had hated his father, but that's why she'd acted for sure. What was nudging at him though, was the fact that his mom had participated in killing her husband! No matter how much sway the doctor had over his mother, trying to get her to act against his father, his mother had let herself be convinced to kill! For that to happen his dad would have had to have acted pretty bad.

The doctor hadn't sounded like she was out to get his dad. To listen to her tell it, she just couldn't stop him from being violent and no one around Wegebow would help. The truth was that he knew this place, knew how much was covered up, and what the doc said sounded too believable.

It had given René a good deal of satisfaction to have acted in support of his parents — it was a way of reaching across the years to show solidarity with them — and he still felt that way, but the journal was making him question whether the story he'd grown up with had been the true version of events. It left him confused. He didn't feel the same degree of certainty about his actions as he had the day before.

ROBERT GOT OFF THE westbound train at the Wegebow train station, at 9:00 a.m. and went straight to the auto repair shop. Days before, he'd called and gotten the address and phone number from the operator. He refused to note anything about the houses he passed because he didn't want to be looking at the town, making comparisons between things now and then. He hated the bloody place and it wasn't as if he was a tourist.

As he approached the garage a young guy stepped out into the sun, took in Robert, and said, "Hello."

"You René Gagnon?"

"Yeah."

He wasn't a big guy like his old man, Robert thought. Not small like his mother either though. Rob said hello and went into a story about how his car had broken down just outside of town.

"Uh huh, uh huh," the guy said, listening. He asked a few questions about the problem, then said, "Could be a few different things."

"Do you have a tow truck sos we could get it?"

"Naw, but I got a pick-up and some chains. We can tow it in. Lemme get my keys."

Stepping inside the garage to wait, Robert scanned the tools on a wooden workbench.

"Okay, let's get going," said René, coming up behind him, wiping his hands on a rag.

Turning, Robert's hand, holding a ball pein hammer, dropped down by his side. With a vicious uppercut he drove the hammer into the guy's testicles.

René fell to his knees clutching his groin and then on to his side with his knees drawn up in front of him into a fetal position.

"Fuck! Fuck! Fuck!" he screamed, gasping for breath.

Robert straddled him, grabbed the front collar of René's shirt, and shoved the hammer upward pushing the young man's mouth closed and his head back so he had no choice but to look him in the face.

"You don't look like your old man but you're stupid like him. What did you think was gonna happen? Think you'd get away with it?"

"What the fu…" was the strangled response.

"I'm Rob MacQuigau. My wife was Dr. Madeleine MacQuigau, the same woman you murdered." He was getting louder.

There was no attempted rejoinder. René stared back, wide-eyed.

"Yeah, you weaselly prick, I know what you did."

"The bitch…"

Robert drove the hammer into the guy's mouth, smashing in most of his teeth.

René sobbed and struggled to breathe.

"You are only alive 'cus of the woman you killed. Your old man was this close to killing your mother and maybe you. Do you remember the present of the broken arm he gave you? The rifle he was waving at you? Maddy acted for one reason, to save the two of you, and all she got was grief for it from you and your damn mother."

He didn't know whether the kid heard him through his pain or not.

He raised the hammer again.

## *Lawrence*

I got up in the morning, went to the restaurant for breakfast and watched the 9:00 a.m. overnighter crawl by on its arrival from Toronto; the same train that I'd been on the morning before. In just over an hour I would head for the station to take the eastbound train back to Toronto. I felt positive. Leaving my mother's journal with René was a victory for pacifism; a moral victory over violence and retribution. It might be a long time before he'd read it, but I was confident he would, and in time recognize what he'd done.

René Gagnon would live, not from fear or any failure of resolve on my part, but because I was convinced it was what my mother wanted. She had sacrificed her life to end the cycle of violence—maybe she thought of it as her punishment—but it was her decision and I had to respect it. Knowing that René would come to realize the truth and undoubtedly alter his feelings about my mother helped me to get past the idea that a few minutes away was the man who had killed her and I was going to do nothing about it.

At 10:40 a.m. I boarded the train for Toronto.

I watched an older woman in the seat across from me. Plainly dressed, she had a new perm and garish red lipstick. This trip—up the track to visit some relative or whoever—was probably a big outing for her. As the train pulled away from the station she squirmed in her seat, anxiously pressing her face against the glass, looking left and right.

"There you are!" she called, spotting a young guy swaying back and forth, clutching the corner of the seats while walking up the car. "I thought that you were going to miss the train."

"There was some excitement," the man burst out as he strode forward, looking flushed, "a murder on First Avenue a little earlier."

"Sacre…who?"

"René Gagnon. You know the young guy with the garage."

"Of course. Oh my God!" She clasped her hands over her mouth in shock, her eyes huge, expressing questions and fear.

I stared at her son too (if that's who he was), feeling similar emotions, waiting breathlessly for the rest of the story.

"What happened?" she eventually asked.

"Some guy beat him to death."

She gasped. "Oh, how awful."

"They said it was a guy named MacQuigau. Ever hear the name?"

The old woman shook her head and we both stared back at the young guy, waiting for more.

"I never heard of him. Robert I think they said. He killed himself after."

I sucked in my breath and felt a sudden tumult of nausea, adrenaline and grief. My hand squeezed the arm rest. I wanted to attack the messenger, to throttle him. I turned to look out the window and avoid the temptation of his presence. Wegebow was gone and the train was speeding up. Should I get off? Stay here? The questions sped through my thoughts but this was too unreal to know what to do. I leaned my forehead against the window.

The chatty couple, with something now to talk about, pressed on.

"Why would someone do a horrible thing like that?" I heard the old lady saying. "It's unbelievable, he was such a nice young man. And he has that lovely young wife."

"They said it was some sort of fight. Must be over money."

"You know those kind of things happen in the city but you don't expect them to happen here…Should we still be going to Grandma's."

"I don't know why not. It's got nothing to do with us."

"It seems kinda disrespectful somehow. His dad was a second cousin of mine, so he would have been…I don't know, something."

For a long time I stood between the cars of the train and smoked. I stared at the blur of trees going past, still numbed by the news, not yet in shock. No tears. But I couldn't sit in my seat and listen to that damn couple go on and on about the killing. People came and went, shot the shit, insisted on telling me the incredible news. You had to nod and grunt, but if you kept staring out into the bush they didn't stay long.

I didn't want to get off the train and go back to see the scene in Wegebow or my father's dead body. As is often the case, I found a way to rationalize what I wanted. I was sure the cops would find it suspicious that I was in Wegebow. I wasn't likely to just be in the neighbourhood. They might assume I had come with my father and was complicit in what he did. I had used an assumed name at the motel — Frank Cenci — so the way things stood there was no reason for anyone to associate the person at the motel with what my father had done.

My father had acted like my father. What he'd done was brutal and real. He had been in the war, undoubtedly knew what he was doing, and wasted no time. I had never known anything but a comfortable life. Even if my thoughts had been different and I'd decided to go through with revenge I wonder if I could have done it. I was never much like him in many respects. He'd learned things through experience.

I finally returned to my seat and found the old lady across from me dozing. All this brutality had been nothing but a disturbing rush of excitement to now be slept off. I sat, closed my eyes and feigned sleep to discourage conversation from the kid sitting beside her. The police would visit Martin, tell him what had happened and he would try to figure out how to arrange to get my father back home for a funeral. He'd be looking for me, calling everyone in my life trying to find me, and I felt guilty about that.

I thought about what my father had done. He'd gotten his revenge and then taken reciprocal revenge on behalf of the Gagnon family. There was now no reason for them to exact retaliation on my family. My father had taken care of it for them with a certain perverse logic. My mother thought she'd ended the cycle of violence but my father had brought it full circle before ending it in his own way.

PART 4

# *Lawrence*
# 12 Years Later

In 1822, at age 29, Percy Bysshe Shelley left from Livorno, Italy in a boat, the *Don Juan*, to return to Lerici. A sudden storm came up. Shelley was an experienced boatsman but couldn't swim. Death by reckless foolhardiness. A few days later his body washed to shore. He was cremated by Edward Trelawny, Leigh Hunt and Lord Byron. At the last moment, Trelawny pulled the heart from the fire and Shelley's wife, Mary, carried it with her for the rest of her life.

Shelley had died at the height of his powers. His convictions never having wavered with age.

By contrast, my premonitions of an early death have not proven true. I am 36 years-old, teach in a small college, have published only 3 poems, all written in my youth, and struggle at times to maintain my idealism.

WHEN I FINALLY OPENED up my eyes that day, on the train headed for Toronto, I realized that one of the stops we'd made was at Harris. I considered jumping off at the next station but the logistics of finding my way back there seemed too considerable. Small, unexpected things like this change your life. I never saw her again. It's the great 'what if' of my life. I have had two constants in my life: beauty and violence. Given the latter, I don't regret succumbing to the former. I always chose beauty.

I OFTEN THINK OF my parents and what happened is still overwhelming in many ways.

I no longer feel judgemental about my mother. When I recall her, I remember the kind, nurturing person. I realize that she gave up much for her family and that my judgements of her at the time were harsh. She had acted to try and save lives, but the Gagnons were a doomed family and 3 of them still died violently, as did both of my parents.

My father's selfish actions that day in Wegebow stripped my family and myself of something. I had quelled my anger to act in a way consistent with what my mother would have wanted — and after all, she's the one who lost her life and deserved to have her wishes followed. I acted in a way, when I left the journal for René to read, that was moral. My father took that away from me and I resent it. In the name of family, he had the self-satisfaction of brutalisation, but his actions were based on rage and his own sense of loss. (Acting for 'family' justifies all manner of sins.) For myself, instead of self-applause for overcoming base instincts I now only question whether I should have acted decisively. I endlessly ask myself whether I am a coward and if that's what motivated my decisions.

THE LOSS OF MY parents has left me with a lack of support and a realization that I am alone in the world. My mother's encouragement allowed me to accomplish things because I believed in myself but I realize my father's brutal ways helped to undermine my self-esteem. He turned that same violence, that he directed against others, against me, a member of his family. Violence was just his way of handling things.

I wonder if Marcel's violence was rooted in a similar lack of self-esteem. That he felt he didn't deserve love and was terrified by the idea of losing it. His violence was weak and pathetic. Or if René's actions were intended to overcome the sense of being alone in the world; to unite him with his parents by directing hate at who he had learned (through lies) were the objects of their demise. Strangely, perhaps, I feel a certain bond with René because we both lost our parents to the same cycle of violence.

JUNE LEFT 3 MONTHS ago. She says that she can't handle my infidelities, which I understand. I had the same difficulty with Dee, with my jealousy, despite my opposition to monogamy.

I tried to speak to June about my feelings, many times, but she was unconvinced. I explained that I felt that monogamy was an attempt to own a person; their emotions and their body. But she came back to me after a time and argued that, in reality, I was embracing some sort of post-war consumerism with my affairs; following a consumer ethos which says that more is better and everything is disposable.

What June has never understood was that, for me, my affairs were acts of love and that we can love more than one person. My actions were never a betrayal of her or my commitment to her.

So, I don't regret the preoccupation with ardent pursuits that has always characterized me. Some of the affairs cause feelings of guilt because of their effect on her, but I saw them as the embracing of life and experience. They were about fully living a radical life.

I HAVE WRITTEN DOWN the events of my story and packaged it with my mother's journal for Bea to read. I hope the day will be soon. She is 14 and angry at me for some ill-defined reason. I think it is a level of contempt. She accuses me of being an embarrassment, a burned out hippie who spends his time chasing women and accomplishes nothing. I wonder if my sense of failure has led to a degree of self-contempt that she has picked up on. I feel helpless and lost with her. It undermines my self-esteem even further. What have I accomplished in life? If it ended today there would be no one who would remember me fondly.

This morning she stormed out of the house. (She came to live with me when she was 4 after her mother grew weary of being tied down.) Her boyfriend was waiting outside on his motorcycle. She seems attracted to that; to machismo and implied violence. I hope that reading about her family's past and seeing where violence leads may make a difference in her life, and that her family's future will be better.

ಸಂ

CPSIA information can be obtained at www.ICGtesting.com
226914LV00001B/8/P